ADVANCE PRAISE

"Sharyn Haddad Vicente's dark debut is a harrowing tale of obsession and twisted love that elicits, even amidst the horror, an undeniable sympathy for the savages among us. This is no easy feat. Vicente shows a sensitivity to the tragedy of mental illness and the power of human connection that make *Love Me* a page-turning thriller that will stay with you for a long time."

> Heather Young,
> *Strand award-winning author*

"*Love Me* is an intricately layered thriller that grabs you by the throat and doesn't let go. The story explores the dark human psyche, and the deception and intrigue is quickly addictive."

> Robert Dugoni,
> International Bestselling author
> of *the Tracy Crosswhite series*

LOVE

ME

LOVE

ME

SHARYN HADDAD VICENTE

Text copyright © 2021 by Sharyn Haddad
Vicente
All rights reserved.

ISBN: 979-8537004707

Cover design by Kaitlyn Vicente

Second edition

To Joe, my eagle eye, for always letting me be me, to Kaitlyn for being my creative muse, and to Nick for forever helping me to see the big picture.

deep down
you just want to be loved
in a way that calms your soul
r.h. Sin

ONE
The Past
James

James Lowden stared helplessly at the empty swing as it made its rhythmic movements back and forth like an evil pendulum. James knew three things. The first was that he would never let his best friend swing that high ever again. The second was that he didn't like it when she cried. The third was that he would always love and protect Paige Vale.

The empty swing next to him still swayed back and forth, taunting him with the fact that he let it happen; he didn't stop her in time. He followed the trail of blood that led to her deck at the back of the house. The droplets announced her trek up the cedar stairs and in through the sliding glass back doors of the house, which he knew, led into the kitchen. He had been there many times. He liked this house much more than his own. This was a massive house with so many rooms, he was afraid he would get lost at times. He often wondered how they could hear each other when the family was scattered throughout and was told that the house was equipped with an intercom system.

Looking up at the vast sky strewn with pastel-colored strokes, drawn by a majestic and benevolent painter, James realized that he liked the color on the outside of the massive Colonial the most. It reminded him of the buttercup flowers that Paige liked so much. The house had so many windows that were all trimmed in a white scallop design; it reminded him of a decorated cake. You could walk into the kitchen by opening a door from inside the attached garage. The garage alone was big enough for him and his mom to move into and be comfortable. His favorite feature was the farmer's porch. Many afternoons he would walk the length back and forth while waiting for Paige to get home from school. He knew it would take 46 to 48 steps to walk the entire length and would take two or three passes before the school bus would stop in front, depositing Paige in her plaid uniform.

He was not used to such lavish things. His house was slightly larger than the Vales' garage. His mother used to mock the Vales' saying that they were snobs and that they thought they were special. James didn't think that. He liked being here. Paige had a sandy-haired little brother, Timothy, and a grey labradoodle named Jasper. She lived with both her mom and dad which made him feel as though he were watching a movie since his life was in stark contrast.

James stood looking through the sliding French doors into the kitchen. He heard Paige sobbing quietly and her mother, Sloane, consoling her.

"It's gonna sting, Mom!"

"I need to spray your knees and elbows to clean out the cuts, Paige. Look, the bottle says it won't sting. I'll spray it and then blow to make sure it won't hurt too badly."

"Okay, but I know it's gonna hurt, I know it!"

"Paige, stop saying gonna!"

James noticed the box Sloane had on the table full of gauze, ointments, and bandages and thought she was amazingly prepared for anything. He was gazing at them through the screen door when Sloane called to him.

"James, why are you standing out there? Come on in."

He opened the door slowly and walked into the kitchen with his head hung low staring at his worn, tattered sneakers that were quickly becoming too small. "I'm sorry, Mrs. Vale."

"Why are you sorry, James? Did you push Paige off her swing? Did you tell her to try to break a world record?"

"No, no, I would never do that. I only want to protect her." He raised his head and looked at Sloane with wide, intense eyes.

She knew this was no hyperbole; he meant every word. "I didn't think so, James, so stop the sulking. The blood is cleaned up, so there is no reason to be lurking around."

"I tried to get her to slow down, I, I knew it was too high. I knew she would get hurt. I tried to make her stop. I'll do better next time, I promise."

"James, I know better than anyone that our Miss

3

Paige here has a mind of her own. She needs to take responsibility for her actions. These scrapes will remind her of that for a little while."

James heard what Sloane had said but thought that she couldn't be more wrong. He made a promise to himself long ago to always be her protector, to keep her safe so that they would be together forever. A bead of sweat slowly rolled down his brow, into the corner of his emerald green eye, and dripped off his long, greasy nose onto the floor.

It was warmer than it should be for October. He thought he remembered his teacher saying they were having an Indian summer. He had no idea how Indians could make the weather warmer but thought back to some movies he had seen where Native Americans were dancing in an attempt to make it rain and thought there must be a connection.

Sloane looked at James and said, "Help yourself to a cold drink in the fridge. There are some chips in the cupboard too. She will be good as new in a few minutes. It is time for homework, but if you promise to sit quietly, you can stay until Paige is done. Please be careful of my tiles though, I'm working on inking some new designs for the counter backsplash. Better yet, don't you have any homework of your own, James?"

James went to the public middle school in the small town of Cumberland, Rhode Island, while Paige went to a private school where everyone had to wear the same uniform. He knew the kids that went to that school were rich and smart, not like the kids

4

at his school. There were some smart kids there, but they were just smart—not smart and rich. James came from the *South* side of the town, while Paige came from the *North*. He had asked his mother why there was a difference, and she said that was just the way it had always been. Those who lived there only knew of the divide between the North and South parts of town. It was an underlying knowledge that the haves came from the North, and the have nots came from the South. She told him that as far as she knew, that was the only town in Rhode Island where they thought of each other in that way.

James told Sloane he would go back out, retrieve his backpack, and do his homework. Leaving the house, he was once again surprised by how warm it was for a mid-October afternoon. He trotted over to the swing set where they had been together just minutes ago. The trees that lined the Vales' property were well past peak and the leaves that had fallen, like multicolored tears, were huddled together on the ground beneath him as if they were trying to unite in hopes of escaping the inevitable raking. Once vibrant reds, oranges, and yellows were now becoming a muted assortment as if he was viewing them through a dirty window. There were so many trees on their property. Too many to count—he had tried once. They were of different varieties and sizes and they made James feel small. People told him that he was big for his age, but being in the presence of these trees, he felt insignificant.

James retrieved his backpack from the back of his

bicycle and made his way back into the house. Sloane turned to watch him approach. She never knew what to make of him. Once he caught her eyes, he lowered his head so that all she could see approaching was his large, thick frame trying to crumple in upon itself and disappear. His dirty-blond hair was unkempt as usual. Once he came through the door, she could tell that he was truly troubled over Paige's accident. He finally looked up and met her gaze. She thought it odd, it really was not a big deal, but it was also odd that the piercing eyes, the color of jade that normally shied away and were impenetrable, were now beckoning her, seeking a pardon. It made her want to comfort him as well as her daughter.

Paige broke the silence, truly unaware of the thoughts in her mother's head. "James, could you get me a diet and bring the chips over here?" When he didn't reply, she looked up and noticed him intently watching her. She rolled her big blue eyes. She playfully mocked him telling him that when he looked at her like that it reminded her of the dumb romance novels her mom read. James laughed carelessly but was secretly happy that she thought of him and a romance novel in the same thought.

They each worked together in silence at the kitchen island, tackling their respective assignments, for what seemed like hours. The only time he ever actually did his homework was when he was with Paige. She always made him accountable for his *future*. She said that good grades were the catalyst to a good job and a bright prospect ahead as an adult.

She worked hard and had many plans for her future. He just hoped they included him.

Paige was almost finished with her homework and tried to glance nonchalantly at James's work to ensure he was making a valiant effort. She worried about him all the time. He was her best friend for over three years now. They met when they were eight while taking guitar lessons at a music store in town. They had an instant connection when they both grew bored with the instructor's assignments of ancient show tunes and asked to learn "Only Wanna Be with You" by Hootie and the Blowfish, simultaneously blurting out the song title and sharing a fit of laughter.

That gave her an idea. "James, we should break out the guitars and play a few songs."

He agreed. They put away their schoolwork and moved into the living room. James made himself comfortable on the oversized cream-colored couch, while Paige went to retrieve the guitars. She grabbed the instruments from the music room. She kept on talking as she made her way over to James and now stood before him, both hands holding a guitar. Her head was cocked to the side, which made her look self-confident, and she blew a puff of air out of one side of her mouth to move the dark hair out of her eyes. It was then that he noticed how alike they were. Paige had the same flawless alabaster skin as Sloane. She also shared the same jet-black hair and crystal-clear blue eyes. When he first met Paige at their music lessons, she reminded him of Snow White.

She handed one guitar to James and then sat down with the other. They tuned the instruments and began playing. As always, they never needed to speak, but moved fluidly from song to song in sync with the other when it came to music. It was always that way. They played for a while when, huffing and puffing, Sloane came into the room with two bins in her arms, Timothy following behind her. James placed his guitar on the couch and jumped to his feet to assist her.

"It's time!" Sloane announced.

"Awesome!" Paige ran over to the bins and began opening them. They were filled with Halloween decorations. Timothy dug into the bins, relishing in the decorating tradition. Seeing this reminded James that Halloween was by far the most cherished holiday in the Vale family. The family put a lot of time and effort into decorating the inside and outside of the house, but nothing compared to creating their prize-winning scarecrow each year. Paige was eager to get busy making the one for this year.

"You know your father will be very upset if you don't wait for him to come home and help with that."

"I know, Mom, I'm just getting everything we need together. Dad promised he would get the hay on the way home from work."

"Okay, I don't want anything ruining our hard work. By the way, since he is four years old and can understand the concept, this year it's Timothy's turn to name him." As soon as she finished saying that,

Timothy looked up with a Wizard of Oz Tin Man mask on his face from his dad's costume last year.

Tim squealed, "I want to call him, Bob!"

Sloane chuckled and gave him a kiss on his forehead. "Bob is a great name, buddy." She tickled his pudgy belly and sent him to play with Jasper while she began getting dinner ready.

"James, will you be staying for dinner tonight?" Sloane asked. He declined, saying that he needed to get home and get dinner ready for his mom for when she came back from work at the local casino. Sloane knew what that meant—popping a frozen dinner into the microwave oven when he heard her car pull into the driveway. She wanted to ask if he would like to take a care package with him but knew his mother would take it the wrong way. Lydia Lowden could be very hard to understand. At times, she was warm and friendly; while other times it seemed as if Sloane upset her just by breathing the same air. She really did feel bad for them. She knew that Lydia did her best for her son, but being a single mom, it wasn't always easy. It was well known in town that her husband left them high and dry when James was young. She gave the mother and son a lot of credit for working hard and always being there for each other.

Sloane heard Jasper begin barking happily and wagging his tail like crazy as he and Timothy ran over to the window. That could only mean one thing—Mitch was home. As soon as Paige heard the commotion, she ran into the kitchen and bolted through the door and into the garage with James at her heels.

"Did you get the straw, Dad?"

Timothy tried to copy his big sister and in his toddler's voice, said, "Yeah, did you get the stwaw, Dad?" Jasper pounced on the car beckoning him to get out and play.

Mitch opened the car door and like a contortionist began uncoiling himself to exit the sports car. It was hard to believe that his 6' 4" frame could fit behind the steering wheel. With his chiseled features and sturdy jawline, he looked like an action figure. Teasingly he answered, "Was I supposed to pick that up today?"

Paige gasped theatrically as she clasped both hands to each side of her face. "Well dad, you know what that means; you don't get to help us with the scarecrow. If you can't remember the most important part, you have to watch us have all the fun from the sidelines!"

He walked over to the back of the jet-black car and opened the trunk. He said, "Well I guess I am lucky I remembered after all!" With a gleam in his eyes, he lifted the bale of hay out of his trunk and placed it on the floor of the garage. Paige smiled from ear to ear and Timothy immediately began to climb the straw cube that was about the same size that he was.

"Hi, James." Mitch looked at James who was watching the family interactions with an expression he couldn't quite make out. "Interested in helping us make this year's prize-winning scarecrow?"

"Hi, Mr. Vale. Thanks, but I have to be getting home."

"I can give you a lift. It's getting dark out earlier and earlier these days. And my nose tells me that dinner isn't quite ready yet."

"Is that a fact?" Sloane teased as she came into the garage wiping her hands on a paper towel. "How much time does your nose think the casserole needs before it is fit to be consumed?"

Mitch walked over to her and dramatically dipped Sloane as if they were ballroom dancing. He then scooped her up and planted a kiss on her lips—much to their children's revulsion. "About 13 minutes—just enough time to bring our friend here home and for me to return to this very spot."

James felt funny accepting a ride and didn't want them to go to any trouble for him, so he declined. He liked to ride his bike. It gave him time to think and plan the things he wanted to do. Paige said that she would walk him out to the front of the house, and they were off. Being a Thursday, they made plans for the soon to arrive weekend. They wanted to go to their secret clubhouse. It was buried in the woods, in the back of her property, near the Diamond Hill Reservoir.

They had been collecting leaves and other items deep in the woods behind her house for a science project that Paige was working on one day when they stumbled upon it . . . literally. There was an old stone structure protruding from out of the ground.

Stones were arranged in what was once an elaborate circular formation, but would now only be mistaken for a random pile of rocks. It no longer had a covering, but there were still steps that led down, from the open center of the circle, to the inside of what looked like an ancient underground food storage cellar. James made Paige stay above ground while he went down to investigate. It was dark, but he always carried a flashlight and used it to see where he was going. He descended, carefully placing each foot on what was left of the stone steps. The stones that remained were jagged and loose, but each step had room enough for his foot to make purchase. The cellar smelled damp and musty. The air felt cooler down below than above ground. James directed his light up and saw an estimated six or eight large logs; some still had visible traces of bark in places. They lined the top of the space, which was much longer than it was wide. Other logs were running the opposite way connecting the earthen walls. They were being propped up by yet more logs, off to the sides, standing as straight as a palace guard, supporting the whole structure.

When he deemed it was safe, he went back up and helped Paige down to have a look. He guided her down slowly and protectively which got on her nerves.

She was in awe at what she observed. James pointed out how it had survived so long by directing her attention to the log beams and how sturdy they were. As she perused the space, she noticed that, to the right, there were at least two dozen crates all neatly lined up against the wall. There was also a long, narrow table made of wood up against one side of the earthen and log-laden walls. The table was strewn with random tools, several mason jars, and various bric-a-brac scattered about; some jars had contents that were fully sealed and some were empty. There were large covered white buckets underneath the table that were neatly stacked up and labeled. The labels were very faded, and they were barely able to read them. They read the label of one bucket as containing *Turnips*. James pulled that one free from the rest and looked up at Paige who gave an encouraging nod for him to continue the investigation. He needed something to pry the lid open and found a screwdriver on top of the table that proved to do the job. He handed the flashlight to Paige to free his hands. He began to pry open the lid. Before the lid was completely off, the two were knocked backward from the horrid stench that emitted from the bucket. It offered as powerful a punch as a prizefighter hitting a KO victory.

Paige immediately blocked her nostrils with her fingers. "What the hell? It smells like something died in there. Cover it fast!"

James was already covering it before she said the words and quickly used his sweatshirt to pull up over his mouth and nose as a barrier against the putrid smell. He grabbed Paige and pointed up and over to the steps. She understood, returned the flashlight to him, and followed his lead up and out of the cellar. Once up in the fresh cool air, they could finally breathe again. They looked at each other and began laughing so hard they fell to the forest floor until their fit subsided.

"Do you think there was a dead body cut up in that bucket?"

"No, I think they were turnips at one time. It must be wicked old, Paige. I bet there was a house nearby that is gone now. Maybe when whoever owned it died, no one knew about the cellar and just tore down the house."

Paige announced, "Well, I'm not going back down there for a long time!"

"We should make it into a clubhouse!"

Paige wanted to know how they would ever get all that smelly junk out of there.

James was excited. "We need to bring some supplies and make a plan. It's almost time to go home anyway. I'll walk you home and head to my house then we can both get busy making a list of everything we will need to get the job done."

"We are going to need some major supplies. What are we going to tell our parents?"

James considered this. "We can each tell them we are helping one another with a science project or something when we want to meet here. You say you are going over to my house, and I'll say I am going over to yours. We will meet here—that way it will save time."

Paige pondered this. "Why can't we just tell them about it?"

James looked at her for such a long time; she was beginning to feel uncomfortable. He finally said, "This should be our secret clubhouse. You know how I need to get away once in a while. It wouldn't be any good if our parents knew where we were when we wanted to be away from them."

She thought about that, decided that he was right, and felt that the plan would work.

James was startled back to reality when a neighbor beeped allowing him to cross the street safely. Enjoying his memory, he waved a thank you and went back to thinking.

Quickly returning to his memory, he thought back to the following day when they met as scheduled. Paige had all the equipment ready when he arrived. James took a wheelbarrow, large trash bags, masking tape, water, and camping lanterns. Paige took gloves and snacks for the two of them, a plastic wagon that her brother played with, batteries and some seat cushions and tablecloths that were old and wouldn't be missed. They brought the contents down.

They began lugging the tubs up the steps and onto both the wheelbarrow and the wagon. Once they were both full, James tested the weight and put more of the tubs onto his making Paige's lighter. She objected, but he just ignored her. He was the biggest kid in the sixth grade of all the local schools. With his broad shoulders topping his 5' 8" frame, he looked more like a high school senior than an 11-year-old. They pulled the refuse through the woods toward the reservoir. There was an old narrow dirt road about 400 feet east where James had seen a dilapidated shack and some big dumpsters. They deposited the tubs of old decaying potatoes, turnips, carrots, beets, onions, and other unidentifiable ooze inside it.

After several trips, all the tubs were removed, and Paige grew grateful that James had insisted on lightening her load but would never admit to it. They stayed outside the clubhouse and had a well-deserved break while eating some of the snacks and drinking some of the water before descending into their new haven. Once finished, they each agreed that they would next tackle the crates and hoped that there were no additional malodorous contents they would need to deal with. Fortunately, there were only books, utensils, plates, napkins, cups, pillows, blankets, undergarments, flannel shirts, and farmer jeans. There were ropes and twine, along with rolls that were labeled "sausage casing." Clearly, this cellar was meant to be used in an emergency. They salvaged what they thought would come in handy and kept the crates that were in good condition. They used the push brooms that were there as their final task and then took up the waste and brought it all to the trash dumpsters.

They went down one more time before having to be home. She put seat cushions on top of two crates they would use as seats and then moved two next to them to be used as end tables, strategically placing the camping lights on each one.

Looking around at what to tackle next, she

spotted some hooks jutting from a log at the far end of the cellar. "James, what do you think those were for?"

He looked in the direction she pointed to and said, "I think it might have been to make sausage, jerky, and other salted meats."

"That's so cool! They could be very self-sufficient here."

He nodded in agreement.

Paige then set out to clear off the top of the table and picked up a full mason jar. There was a label that read: "Peach Preserves—August 1940."

Paige held up the jar, "Hey, check this out!"

James came over and looked at the label in awe. "I can't believe how old this place is!"

Paige said, "Our grandparents were probably little kids in 1940!"

James seemed to be doing the math in his head. He grinned. "Awesome!"

Paige then placed each full jar into a trash bag—very carefully, and then disposed of everything that would be of no use. She placed all the empty jars and buckets, tools, and what she thought they would be able to use at some point, into some of the empty crates, and then placed them under the wooden table.

Once the table was cleaned off, and the tablecloth placed on, they decided that they were finished until the next time they could retreat to their secret hideaway.

James had almost ridden right past his house

because he was so lost in his thoughts, reminiscing about the first time that he and Paige were ever in their secret clubhouse.

TWO
The Present
Paige

Six Octobers later and it was still the same—days were growing shorter and the evenings had a crisp chill in the air. The Vale family loved the fall; it was the only season where you could experience every weather pattern and all temperatures—all at once. One day it could be 90° Fahrenheit, the next, 55°, and the next, 70°. There was a saying in New England: "If you don't like the weather, wait a minute." That was one of the main reasons they loved living here. The neighborhood they settled in was quaint and their street was on a cul-de-sac right out of a Norman Rockwell painting. Their house was in the center of the half-circle and was surrounded by a lush, thick lawn that looked like a welcoming carpet of green. Gardenia and holly bushes edged the circular driveway and beautiful purple, pink, and white azalea bushes framed the wrap-around farmer's porch. Weeping willow trees stood guard protecting the home from direct sun during the day and offer cool breezes at night. Several different species of trees that explode with a kaleidoscope of vibrant colors during the fall surrounded the property.

Today, several families were outside, just past the crack of dawn, decorating for the neighborhood harvest *Dec-off*. Each fall, the neighborhood families decorated their houses and yards and would award prizes for many different categories. Each neighbor tried to outdo the other. The Vale family always won for the best scarecrow. Neighbors always commented on how perfectly detailed they were and begged them for their secret.

Inside, Sloane was preparing breakfast and was stealing a glance at Paige while trying not to be noticed. Seventeen-year-olds prefer to be cloaked in mystery. She was admiring the young woman before her and grieving the child that used to be. She loved the relationship they now had but ached for the days when Paige would dance throughout the house, never walk—flint-colored ponytail flapping behind her.

Paige, as if feeling her mother's eyes upon her said, "Is there a reason for eyeballing me?"

Sloane just walked over to her and hugged her.

Paige reminded Sloane that she had cheerleading practice after school.

"Please make sure you inform James of your plans. I can't stand to see him skulking around here waiting for you all the time. It breaks my heart."

"It's not my fault, Mom. I've told him my schedule is pretty full and that I'd let him know when we could hang out. He's relentless; he left me two voicemail messages and like 14 texts yesterday. He's always waiting for me after every class, and I think I even caught him spying on us at Jenna's house."

Those words sent an eerie feeling through Sloane's body, but she quickly brushed it off. "I'm sure he means well, Paige. He doesn't have many friends. Can't you include him when you're with your other friends?"

"Seriously, Mom? I've tried, remember? He fits in about as well as a toaster in a bathtub. I've tried to make it work by seeing him when I can, but it is getting too hard and I'm not sure it's worth it anymore, we've sort of grown in different directions."

"You've been friends for a long time, and I know that he was very happy to finally be attending the same school. I hope you aren't making a mistake. Even if you just make time for him once in a while, that's still something."

"I see him in school at lunch and we have PE together next session. He tries to walk me to my classes, but we are in totally opposite ends of the school and I know he's gotten detention for being late, so I've asked him to stop."

"I'm sure you know what's best. Just be gentle with him."

Almost as though he were listening to the conversation, Paige received a text from James:

Meet me at our spot after school. Impt.

Paige exhaled loudly. "See, this is what I'm

talking about—it's him. Again. I'm heading out." As Paige ran out the door, she yelled, "I have cheerleading practice right after school; I'll be late for dinner, save me whatever you're making. Love ya."

THREE

James

James hit send and hoped Paige would reply quickly. He turned the volume up on his phone so that he'd be certain to hear the second her reply came through. He was tossing around the thought that he should stay home from school because he didn't know when Paige would get around to answering his text. She had become less and less communicative with him lately. He knew that she was busy with after-school activities and he knew that her friends didn't like him much. She assured him that it wasn't true, but he saw the signs.

He always knew what people were thinking of him as soon as he looked into their eyes. After his dad left, most people around town saw him with a mixture of pity and condescension. He would never forget the day his father walked out of their lives. It had always been the three of them—they were the three musketeers. His mom, Lydia, worked part-time at the elementary school he attended, and his father, Carl, was a sergeant of the police force in town. The police station was the building right next to the school, so the three of them were always in the same area. They were never too far away from each other.

Ever. He hated his father for messing that up.

Whenever James thought of that time, he would remember the pain he felt. At times, it was so bad that he would try to scheme to bring his parents back together. He believed that if he helped out around the house more, his mom would notice and be happier. He would take out the trash before being asked and tried to fix the beat-up lawnmower they owned. He even made deals with God. Every time these things failed it broke a piece of him. He was never able to put those pieces back together. James referred to those times as the *Red Times* because when the pain would be at its worst, he would see red.

James couldn't believe how much time had gone by while dragging himself out of those harrowing memories. He certainly was not going to school. It was well past lunch and he realized that he was starving. He also realized that Paige had not yet replied to his text. That made him feel overwhelmingly angry and alone. A wave of *Red* swept over him and he consciously struggled to push it away. He made a quick peanut butter and banana sandwich and decided he would go to the hideout to await a reply or better yet, to meet up with Paige.

As James was biking through the woods, he was trying to clear his mind by listening to the rustling of the tall trees, the rippling of the water, and the musical songs of the birds. It was much easier to get around when his truck was running but he enjoyed the peace and solitude of riding his bike.

When he arrived, he was happy to see how well their entrance disguise had held up. Early on, they knew they needed to do something so that others who passed by the area would not interlope in their private hideaway. There were always people fishing in the reservoir and hiking in the woods.

Paige and James went exploring close to the water and found remnants of an old campfire made of large stones and boulders. They brought some of the scorched wood to the opening of their sunken refuge. James then nailed the charred pieces to a circular piece of plywood, screwed a handle underneath the wood, and then covered the entranceway. The pair moved the large rocks to fill in the existing circular pattern around the entrance to make it resemble a fire pit. Each subsequent time they arrived, all that was needed to be done, was to move the piece of wood aside and climb down, grab the handle to reposition the wood, and enter their private sanctuary.

Being there now, in seclusion, felt so different. James had been there plenty of times on his own, but somehow this felt wrong; it felt like it was the end. When he was on the verge of being consumed with the *Red*, he got up and walked around as if he were a boxer in a ring anticipating the clang of the bell. He jumped in place, punching his fists together and shaking his head. That only worked for so long. He decided he would go exploring while he was on his own. They each had their own area that was *private*. Grownups were always snooping so they knew they could trust each other to respect one another's privacy.

He looked around at the old, faded crates and chests that were in his designated area. They each had six shelves that were located on opposite sides of the hideaway. James took one of the larger crates down and blew away the thick, sticky cobwebs, and wiped away the dust that had accumulated on top. He opened the chest and found its treasures that had once been very beloved. They held little meaning now that he was older, or so he thought. As he rummaged through the box, he realized that his grandfather gave most of its contents to him.

As he unenthusiastically hunted through the contents, he came across something that caught his eye. It was a red metal toy truck, much like the one his grandfather used to drive. James and his grandfather were very close when he was a young boy. His grandfather picked him up after school on days when his mom had errands or appointments and they would go fishing at the reservoir or hiking in the woods. James loved to fish. It was something that came naturally to him. His favorite memories were of fishing trips when he, his father, and grandfather would all go together. His grandparents had a log cabin in New Hampshire and the family would go whenever his father could get away. Since his granddad was on his own at the end, James tried to spend as much time as possible with him and loved driving with him to keep him company.

When James thought back to the cabin vacations,

he remembered that they weren't all happy memories. He was eight years old on one of the last vacations that the family took there. One-night, thunderous shouting coming from below, awakened him. He was sleeping in the open loft above the living room. There was a four-foot-high wooden railing for protection. He was about to get up and investigate, but it sounded serious and it frightened him so much that he was frozen in place. He also knew that if he went down, they wouldn't continue the heated conversation in front of him. His fear squelched, he quietly crept out of bed and went to the railing. His mother, father, and grandfather were all arguing. He could barely understand his mother because she was talking funny. At the time, he thought she was ill, but now he realized that she was drunk. He vividly remembered what his mother was shouting at his father:

"You have destroyed our family, how could you? Weren't we enough for you? What about James? He's never going to understand this. I hope he hates you forever!"

His father was crying while mumbling something inaudible and his grandfather was shouting at his son about what a disappointment he was. From what James could make out, his father was leaving them for another family. That was the first time the *Red* appeared.

He remembered a throbbing taking over his body and with each pulse, his vision went blurry, and then all he saw was red. There was a ringing in his ears, and he could actually feel the *Red*—the heat of it. He could smell it, taste it; it was in every molecule of his body. And then, in what felt like one moment, everything went from red to black.

He awoke at the top of the wooden stairs to his mom shaking him and calling his name. He had no idea how long he was out, but they were all being civil to one another by then. Not another word was said in anger in his presence. The following day they returned home from that vacation and he never saw his father at home again. When James went to his room to unpack, he found the truck he now held in his hand on his pillow. His father had left it there for him before leaving the family home.

Shortly after they returned home from that trip, his grandfather passed, and the truck that his grandfather cherished was left to him. It wasn't much to look at, but it drove faithfully; rust, patches, and all. It was all that was left of his grandfather. James was sure his father was the reason his granddad died. His grandfather was so upset that night, and he was so old, it wasn't healthy for him to be so worked up. James missed his granddad so much it hurt.

Coming back to the task at hand, James put the truck back and checked his phone. He realized that it was getting late and that Paige probably wasn't going to show. He couldn't understand how or why she could abandon him like that. He thought there had to be an explanation. He considered their last encounters and conversations, racking his brain to see if he did or said anything wrong, but he couldn't think of anything.

James was just about to call Paige but then thought better of it. He threw his phone on the table, pulled at his hair, and screamed in a rage. As he was leaving, he spotted a crate slightly out of place in Paige's area. He felt that if she didn't respect him enough to show or reply, then he was going to go through the box in hopes of finding some answers about how to reach her in the new world she had created for herself. He could remember several times when she would doodle in each of the many journals that were kept in that box.

He fumbled through assorted colored pencils, Tamagotchi Virtual Pets, a copy of Romeo and Juliet, Koosh balls, gel pens, and markers, and found the journals. There were four of them—each cover decorated in Paige's artistic style. She was so talented and could do anything she put her mind to. The journals each had a one-word title. The first one was "*DREAMS*," the next one was "*VACATIONS*," the third was "*FUTURE*," and the last, "*LOVE*."

He checked the one titled "*FUTURE*" first because the black pages drew his attention. He could remember Paige and all the other girls in his school a few years back were always doodling on the black paper with bright neon-colored gel pens. It was all the rage.

Thumbing through, he saw that there were pictures of celestial moons, suns, and stars, lyrics to partially started songs, and her plans for the future, which changed from page to page. Paige's aspirations went from being an actress to a singer, to a fashion designer, and more toward the end of the journal, a psychiatrist. She had plans for her family's future as well. She wrote that her mother should focus on her art and open a gallery. Her father should concentrate on starting a handyman business and her brother should be a writer—there she added that it was because he was always telling stories. She even added the hopes she had for James's future and said that she thought he would make an excellent veterinarian.

A wave of euphoria came over him. He was elated by the fact that she had even mentioned him in one of her writings. He decided to pour through the other three journals to glean more insight into her true feelings. He was so engrossed that he didn't even realize that the sun had long ago set giving the moon its turn to keep watch over the small New England town.

He loved that she thought he was good with animals. It was a dream of his, but he lacked the confidence needed to pursue any such endeavor. With this new revelation, he decided to go to the local animal clinic right after school tomorrow to see if he could begin to volunteer.

The next day he did just that. He called ahead and was given an appointment to meet with Dr. Dustin Hogan who was the owner of Dr. Doolittle Pet Care. He and the doctor hit it off right from the minute they met. James felt like he was someone he could look up to and learn a lot. They agreed that he would volunteer three days a week to start and see how things progressed. James was so elated; he wanted to run and tell Paige. It was then that he remembered she never contacted him. Like the flip of a switch, his mood changed and he needed to quell a wave of rage.

FOUR
Paige

Paige arrived home later than expected Friday night and was exhausted. Practice was grueling. The coach was upset because so many of the girls still did not know their choreography for the routine. Paige herself was angry because competition was creeping up on them. She worked hard practicing often and it was evident her teammates didn't take things as seriously. It would help if the coaches didn't constantly make changes to what they already learned. Before she could decide what to say, another cheerleader spoke the very same concern.

The coach insisted that every change made would help to ensure they would win the State Championship. She certainly didn't like being questioned and Paige was happy that the challenge didn't come from her.

When Paige came through the door, Sloane yelled from the living room that her dinner was keeping warm in the oven. She heard Paige open the oven door and Sloane yelled out for her to wash her hands first.

Paige was trying to stay awake while she was eating, after the extra-long, grueling practice, then she remembered that she never contacted James. She made a mental note to have a long talk with him tomorrow.

+++++++++++++

Paige woke up Saturday morning and was famished. She slept later than she intended and noticed that she had eight text messages from her friends. They were all trying to plan on a time to get together to make signs for the upcoming pep rally. They needed to meet at Brooke's house because she had to be home to accept a furniture delivery for her parents. They mentioned that they planned to go shopping for outfits for the pep rally and the party afterward. She also remembered that she wanted to meet up with James at some point during the day and she wasn't sure how she would fit it all in.

Paige pulled the covers off and was instantly chilled to the bone. She made a mental note to tell her parents that it was time to turn up the heat. The view outside her window was very deceiving. The sun shone through and looked as if it should heat the room with its warm-looking rays, but the golden beams couldn't penetrate the nip in the air.

She ran into the bathroom. The deep purple curtains and rug seemed to emit the lavender scent her oil reeds gave off. She quickly assessed the bags under her eyes in the mirror above the pedestal sink and thought they were almost as dark as the accents in the room. She started the shower. When she turned around to get in, Jasper came barreling through the door thinking it was bath time and she had to deal with getting him out. She then quickly showered, dressed, and raced down the dark cherry stairs to see if her mom made smoothies. She had! She put the cover on her travel container and grabbed a protein bar to hold her over until lunch.

As Paige was about to yell out to see where her mom was, her mother came into the living room with a laundry basket of clean clothes. Paige notified her that she was heading to Brooke's house to work on the pep rally signs and then heading to the local mall to go shopping for outfits.

Sloane thought about how grown-up Paige was for her age and felt that it was such a blessing. Her friends were always complaining about how immature their kids were.

Once Paige had given her mom a quick rundown of her plans for the rest of the day, Sloane asked, "Paige, have you forgotten about making the scarecrow?"

"Oh crap! I totally forgot that was today. Can we do it after the mall? Oh wait, I promised James that we would get together, ugh!"

"Why don't you invite him to dinner? It's been a while since he's been here, and he can help us."

"Okay, that works—you're a lifesaver. I'll let you know when we're finished at the mall. Love ya, bye." Paige grabbed her tote bag with the poster boards, supplies, smoothie, and snack, and ran out the door.

As Sloane stood in the doorway saying her goodbyes, her beautiful daughter was framed in sunlight. Sloane locked up after her. She was worried that Paige was being spread too thin. It wasn't like her to forget about making the family scarecrow for the yearly neighborhood contest. She thought that this must be normal for a 17-year-old, but it was still worrisome.

+++++++++++++

Paige sent James a text in the car and told him to go to her house at six o'clock, that she was with her friends, and that her mom was cooking dinner. She groaned when she thought about her busy day.

She arrived at Brooke's house the same time as Jenna did. As they were walking to the front door, they heard voices out in the backyard. They changed direction and headed around the massive white Victorian house, through the gate of the lofty picket fence, and over to the patio where the rest of the group was playing with the family's two Cocker Spaniels—Mulder, and Scully.

Once through the gate, they found Brooke and Amber throwing balls to the dogs in the large, shaded yard. At first glance, it seemed to Paige that the lawn's dimension of colors looked like an ombre. Where she stood, the grass was lush and dark green. It became less rich and a lighter green toward the middle and at the very end of the yard, there were mostly raised roots, discarded needlelike leaves, and bare earth due to the greed of the thirsty white pine trees that stood sentry at the end of the property.

Brooke was throwing a tennis ball to Scully, a beautiful white and cinnamon spaniel while Amber was throwing a blue rubber ball to Mulder, a mostly cinnamon spaniel. The pair of dogs were thoroughly enjoying the attention. When the girls saw Paige and Jenna, they threw the balls one last time and came over to the patio.

Brooke greeted them, "Hey, ladies!" Paige and Jenna set their supplies down to pet the dogs.

Brooke filled the dog's water bowls and then brought out the materials she had. "We can get started. Karol and Sade will come here right after their morning shift."

The four girls sat at the patio table and began to combine their supplies when they heard frantic yelling, "Jacob! Jacob! Where are you?"

Brooke said, "Oh, no. That's the little boy next door."

The group got up and followed Brooke to her neighbor's front yard.

Brooke's neighbor spoke frantically, "Brooke, did you see Jacob? I can't find him!"

"No. I've been outside for about 15 minutes now. I haven't seen him at all today, but the dogs were scratching at the fence the way they do when they know he's outside. We'll go around the neighborhood and look for him."

They separated—Jenna and Amber went to the left while Paige and Brooke went to the right. They walked around the block searching for the boy and calling to him but met back at the frantic mother's house empty-handed. She was beside herself with worry. A minute or two later, a police car arrived with its red and blue lights flashing and siren blaring.

Two people exited the police car. Paige noticed that the man was James's father, Carl. She had met Sergeant Lowden only a few times before; James and his father did not have the best relationship. He was a very intimidating-looking man. He was extremely tall and had massive muscles and a linebacker's shoulders. Her parents nicknamed him *Rambo*. His partner also exited the sedan. She was a beautiful black woman with distinct features that made her very attractive. She was small in stature but held herself in a way that exuded confidence.

"Hello, ma'am. I'm Sergeant Carl Lowden and this is my partner, Detective Arabella Luthor. You called about a missing child?"

The boy's mother nodded in agreement, her voice catching in her throat. "Yes. He's just four. I don't know how this happened."

Carl looked at Arabella signaling her to take over with a warmer touch. "Tell us everything from the beginning. When was the last time you saw him?"

"That's the weird thing. We were going out in the backyard so he could play in his sandbox. I opened the sliding door and placed some snacks on the picnic table. Then I remembered that I forgot his juice box so I went back in to get it. I was only gone a few seconds, honest! When I came back out, the gate was open and he was gone. I've checked everywhere for him."

"Okay. Do you have a recent photograph of him? "The woman showed Arabella a picture that she had on her phone. When his mother saw the photo, it made her begin to cry harder.

Arabella snapped a picture of Jacob and sent it to the station. "We'll get his picture out and send some patrols out in the area. First, we need to check the house and yard."

"Sure. I've already checked everywhere."

Arabella said, "You'd be surprised how many times children think it's just a game they're playing and hide really well." She entered the house while Carl went through the gate to look around in the yard. The girls stayed with Jacob's mother.

Arabella came out after a while and did not find him inside. Carl came around the corner and signaled the group to follow him. He brought them to the side of the detached garage. There was a light blue kiddie pool propped up against the side of it. He put his finger to his lips for everyone to be silent. They could hear a crunching sound. He slowly tilted the pool away from the wall and there was Jacob eating a bag of potato chips. The boy stopped mid-chew and looked up at the ogling crowd, eyes wide, and began to wail. Everyone breathed a sigh of relief while his mother scooped him up in her arms and smothered him with kisses. She apologized profusely.

Carl said, "Don't you worry, we're happy the little guy was here." They left and the girls went back to

Brooke's house.

Jenna announced, "Now that the excitement is over, we can get started."

Paige and the girls took the inured lead from Jenna who always assumed the role of the group's boss. She passed out the supplies and of course, Amber and Brooke switched with each other right away. Paige smirked when she saw *the look* from Jenna. Karol and Sade arrived just as they were getting started. They had finished their morning shifts at a popular coffee bistro in town. They were filled in about the missing boy as the pair sat down and began to help to create the signs. They were very happy with the posters they produced and decided it was time to call it quits and head to the mall for some shopping.

They arrived at the mall and headed over to their favorite shop situated across from the food court. The redolent mix of Asian, Italian, Mexican, and Indian foods were all competing for the foremost aroma and it was less than appealing.

They eventually selected some outfits and decided to swap some additional pieces with each other later.

FIVE
Paul

The room smelled of mildew. The musty stench permeated every element of his unclothed body. It was so strong that he couldn't breathe properly. He had no idea where he was or how he got there. He realized that his breathing trouble wasn't only because of the smell, but because his arms were stretched out tightly on both sides of him. It was constricting his lung capacity. He was on the floor in the Fowler's position with his back against the wall, and there were chains cuffed to his wrists, waist, and ankles. He tugged at them to no avail.

The bound man couldn't tell if it was day or night. There was no light but for a slit of gold streaming in on the floor across from him. He thought it must be from below a door. He could hear rushing sounds like cars zipping along on a highway.

Lightheaded and fighting to stay conscious, he tried to yell out but couldn't get enough oxygen to make a sound. He knew he would never leave this place alive; he just didn't know why. He thought to himself; my name is Paul Cooper; I am 32, and my life is over.

SIX
James

James was in his yard working on his grandfather's truck at the back of the house. He was underneath it when he felt and then heard that he had received a text message. He was trying to get out from under the vehicle when two of his black labs ran to him. They were very frisky and wanted to play.

He brushed them away and retrieved his phone. The message was from Paige:

> **At the mall w mean girls**
> **Meet my house @6**
> **Mom cooking**
> **Making scarecrow**

He was so happy to finally hear from her and couldn't wait for six o'clock to arrive. He still had time to fiddle with the truck, so he went back under and tried to focus. He thought it was funny that she still called them *mean girls* and continued to be their friend. He liked having that between them.

The term started when Paige tried to introduce James to her friends and have him be integrated among them. He was met with a frosty greeting and he could tell that they had already made up their minds that he would not fit in with them and was not welcome. Paige told him not to worry about them, that they each had a role to play within the group—just like the *mean girls*. She promised him they would come around.

When he finished with the truck, he went into the house and showered. He put on some clean clothes and went into the kitchen to make sure his mom had something to eat when she came home. He left her a note telling her where he would be and set out for the Vales' house.

SEVEN
Lydia

Lydia came home from work to an empty house that was never really empty. There were always four happy tails and soft wet noses to greet all who entered their humble abode. She loved the fact that James had importance in his life. His love of animals was so great, that she knew it gave him purpose. He had always taken in hurt and homeless creatures big and small.

Feeling the energy draining from her body, she couldn't decide if she had ever been more hungry or tired and decided—she hadn't. She didn't know how much longer she could keep up this pace; long, late hours at the casino and still working at the elementary school five days a week was taking a toll.

She went into the kitchen to see what she could rummage together to eat before she got some shut-eye. There was a note from James. He told her about her dinner and that he would be out for the night with friends. She was glad that she did not have to worry about what she would eat. He tried so hard to take care of her. She felt a pang of guilt because he had to be on his own so much.

Friends? She knew he meant Paige. Lydia was still

not sure if having her in his life was good for him, but she knew that he didn't have many other friends and the Vale family were pretty decent to him. She used to think less of them but felt better about the family now. It seemed to her that he didn't see Paige as often lately which could explain his recently withdrawn demeanor. She put the food he left for her in the oven and took a quick shower. After she ate, she climbed into bed, adjusted her pillows, and fell into a deep, all-encompassing sleep.

EIGHT
Paul

Paul Cooper was shivering and hungry. He needed to void his bladder and his muscles were spasming. He didn't know how long he'd been chained up. He felt as though he was hungover. His breathing was becoming more and more labored. He felt as if the mass and energy that was keeping him alive were slowly being drained into a deep, dark void. He thought it would be good to just acquiesce and let the void swallow him whole. Just as he decided to let go, he heard a noise.

The room was humid and there was a suggestion of light coming in from outside now. There were still intermittent rushing sounds. He also heard night birds sing in the distance while the crickets joined their tune in harmony.

He looked up and before him stood a man. His entire tall, bulky frame—from head to toe, was covered in clothing in one form or another. He had on what seemed to be fishing waders that came up to his waist and were suspended and fastened over his shoulders. He wore a long-sleeve shirt with a high collar underneath this and he had a motorcycle helmet on that covered his whole face.

The speechless man carried in a sack and put it on the floor. With his gloved hands, he unzipped the sack and withdrew a large black cloth. He laid it out on the floor beside Paul. He unwrapped a satchel that contained several different kinds of nefarious-looking knives, tools, and other implements, removing each one and placing them on the cloth.

Paul was so confused. He had no idea what had happened before he ended up in this place. His memory was very sketchy and he could only put together bits and pieces of what had happened. He certainly didn't know who was there with him or why he was unleashing this terror.

The fog-like hangover feeling came and went and he was getting fragments of memories—or what he thought were memories. There was a vision of a woman dressed in black with very pale skin and blond hair floating as she descended a staircase. He racked his brain to remember who she was but realized it was only from a movie he had recently watched. He felt himself again succumbing to darkness and saw bright lights and heard music and bells and other loud noises behind his sealed eyes. Again, he couldn't tell if they meant anything of importance or if they were even real. Then he saw a woman and opened his eyes with a start.

His eyes focused on the man before him, which startled him back to the present. The shock and adrenaline of the situation made things much clearer. He remembered that he was at Ocean State Casino in Lincoln, seeing the Beaver Brown Band with his brother on Friday night. After the show, they decided to try their hand at blackjack, and he was on a roll. He saw faces all around him—people from all over stopped what they were doing and stood around the table to cheer him on. One woman, in particular, caught his eye. She had flawless creamy skin and both her hair and eyes were as dark and shimmering as obsidian. She was far from beautiful but had a reckless abandon that was contagious. Paul remembered that he thought she was his lucky charm. He remembered a name—Rosa Marie.

He recalled that he won several hands but felt that continuing to tempt his fate was a bit too risky; he decided he was ready to call it a night while he was still ahead. The group members supporting him voiced their upset. They dispersed and his lucky charm stayed behind. He searched for his brother. Someone told him that he had left the table earlier.

More noise and unfocused images flooded his mind and he saw his brother with an unfamiliar woman—a leggy blonde.

"Randy, I'm heading out; can you get a ride home?"

The blonde looked up and told him that his brother would be fine. Randy winked and said goodnight to Paul.

Paul went to the exit and met Rosa Marie. He remembered that they drove to his place and opened a bottle of wine. The sex with Rosa Marie was wild and spontaneous and he remembered feeling free. But that was it. That was the last of his memories until waking up in chains.

The strangest thought went through Paul's mind—he was happy that the last memory he had was that of him having sex. He had always heard that right before the end your life would flash before your eyes. He assumed that would mean childhood through the present; seeing his parents and family. He almost felt guilty. He thought about how irrational that was because it did strike him as being funny.

+++++++++++++

Consciousness returning once again, Paul took in his surroundings. He knew that he was weak and probably working off the remnants of being drugged, but even with all that, what he was seeing made little sense. The room was dark, but there was enough light streaming in that he could finally see. The room looked as if it had been abandoned for quite some time. There was evidence of people being there recently; most likely partying teenagers or the homeless trying to get some shelter. He could smell the sulfur from long-ago candles mixed with the stale smell of mildew. It was a small area, but it seemed to be a square room with a round section protruding outward. In the dim light, he thought his eyes were playing tricks on him, but he realized that was exactly what he was seeing.

Before he could register his surroundings, the hulking figure approached Paul with a very sharp-looking implement in hand. Wordless, the man set to work liberating Paul from his manhood. Once he held the dislodged member in his hand, he sliced the inner thigh on Paul's left leg. He still uttered no words. Paul wondered if there was some mistake; if the man mistook him for someone else. The pain was immense. He couldn't imagine why this was happening to him.

He saw shards of fire red, yellow, and orange behind his eyes and could no longer keep them open. Darkness enveloped him and he wanted nothing more than to let it take over; then it did. His eyes opened once more, and the looming man was gone. Paul was terrified to look down, mostly because he could no longer feel anything. He heard a whooshing noise that resembled the rolling ocean tide. He realized that it was his pulse he was hearing. It was slowing down. He had become very light-headed and at once, he realized that he needed someone to find him soon. He could smell the metallic scent of blood and knew there must already be a copious amount that evacuated his body.

He wished that the man could have ripped out his memory along with the humiliating dissection of his member. The memory brought back the agony he had faced. He was grateful that the tool used to do the deed was as sharp as it was. The job took all of four swift slices. He began to shake, either due to the memory or to the fact that he was in shock. He was very cold and knew that he would lose consciousness. This elicited some atavistic fears within him that he didn't know existed; especially when he thought that the man may return for more carnage.

NINE
James

James rang the doorbell promptly at six o'clock. Timothy answered the door with an exuberant tackle to James's legs. The two began having a wrestling match that announced to the rest of the family that James had arrived. The next one to greet him was Jasper. When Paige entered the foyer, James was crouched down, playing with the dog and her brother.

"I swear sometimes I think that dog likes you more than anyone in the family. You really are the original *dog whisperer*."

"Hi, Paige." As he was continuing to give Jasper's belly a vigorous rubbing, he added, "You just have to know what they like. I pay attention more, I think. Dr. Hogan says that some people can understand animals more than others and that he thinks I'm one of them."

"I have to agree."

Remembering what he had read in the hideout, he asked, "Did you always think that, Paige?"

"For as long as I can remember. How are things going at the clinic?"

"Great. I'm getting to do more and more. I started

out just feeding and bathing the animals, now he is letting me watch the examinations, which is cool."

Tim yelled, "I'm bored!" and ran into the living room.

"I'm going to see if my mom needs any help. Head into the kitchen when *Cujo* releases the trance he has over you."

James found Paige and Sloane busy getting everything ready. He quickly began helping Paige set the table. He really liked the style of the interior of the house. He felt that it was homey, clean, and modern all at the same time. They had an island in the middle of the kitchen that had high-backed stools around it and the top was a cool-looking swirl of gray, black, white, and maroon. The whole kitchen was set in that color scheme. He knew that Sloane decorated everything herself. She used something called alcohol inks to do a lot of the tilework and the artwork herself. He wondered if many other people decorated like that.

"Thank you, James, but we didn't invite you here to work. Why don't you get a soda and watch some television? Mitch should be home any minute and we'll eat right away. I know everyone is excited to begin making this year's scarecrow."

Timothy had been sitting at the island coloring Halloween decorations and perked up when he heard that. "Can we make the scarecrow before we eat, Mom?"

"Tim, you know the rules. Dinner, scarecrow, bath, and bed. And by dinner, I mean you eat it all and wait for everyone to finish cleaning before we begin; no whining allowed. We're eating extra early tonight; that's the best I can do."

"But, Mom!"

"Excuse me, young man; did you just call me *Butt Mom*?" She laughed at herself and rumpled his light brown tuft atop his head. He gave her the obligatory eye roll at her lame excuse of a joke and went back to his crafts.

During dinner, Sloane checked her list, oh, how she loved lists, and announced that it was Mitch's turn to name the scarecrow this year. He suggested that since James had taken part in a few of the creations, he should have a turn. He vehemently declined and Mitch didn't push the issue. James said that he enjoyed helping to pick out his clothes, and that was enough. Following the routine that she began since the first neighborhood contest, Sloane had kept Mitch's damaged or unwanted clothing that would work for a scarecrow. That way, he would be sure to look unique each year.

After dinner, they made their way out to the garage where the boxes were brought forth for the annual tradition. The garage displayed a vast array of every tool imaginable. Everything had a place and there was a place for everything. There were massive tool chests and machines that James had never seen before. Even with all the equipment and three cars, there was plenty of room for workout equipment to the left of the garage and an area for Paige to practice her cheerleading and dance moves. Sloane had her craft area set up at the other end. It was alongside the family's stored beach umbrellas, ski equipment, and patio pillows. The thing that struck James the most was how clean it was. He had been in many garages but nothing that looked like this. This family was truly one of a kind.

Everyone contributed ideas and assisted in one way or another, and finally, Bond Vader was created.

"Bond Vader, really, Mitch?" Sloane raised her eyebrows along with the rest of the family.

Paige turned to James and asked if he could guess which movies her father watched the night before. They laughed and started to clean up the remaining supplies.

The scarecrow was transported to the front of the house and placed in the holiday scene that was constructed over the past few weeks. It included a plethora of mums, corn stalks, pumpkins, and gourds along with bales of hay arranged in a spectacular fall scene. Everything was intertwined with white, yellow, and orange festive lights. Bond Vader was the finishing touch to a display that was sure to win again this year. The scarecrow sat in a chair with his red plaid flannel shirt beneath a tuxedo jacket and crossed legs clad in denim. Mitch had even placed a black welder shield over his face and beneath his straw hat, but the piece de resistance was a martini glass secured to his hand; olive and all.

"Very nice, Mitch. I'll just make some minor adjustments later, so he fits the theme better."

Mitch grabbed at his heart and gave an overly

theatrical performance that feigned being hurt while winking at the kids.

Paige looked at James and then at her parents. "We're going out. I'll be back early."

"Early it is. It is a school night. I need to go to the hardware store. Do you want a ride anywhere?"

"No, Dad. Thanks though."

The two left and headed to their hideout. They walked along in a comfortable silence listening to the rustle of the leaves and the chatter of the nocturnal critters that inhabited the woods surrounding the reservoir. Paige thought about how she loved the smell of the dead foliage mixing with the damp evening air. At the same time, James was thinking that he loved the way the buttery light filtering in through the thinning trees made his friend glow. They made good time and entered their shelter happy to find nothing disturbed.

"James, we need to talk. I know we haven't been able to hang out as much lately. You have to understand, I am trying to make sure I do all I can so that I get into a good college. I am trying to be a well-rounded student and that means getting involved in extra-curricular activities. You need to know that I also have different friends, James. It doesn't mean we aren't friends just that we can't hang out as much."

She tried to read his eyes through the curtain of fringed bangs that covered them. He was silent for what seemed too long, and his expression gave nothing away.

"I get it, Paige. I know you have other friends you

like to spend time with and lots of stuff to do. I just like to make sure you're all right and to hang out when you're free."

"I promise I'll try to make more time for you, but you can't text and call me day in and day out. We need to come up with a solution that will work for both of us. Unless it is something urgent, only one text a day. I promise I'll do my best to return it as soon as I can. How does that sound?"

"I can live with that. I know you've always wanted to plan for your future, but do you think the things you do now will matter when you go to college? It's a year away."

"James, admissions officers look back at freshman grades all the way through your senior year. That's why I've always tried to get you to be serious about your grades. If you are serious about veterinary school, you will need to buckle down."

"I know Paige. I have been doing better. My counselor, Ms. Zunen, said that she's going to help me apply for some scholarships soon. Working with animals is the only thing I want to do other than work on my truck. I really hope it happens. I'm volunteering at the vet clinic. I have been doing everything you told me, and my grades are getting better. Do you think if they see I'm improving, they won't pay attention to my grades when I was younger?"

Paige thought back to when the pair were younger. She had always been religious about her studies. She was very organized and enjoyed going above and beyond when it came to her schoolwork. She was always happiest when her parents and teachers were pleased with her. She did not like it when anyone was unhappy with her for any reason. James, on the other hand, would eventually do his homework, received average grades, and he was always happy with that. They once received a very similar assignment in history class. They each had to write about a historical figure whom they would want to meet. It had to be between three to five pages. Paige turned in a six-page report, and James submitted one that was barely three pages. He always gave minimal effort to anything unless it involved animals or his truck. Come to think of it unless it involved her also.

She was very happy to hear him speak so passionately about his future. Seeing James looking intent on her answering him, she said, "I'm sure it will all work out. It's never too late." She hoped that was true and that his newfound ambition would allow him to succeed.

Paige added, "Listen, the pep rally is in two weeks. Jenna is going to have everyone over after. Her mom will be away, and her sister will be working. Why don't you come by so we can all hang out together? It's not a big party, probably just a dozen of us getting together."

She knew that James didn't like big parties and liked her friends even less, but she hated being in the middle of both sides. She felt like she was always deflecting for the other side depending on whom she was with at the time. It could be exhausting and very upsetting at times. She thought this could be a step in bridging the gap between both sides.

"I don't know, Paige. You know they don't like me, and the feeling is mutual. We have absolutely nothing in common. I was planning on going to the rally and game—it's with our rival after all. I hope we cream Woonsocket." Seeing the hurt look on Paige's face was more than he could stand. Sighing, he told her that he would think about it. He thought he could use this opportunity to make her happy while keeping an eye on that group. He didn't want her there without him.

They decided that it was time to get home so they left their secret fortress. Walking back through the woods, Paige was glad James was with her. The night turned overcast with numerous gray storm clouds looming above threatening to wring themselves out and release their contents at any time. Not a star was to be seen in the sky. It was darker than usual and having James with her made her feel better. As they walked among the dead leaves protesting under each footfall, they heard the scurrying of woodland creatures who were not happy to have their slumber disturbed.

The pair arrived at her house and were happy to see that Bond Vader still donned his tux jacket, welding shield, and cocktail. James laughed. "I'm glad your mom didn't make him an ordinary scarecrow yet, I meant to take a picture." He pulled out his phone and snapped a photo of the porch scene. "I thought about it, and I'll go to Jenna's after the game."

Paige smiled and kissed him on the cheek. "I'm glad. You'll see. It'll be fun. I'll make sure everyone is on their best behavior. See you in school tomorrow."

James got on his bike and headed home.

++++++++++++

On his way back home, James received a text. It was from his father. He wanted to meet for pizza after school tomorrow. James still had some very conflicting feelings regarding his dad. Ever since he left, it was hard to feel the same. The unfaithfulness always seemed to come to the center of all his negative emotions. His dad leaving caused a storm of bitterness and betrayal that he had never outgrown. It was especially hard to accept his leaving because he thought that they were all so happy together. Carl was a prominent figure in the community and everyone looked up to him. He loved his father very much, then all at once, he was gone, and there were only memories that turned into the occasional holiday and sparse plan to get together every now and then.

His mom always made it seem like it didn't bother her, but he knew better. He would hear her crying at times. He would hear her talking on the phone when she thought he wasn't listening. She would talk about how hard her life had become. Having to work two jobs was aging her before her time. She would say how she detested the advances from drunken men at the casino, slurring their vulgar innuendos with their alcohol-laden breath, and pawing at her with their liver-damaged hands. He was grateful that she had family and friends to help her through this dark time in her life. He wanted to help more, but he could never find the right words. He knew she was strong and would overcome the shock of abandonment, but James vowed to do everything in his power to help her every way he could, and he has. He had overheard her say that it was a double betrayal because he left her for a friend. Now, their friendship was no more.

The worst part was how it changed both of his parents. While his father was absent, the times he came around were riddled with strained conversations and neither parent being comfortable around the other. Carl always tried too hard, not finding the level spot in the middle.

His mother was always the bright light in any situation. People always gravitated to her. She had a kind face that spoke volumes with every expression it showed. When she worked at the school, all the students ran to her as a safe haven from whatever uncomfortable situation might be unfolding. She was usually the life of any party. She loved to sing and hummed without even realizing it. There was an abundance of joy in being in her presence.

Now, she was a mere shell of herself. She never saw friends. She never went to parties. Her family would make sure that she at least made it to holiday events and took part in special traditions. It just wasn't the same. The spark left her eyes and her smile never reached its fullness. James blamed it all on his father.

James responded to his father and said that he would meet him. They decided on meeting at A Slice of Sicily pizza place. It was close to where James would be once he left Dr. Doolittle Pet Care. As James entered his house, he saw that his mom was home and already in bed.

TEN

James

Sitting and eating pizza with his dad, James was surprisingly comfortable. The conversation flowed freely and he even lost track of time. He was about to ask his father if he was going to be on duty at the pep rally when Carl's cellphone vibrated. He told James that it was the station and that he had to take it. He went outside to the front of the restaurant to take the call and when he came in, he was visibly shaken.

"I'm sorry, James, but they found a body in North Smithfield and they think it's someone I know. Can you call someone for a ride?"

"Sure, Dad. Who is it?"

"I'll know more later. I'll call you tomorrow." Carl placed money on the table and exited the restaurant, his police car speeding out of the lot with the light bar flashing and sirens blazing.

James actually felt saddened by his father's sudden departure, which was a new experience for him. He was conflicted by this feeling. He felt he was betraying his mother every time he met with his father. She claimed that she didn't mind, but he felt the conflict behind her words. This only compounded his feeling of guilt for enjoying pizza with his father.

Thinking of how he should spend the rest of his evening, he decided to go to the hideout because it was the first time he wasn't expected anywhere in a long time. He thought he might try his luck and text Paige to meet him.

Hey, busy?
Heading to the place

He checked his phone the whole way there waiting for her reply. He entered the spot and began his descent. He finally felt the welcome buzz of his phone. He checked the display, which read:

Can't, sorry

He wasn't all that surprised that she couldn't meet him. With that out of the way, he looked around to see how he would spend his time. He had been itching to look through the other journals but was feeling guilty about it. As he looked through his boxes yet again, he quickly grew bored and frustrated.

He went to Paige's box and rifled through her journals once more. He picked up the one titled *"LOVE."* He suddenly felt trapped in the small space and needed some air. He knew it was a risk, but he left the hideout with her journal in hand. Riding home helped to quell his feeling of frustration, but living in this Podunk town, he constantly had to fight that feeling. He repeatedly attempted to ease his mind.

When James got home, he took the dogs out and played with them a bit. After feeding them and giving them fresh water, he went to his room to read the journal.

James looked around his cramped room. He hadn't taken stock of everything held within the four walls in some time. Almost everything he saw brought him back to a time when he was young. The room didn't look juvenile, per se, but it certainly did not reflect the adolescent he had become. He was much too big for the twin-size bed. The small bureau was strewn with fishing lures and things that he couldn't even remember accumulating.

The deep browns and blues that the room was decorated in made the small room look even smaller. His light brown pile carpeting was stained in spots and had certainly seen better days. The posters that covered the ancient faux wood paneling were of bands from his childhood. While he still enjoyed listening to them occasionally, they should be removed or updated for sure. He made a mental note to get to it at some point.

James sat on his bed and held the journal as if it were sacred. He tried to touch it as little as possible. He flipped the pages of the journal and read the very personal words that were printed upon them, not meant for his meddling eyes. Paige had listed all of the important people in her life. She added how and why she loved them. Conspicuously missing was his name. James started again from the beginning and made sure that none of the pages were stuck, re-reading them, but again, he was not there. A sound escaped his mouth that he never heard before. It was a noise somewhere between a moan and a howl; it was inhuman. James felt a strange lightheaded sensation and his muscles tensed. He couldn't breathe and had to struggle for air. How could this be? Why was his name not among the pages of those whom she loved? He grabbed his guitar and began to try to suppress the *Red* that had not reared its ugly head in some time. Just as he was plucking away at the strings of his guitar, the strings of sanity within him were threatening to snap.

ELEVEN
Rosa Marie

Rosa Marie Hoover walked into the Searchlight Bar at the Ocean State Casino once again. She sat at a vacant chair and ordered a cocktail. After a while, another woman came in and sat beside her. They started talking and Rosa Marie quickly learned that her new friend was extremely voluble. Rosa Marie did not want to listen to her incessant ranting any longer. She suggested they try their luck out on the floor. The pair left the bar to play some slots. They played and consumed more and more libations until they spent all the money they brought; they became happily inebriated and decided to go to the woman's apartment to continue the party.

TWELVE
Paige

Paige was at Amber's house that afternoon with the rest of the *mean girls* and some other friends. They all brought over clothes to share and decide what to wear to the pep rally. They swapped outfits so frequently, that no one could remember what items belonged to any of them. She felt bad for Amber because she had just had an argument with her mother in front of everyone. Paige never fought with her mother. When she told that to some of her friends, they made her feel like an outcast. She already felt different and set apart from her peers. Paige thought back to a time during music class when Brooke was in tears over a blowout with her parents. Paige made up a story about a terrible fight over her curfew just to fit in. It was then that she realized that she had many friends but didn't exactly feel connected to anyone in particular. She was one of the rare few who was accepted in almost every clique. For a long time, Paige believed that if someone asked her who her best friend was, she would unequivocally say that she didn't have just one. She had lots of people that she could confide in and reach out to when she needed, but there wasn't one special friend.

She often wondered what her relationship was with James. They've been friends forever, but the older they got, the more different their relationship became. She had always considered him a project; someone she was trying to take care of and transform. He was so broken when they met.

When Paige met James at the music shop, his parents had just broken up. He was very timid and withdrawn. He needed a lot of coaxing to speak to anyone. The other students just ignored him after a while, but Paige persisted. She wasn't sure if she wore him down, or if he finally started to trust her, but he eventually began to come around. She remembered overhearing a conversation between his mother and the music instructor where she said she thought music could help him channel his feelings. Paige inwardly agreed and thought that there weren't many problems that a good song couldn't help to mend.

She made it her mission to help him reach his potential. He was a friend but so much more—and not more—at the same time. Their relationship was always changing. He had become so needy lately; it was driving a wedge between them. It was with that thought that she realized that her social life was bisected between James and everyone else.

Having a skirt thrown at her head, Paige snapped back to reality and joined in with the outfit search. She was trying to find a way to bring up the fact that she told James to go to the rally and to the party afterward that would not result in an acerbic remark from someone. Knowing no other way, she shouted out, "Hey, everyone. I know you're all going to give me a bunch of crap for this, but I need to tell you something. I told James that he should come to the pep rally and then to the party with us." Paige suddenly knew what the phrase *the silence was deafening* meant. No one said a word for what seemed like forever.

Karol and Sade both yelled, "No!"

"It's over and done. I won't uninvite him, so you all need to spread the word that no one is to mess with him. It'll be fine. You won't even know he's there." That announcement over, she contemplated that it wasn't as bad as she thought until she caught the menacing glare coming from Jenna, Brooke, and Amber, and the tiny hairs on the back of her neck stood at attention.

"Look, everyone. You don't know him. And I haven't told you everything about him. When he was younger, he would have these *blackouts* and would be like a zombie for hours, sometimes days. Nothing could get him out of them; no one could bring him back. He was taken to doctor after doctor and they couldn't figure out how to help him."

Now, capturing their attention, she continued, "He loved music so his family sent him for guitar lessons to try and find an outlet for him. That's where we met. Once we met, I learned that he was being bullied. After those instances, and when he would think of his dad leaving, he would get like that. The difference was, I could bring him back. He would listen to my voice and snap out of it."

The girls now looked at Paige with softness in their eyes.

"I know he's different, but I'm all he's got." After that, her friends agreed that they would be on their best behavior.

THIRTEEN
Lucas

Lucas Hoover's large, rough hands trembled as he attempted to use the key to unlock one of the doors on his nightly rounds. His legs felt as if they would no longer be able to support his six-foot, lanky frame. He couldn't get the image of the naked man out of his mind. He was determined to stay clear of any local news reports on television, on the radio, or in the papers. He didn't want to know the man's name or any details about him.

He wondered how this could be his life. He was willing to do anything for her. What started out as a harmless way to keep the spark alive in their marriage, had turned into something sick and twisted.

He thought that he should call out sick from his security detail at Aztec Corporate Park, but then realized that staying home all night with his thoughts would be worse. He also wanted to stay home to keep an eye on Rosa Marie. He knew he couldn't babysit her twenty-four-seven, and she promised that it wouldn't happen again, so he just needed to keep busy.

He thought, how did I get here? How did it come

to this? Lucas thought back to the first time. It was a hot summer evening and he was at work. He felt *off* most of the day, but after making it through half of his shift, he was feeling much worse. He clocked out and headed for home. When he arrived, he found Rosa Marie with another man. She flew into a rage. She hopped out of bed and over to Lucas with her fists flailing, connecting at several points all over his body. He was confused, frightened, angry, and couldn't process what was happening.

She screamed at him to be a man. Told him to protect what was his. He was faced with the reality that she was turning this on him.

"Rosa Marie? Are you crazy? I caught you screwing someone. Now I'm supposed to defend your honor? You don't have any!"

She slapped him across the face and made his head spin to the right so far, he felt something snap inside his neck resolving in a burning, vibrating sensation. It reverberated into his ears and sounded like a snapped piano wire. He saw stars and then felt only anger. No matter how angry he became, he couldn't strike her. He looked to the other side of the bed and saw the man getting dressed. He ran to him and began striking him. It didn't take long for the man to evade Lucas and leave the premises.

Rosa Marie wept and threw herself at Lucas. She thanked him for coming to her rescue and for taking charge. She furnished him with loving accolades for the next few days.

That was the first of many. Each time it would

happen, he would blame himself more. Rosa Marie would chastise him more every time. Lucas didn't know how, but at some point, it became this dangerous tête-à-tête. He thought that going along with her idea to join a swinger's group would quell her unnatural sexual desires and the need to sleep with other men and women. Nevertheless, the more parties they went to, the more she needed.

Now, the most important thing was to replay the night over and over in his mind to make sure he didn't mess up; that there were no traces left behind that would connect either one of them to that apartment. From the time he received the phone call from his inebriated wife until he left the man to bleed to death, every step was relived again and again.

Once he heard his beloved's voice full of fear and remorse that night, he set a plan into motion. He left work abruptly and headed toward the address she gave him just a town away. He parked a block away and took out the large folding canvas cart he had seen the groundskeeper use at the industrial park and then grabbed other supplies that he thought would be useful.

Rosa Marie left the back door open and then locked herself in the bathroom of the man's apartment to wait for Lucas as planned. She had given the man a cocktail of her Gabapentin and Xanax mixed into his drink. He was out cold by the time Lucas arrived. Once he was there, she was able to open the bathroom door and then collapsed in his arms.

He quickly set his plan into motion. He covered his shoes with fishing waders, put on a turtleneck top, a helmet, and gloves, and then went into the apartment and quickly carried Rosa Marie outside and placed her in the cart. He wheeled her to the car and then went back to retrieve the man. When he got to the car this time, he opened the trunk and took out his supplies, folded the cart, and put it and the unconscious man inside the trunk.

He walked back into the apartment with his supplies and quickly removed any trace of Rosa Marie having been there. He scrubbed surfaces with bleach, removed the bedsheets, and took them with him. He used Paul's vacuum and then removed the bag and took that too. When he was certain he had thought of everything, he went back to the car where she was sleeping like the dead. They drove home. He carried her inside and then drove around for quite a while trying to think of the best place to carry out the rest of his plan.

Lucas settled on an abandoned building that was hiding in plain sight. It was small; there was plenty of room to carry out the necessary work that he needed to begin. He found the back entrance and easily forced his way in. He brought in the chains and supplies and prepped the area. He put the man back into the cart and brought him into the building, stripped him of his clothing, and began to chain his outstretched arms and waist to some of the exposed pipes that were sturdy. He also chained his ankles together. He was beginning to make sounds so Lucas knew he didn't have much time to go back out and retrieve the bag of tools he had brought.

When he came back in, the man was awake. Lucas had hoped that he wouldn't be but it was just as well. He deserved to be alert for what was to come. He deserved to feel the pain and suffering that his poor Rosa Marie felt when he took advantage of her good nature.

When the deed was done, Lucas went out to his car and cleaned the sharp knife with some bleach, and then put the knife back in the satchel. The groundskeeper would never know that anything nefarious happened with his things.

Lucas rushed back to work before anyone knew of his evil deed. He was sure to put everything back exactly where he found them. Once everything was back where it belonged, Lucas was able to make one last round in the industrial park before his replacement arrived for the next shift. Replaying this over in his mind, he felt sure that there was nothing that was overlooked.

Lucas was utterly exhausted—both mentally and physically, and he felt as though he needed a two-day long shower. On his drive home, he passed the Imperial Panda, which was the place where he had first met Rosa Marie. They were each there with some friends on a night when they had karaoke. They had both wanted to sing the same duet but did not have a partner so the DJ paired them up. He felt the spark immediately. They sang well together. It felt so natural. He could sense that something was happening. Once the song was over, they hugged and went to their respective tables. He could tell mutual sparks were flying when all of her friends were giggling and looking his way. His friends were taunting him and trying to bait him into going over and talking to her. After one more shot, that sounded like a very good idea. The rest was history.

FOURTEEN
Carl

Carl and Arabella arrived at the Big Milk Can on Rt. 146 in North Smithfield. It had been a great ice cream shop in its heyday. Its claim to fame was that the restaurant was actually shaped as a thirty-foot-tall milk can. Now, it was an abandoned building that had seen better days. He still had no details and couldn't understand why he was being summoned there. It was not his jurisdiction, but his friend from the academy had called him. She knew of his relationship to the victim. All he knew was that a childhood buddy and golf partner, Paul Cooper, had turned up dead and that there was no question that it was foul play.

Lieutenant Natalie Frazee met them at the scene. "Let them through," she ordered the patrol officers guarding the crime scene.

"Thanks for the call, Nat. What do you know?" He attempted to go into the peculiar round building, but she stopped him with her hand to his shoulder. The quizzical look he gave her made his large brow furrow and his light brown eyes begged for answers.

"Look, Carl, I called you because I knew you had

a relationship with Paul and he's from your town.

You need to know that you've been invited to be a part of this investigation, but this is my case. Also, you really need to prepare yourself for what you're about to see. It won't be easy." She looked at Arabella and it was clear that he would need her support once he saw the scene.

When they entered, they came upon a display Carl could never be prepared for. On the ride over, he had imagined Paul being shot or stabbed in some kind of robbery gone wrong. This—this was like nothing he'd ever seen before.

There was Paul. Shackled and chained in a pool of blood and waste. He had never witnessed anything like this. The small towns in the area mostly took care of minor law infractions and petty misdemeanors. He stepped a little closer and saw where all the blood from the body emanated. Paul's penis was severed from his body. He was bruised and had numerous lacerations, but an initial evaluation found that Paul had bled to death. Carl knew that it was a horrible way to go and became nauseated.

"So, he bled out? I didn't think that castration could cause death. Horrible way to go. Poor bastard." It was hard for Carl to finish the sentence without a tremble in his voice.

Arabella nervously stated, "Castration is the removal of the testes. It's a common mistake. He did bleed out but not from the dissection. The killer also cut the femoral artery in his thigh—see, right there.

He knew what he was doing."

Carl looked at Natalie and asked, "Do you think he is a medical professional?"

"Not necessarily. He may not have been sure if the dismemberment would kill him, so he may have cut the artery for insurance. Lots of people know where the arteries are."

She could see that it was a lot for him to take in. "We need to get out of here and let the team finish. I'm going to the family to break the news. I thought you'd want to come."

Carl sighed. There was so much to process. He had just had a beer with Paul at their favorite hangout in town about two weeks ago. Everything seemed to be going great for him. He was happy that the summer was over because he could relax a bit. Paul and his brother, Randy, owned their own landscaping business and were always swamped in the spring and summer. Fall was busy but manageable. They made plans to try and get some golfing in soon.

"Sure, I'll go along. We can start with his brother. Let me send him a text to see where he is. He's a landscaper. He could be anywhere."

"Shouldn't we start with the parents?"

"They moved to Florida a while back. Randy will probably want to break the news to them. We should let him decide."

Natalie gave him a nod and climbed into the patrol car. Carl and Arabella got in and they drove to the address that Randy sent him. His mind was reeling. He couldn't believe this was happening. He was not looking forward to the conversation he was about to have.

When they arrived, Randy was sitting on the back of his truck bed having a drink of water in front of a beautifully manicured lawn lined with topiary-shaped hedges. A flowering bush that displayed large hibiscus-like blooms in varying colors separated each hedge. They were in the middle of a very affluent neighborhood in Lincoln.

Carl approached the truck and Randy got down with an inquisitive look that quickly faded into fear.

"Carl, what the hell's going on? Why are you looking for me in the middle of the day?"

When Randy spotted Natalie and Arabella getting out of the car, he sat back down.

"Randy, this is Lieutenant Nataly Frazee from the North Smithfield police department, and my partner, Arabella Luthor. I went through the academy with Natalie and she met Paul a few times. She called me because she knew we were friends. Look, I don't know how to say this, but it's Paul. He's been killed, Randy." Carl's voice was shaky and he had to lean on the truck for support.

Watching Carl deliver this news to his friend, made the tall musclebound man seem to shrink before their eyes.

Randy looked stunned. He was visibly shaken and was trying to find the right words to formulate all of the questions swimming around in his mind. He sat quietly with his thoughts for a minute or two, feeling the mild breeze on his face and watching the rustling of the fallen leaves with each wind gust. He realized that his brother would never feel that again.

"I don't understand. That can't be. I was just with him on Friday." His mind was reeling. He needed a monotonous distraction. He saw a large black cat across the street and focused on it. The cat was perched on top of an overturned basket spilling an array of different colored mums.

Natalie took over the line of questioning. "Today is Monday. You didn't hear from your brother all weekend?"

"No. I didn't. We were at the casino and we both got lucky. I just figured he was tucked away somewhere with her, too busy to call. His crew said he was MIA today so I called but got no answer. I left him a message, but . . . I can't believe this."

He looked from Carl to Natalie; neither could look at him directly. "You said killed. Was it a car accident? Was he drunk? What happened?"

Natalie stepped close to Randy and began to tell him what she knew.

Randy just shook his head. "I don't understand. He was found in the old round ice cream place? The one on 146 that looks like a milk can? Murdered? It doesn't make any sense. Who would do this? Why?" He put his hands over his face and dropped his head.

Lieutenant Frazee asked, "Randy, did your brother have anyone in his life who had any animosity toward him? Did he mention any arguments recently? Anything you can think of at all?"

"No, not at all. I think the last time I can remember him arguing with anyone was in high school. That was years ago. Everyone loves him. Oh, man. I can't believe this. What the hell am I going to tell my parents?"

Carl was finally able to speak again. "I can contact them for you if you want."

"No, thanks though. I need to be the one. They are going to want details. Was it a robbery? Why was he there? Was he shot?"

Carl started to answer him, but Natalie quickly jumped in, "It is still an active investigation. As soon as we know the details, we will let you know."

"Carl, come on. What happened? Is he still there? I want to see him."

"Believe me; you don't want to see him like this. I can say that my gut instinct is that this wasn't a robbery. It was deliberate. Either he was in the wrong place at the wrong time or he was sought out. He bled to death from a stab wound. That's all we know for sure."

Natalie shot Carl a look of contempt. "Randy, you said that Friday you were at the casino. In Lincoln?"

"Yes. Ocean State."

"How long were you there?"

"I don't know, about three or four hours, I think."

"You also said that you both "got lucky." Please elaborate."

"We both left with, dates. I left with a blonde and he left with a brunette. He didn't tell me her name."

FIFTEEN
James

When James arrived back home, he once again set to work making some food for his mom. He truly worried about the long hours she kept and knew that she did it for him. He liked it better when his mother only worked at the elementary school. He remembered when it was the three of them; some days during lunch, his father would stop in and eat with his mom and him. Those days were easy and effortless. He had a family that he could go home to and they all could count on one another. The times before the *Red* were the best times in his life.

With his mother now working two jobs and very long hours, he was often alone. Alone with his thoughts and fears. He did spend much of his time with Paige and her family, but even that felt like it was coming to an end. She had her own life now. That was evident. There was no place for him anywhere. He was working on a way to get her back and to have things go back to the way they were. He couldn't fix his family, but he was sure that he could fix this.

He turned on the television for some background noise. He learned early on that listening to the TV or radio helped him feel less alone. His attention was sparked when he heard, "This just in. Police have said that the gruesome discovery of a deceased Cumberland man was made by a pair of local homeless men in the North Smithfield area. The Chief there has confirmed that it is an active crime scene and that they will be investigating throughout the evening. Unconfirmed details state that the victim was murdered. We will keep you updated as new details emerge."

James stood in place unable to process what he had heard. There were never murders so close to home, especially not to someone from his town. He thought this was probably the crisis his father was called to. He said it was a friend—he wondered if it was someone that he knew.

His mind shot back to when they were all still together. Just one big, happy family with lots of his parent's friends always gathering. They would have cookouts almost every weekend when the weather was nice and the three of them would go to James's grandfather's house and bring dinner on most Sundays.

During most of the cookouts, his mom and all of the women would make fruity drinks and soak up the sun by the pool. They even had a big fan that had a water hose attached which would spray a cool mist over anyone in the area.

One weekend, during one of these get-togethers, it was incredibly hot. So hot that you could see the waves of heat dancing up from the ground and leaping for relief that would never come. This particular weekend was his dad's friend's birthday. The group went all out. All the adults rode in a limousine and drove to a casino far away in another state. It was even great for the kids. They all had a sleepover and tortured the babysitter. He missed those days.

James knew that his father was too busy to be disturbed so he tried to reach his mother. The call went to voicemail and he left a message for her to call him when she had time. He made sure that she knew it wasn't an emergency.

A few minutes later, she called. "Hi, James, is everything all right?"

He became unexpectedly choked up and found it hard to speak.

"James, what's going on?"

He collected himself and tried to find his voice. "Mom, there's been a murder. It's someone you know. Dad got a call earlier and now the story is on the news. They didn't mention a name. I'm worried about who it could be."

Lydia tried to reassure him and told him that she'd see what she could find out and would let him know. James felt a little better now that someone else knew this information and was eager and able to get more details for him.

Lydia decided to text Carl:

> **Carl, what's going on? James said someone has died?? He's very upset. Can you tell me what's happened?**

Her mind was whirling too fast for her to grasp onto any one particular thought. Who could have died? And murdered? She hoped James had it wrong. Her break was almost over, but she tried to check the internet on her phone for any information. She did find a brief story on a local news website, but it only gave the details that she already knew. There was a Cumberland man found murdered in North Smithfield. Not much else was known. Just then, her phone vibrated:

> **Lyd, Paul is dead. It's horrible. I can't give any details yet. Randy and his parents know. Keep it under wraps for now. I'll call James later.**

She couldn't believe her eyes. Not Paul. It didn't make any sense. She had to get back to work but knew that her mind would be on nothing else.

SIXTEEN
Rosa Marie

Rosa Marie awoke and felt as if her head were being slowly squeezed in a vise. She tried to gauge what time it was by attempting to look out the window but couldn't find one. Her mouth felt as dry as a desert and her eyelids seemed to be made of sandpaper. The smells were all unfamiliar and wrong. She tried to get her bearings but felt extremely disoriented waking in a strange place. She heard breathing next to her and looked to find a stranger. So many feelings came rushing over her in waves. She felt guilt, shame, and fear, but mostly she was angry. Firstly, she couldn't believe she had done this again. Secondly, she dreaded having to tell Lucas. Maybe she wouldn't have to tell him. If she left now, she would only have to say that she just left the casino. She checked her phone and saw that it was three a.m. It might work. She might make it home before him. Finding her clothes, she got dressed and grabbed her purse. She left the apartment and went to get into her car, which she despondently realized must still be at the casino.

A feeling much worse than dread came over her. She would have to explain to him that it wasn't her fault. He would understand. He always did. If not, she would make him.

+++++++++++++

When Lucas saw that Rosa Marie was calling him, he was so happy. He couldn't believe he was the man she chose to spend the rest of her life with. He knew that other men were much better all-around than he was. She could have her pick and he would never forget that she picked him — a nobody.

Rosa Marie was the most beautiful woman he knew. She might not be movie star quality beautiful, but that was not what he needed. She was what his parents would call a buxom woman. He preferred to think of her as voluptuous. It was evident that she liked her figure because she always wore very tight-fitting clothing. She liked to wear stilettos, even though they did a number on her feet, because she said that they made her calves look better.

Her face was long with sharp edges. Some would say that she was a handsome woman. Her skin was very fair, almost porcelain looking. In contrast, her eyes were the darkest brown he had ever seen. It was very exotic in his mind. Rosa Marie had short, dirty blonde hair, but very few people knew this. She had several wigs that she wore, depending on her moods.

Lucas tried everything in his power to keep her happy. He answered the call and was sorry he did.

SEVENTEEN
Paige

Paige critiqued her reflection in the glistening mirror one last time, even though everyone told her this was the perfect outfit for pep rally day. The high school colors were blue, white, yellow-gold, and silver. Each year, one of the colors was assigned to a grade. The students of that grade wore the assigned color to show school spirit. Because they were seniors, they needed to wear blue to show their pride. She had decided on wearing a bright blue top that was gathered at the bustline. It had thick shoulder straps adorned with silver studding. She paired it with some perfectly ripped skinny jeans, a white jean jacket, and her military boots. She had put her hair into two wet braids the night before which now gave her poker-straight hair a subtle wave. She finished off the look with the bullhorn earrings that Bryce had given her. Because Bryce was the star quarterback of the football team, she knew he would be instrumental throughout the day and wanted to stand out and make him notice her.

He gave her the earrings one evening after the pair had practiced at the high school. The football team and the cheerleaders had the same practice schedule. They had stopped and bought a pizza and soda and brought them back to the high school grounds. They settled for the privacy of a copse of trees on the west side of the main building. The center was just large enough for them to sit comfortably and eat their food without any prying eyes. They ate, talked, and laughed. Paige never felt like this before. Her heart was beating so hard and fast, she was sure he would be able to see it if he looked. She could actually hear it internally. She was hoping that she knew how this night would end— with their first kiss amid the welcoming scent of purple clover. She wanted nothing else.

Bryce became quiet and serious. She wasn't sure if this was a good thing or not. She steadied herself and prepared for the worst. She thought, sure, hoping for a kiss, and getting the brushoff in reality, great. No sooner had the thought been formulated, Bryce put both arms on top of her shoulders, looked her in the eyes, and went in for a kiss. She could feel all the doubt and trepidation melt away. She closed her eyes and went with the magic of the moment. It was not too short and not too long; it was sheer perfection. At least she hoped so.

When she opened her eyes, he was smiling at her in that way that only he could. He tucked two fingers underneath her trembling chin and lifted it gently to be kissed again. That was when he pulled away and reached into his letterman jacket and produced the earrings. They were blue and silver bullhorns—the perfect gift. She hugged him and put the earrings on.

She felt inadequate that she didn't think of getting him something. He noticed the look on her face and asked her if it was because of James.

It took her a while to process what he had just said. She emphatically denied what he was thinking and assured him that there was absolutely nothing but a friendship between them. When she told him the reason for her mood change, he kissed her again. He moved her hair behind one ear to see the earring more clearly. When he did, his pectoral muscle danced a bit. Paige gasped and was in awe. "Do that again!" He pushed her hair away once more with a quizzical look. "No, make your pecs dance." Bryce looked sheepish and closed his eyes. "Make them dance for me," she said softly. He did and she felt like the world was spinning.

She hoped that they could sneak away again, at some point today after the pep rally and have another magical moment. As she was thinking about how she couldn't wait for the day's festivities, her mind trailed back to last year's rally. She and her classmates had to wear yellow, which was the hardest color to wear—something about skin tones or whatever. Paige could hear the music playing from the school band—her favorite was Bon Jovi's, "Livin' on a Prayer." She could see all the faces of the students and teachers in the crowds. She'd never get over her four favorite teachers and staff and how they stole the show. Ms. Little, Ms. Pastor, Ms. Butcher, and Ms. Zenun, painted their faces blue, yellow, and white and had silver and blue wigs on.

They had pom-poms and sprayed silly string all over everyone. It was very uncharacteristic of them, which made it even better. She could even taste the hotdogs and s'mores and she could smell the smoke from the bonfire, but her favorite part was being at the top of the pyramid during the halftime cheer routine.

The crisp autumn day was going to be the beginning of a perfect rally this year and lead to an even better after-party. She was still a little apprehensive when she thought about James hanging with everyone, but she was determined to stay positive. Paige grabbed her backpack and then she double-checked that her cheerleading uniform was packed with everything she needed for this year's routine. She would be the one to be catapulted, once again, high into the air from the top of a pyramid. She loved the feeling. It was the closest she could get to flying.

Once at school, Paige met up with the gang on the football field. Amber showed up early and saved space on some bleachers for everyone. When Paige saw her waving her over, she thought that she looked like she was going to erupt. She couldn't imagine what it could be this early in the day. She made her way up and took a seat.

Amber burst, "Bryce was scanning the crowds a minute ago. He was looking for you! I could tell because he stopped when he saw me—then he looked bummed."

"Sure. You can tell all that from a look? Really? You should be a PI, Amber!"

"We'll see. He had to go inside and get into his uniform with the others. Honestly, you should not let James hang with us, it might scare Bryce off."

"We've talked about James. He knows the deal. He isn't threatened by him at all."

Paige wanted to scream she was so excited, but she couldn't let on and played it cool. Her mind was racing a mile a minute and hoping she would get a glimpse of Bryce before she had to go change herself. She let these thoughts take her away to the possibilities of what might happen at and after the party tonight . . .

EIGHTEEN

James

James stood before his streaked bedroom mirror and appraised the reflection looking back at him. His uneven bangs were infiltrating his eyes, which made them feel like mini daggers at times. He noticed how hunched over he was. He was always told to stand up straight or else he would remain hunched over permanently. He tried it. He had to admit, he looked much better. More aware and self-assured, which was the exact opposite of how he felt. His wet hair fell over his eyes reminding him of one of the Fraggle Muppets, he couldn't remember its name.

He scrutinized what he was wearing. No one told him this was the perfect outfit for pep rally day like with Paige and her friends. He never knew what the right thing to wear was for any occasion; and when it came to seeing Paige, this upset him greatly. He only wanted the best for her and for her to want the best for him. His thoughts went to the future; their future. He had high expectations for tonight. Paige insisting that he come to the pep rally with her and her friends, and to want him to go to the party afterward was something he thought he would never in his life attain. He thought that this was the perfect time to make his feelings for her known.

When he got to the field, the sights, smells, and sounds overwhelmed him. There were so many people. It was so loud. People were sitting together in groups according to grade, which was evident by the clusters of colored attire. He almost turned and left, but then he spotted her. His heart was beating so loudly that it drowned out the noise of the crowd. He made his way over to her and climbed up the steps.

"Hi." Nothing. "Paige?" Still nothing. "HELLO?"

"Oh, James, hi."

"Oh, hi? Where were you? Seemed like you were on another planet."

"Oh, I was just going over my routine for later. Here, sit." Paige moved to make a spot for him.

James sat but felt like he wanted to run back home again. He couldn't pinpoint why, but he felt that she was trying to cover up something. He saw her nudge Jenna and Amber out of the corner of his eye and then they both said hello to him. It was worse than just ignoring him altogether.

The crowds started cheering as the football team came running out onto the field with the school's mascot. He thought he saw Bryce slow down and look toward him. No. He was looking at Paige. She was looking at *him*. He immediately thought back to her journal. Even back then, she had a connection to him—or wanted one. She wrote about how she loved the way he looked at her. He tried to think back to what else was written and could only remember that she also loved his hands. Something about the roughness of them. Right then he knew this day would not go as he had planned.

NINETEEN
Lucas

Lucas couldn't believe he found himself in this position yet again. Why do people keep doing this to her? She was such a people person; she was naturally drawn to others. He was also sadly aware that she seemed to be getting worse—it was much harder to reign in her impulses. That's why they all took advantage of her. He knew that he should walk away and leave her to deal with things herself. There was some invisible forcefield that kept him drawn to her side, feeding his obsession for her. He knew that if he were a better man, she wouldn't need to do these things. If he was better looking, smarter, had a better job, she would not seek out these dalliances.

He needed to devise a plan for this mess; one that would not be traced back to them. It should be easier the second time around, but he felt like the life was being sucked out of him and his energy was at an all-time low.

His plan needed to be perfect. He rummaged through the groundskeeper shed once again to get supplies. He went into the locker room to change. He wanted to wear dark clothing again and not his uniform. No one locked the lockers here, so he checked around for what he needed. He found a black, long-sleeve sweater that would work with the other gear. Even better, he found an almost full prescription bottle. He didn't know what it was for but needed to give it a try because Rosa Marie was running low on her "meds."

Once on the road, he needed to clear his head. He put the radio on so he could focus. Bad idea. He heard a news report about the body they found on Rt. 146. From what he could gather, they still had no clues. Spirits lifted, he called Rosa Marie to tell her he was on his way.

He arrived at the Lincoln address and drove across the lawn to the back of the house. He hoped that this would afford them more privacy. Rosa Marie let him into the apartment where the woman was unconscious but starting to come around. Her hands and feet were tied with phone charger cords. Lucas jarred open her mouth and forced some of the pills he found down her throat. She now had a mix of Gabapentin, Xanax, and Vicodin that would soon set to work in her system. Hopefully, it would keep her out long enough. They each took one end of her body, carried her to the car, and put her in the trunk.

The ride to the casino was most uncomfortable. The tension-filled silence within the compact sedan was palpable. When she could bear it no longer, Rosa Marie said, "Baby, I know this isn't good, but I swear it won't happen again. Let me help you with this. It's my fault. But, you know, if you were home more I . . ."

Lucas swung the Volkswagen Jetta over to the side of the road. He got out and began to walk in circles around the car hands flailing, lips moving in objection to her comments. When he felt like he would no longer strangle her, he went back into the car and continued driving. No other words were spoken by anyone. Lucas drove to the casino to drop Rosa Marie at her car. As soon as she exited the vehicle, Lucas sped off.

Lucas drove around thinking about what to do next and found himself in a secluded section of Diamond Hill State Park. He was pleasantly surprised at his subconscious for ending up there. He drove up the mountain as far as he could and got out. He scoped out the area and decided on what to do. He took out the supplies and prepared everything he needed. He carefully opened the trunk—he wasn't sure if the woman was still unconscious or if she was awake. She was still out.

Using his headlights to guide him, he put on his gear and brought the woman to an area where there was a substantially sized stump next to a large tree. He cut away all of her clothing. He then cut the phone charger cord, binding the woman's arms, and used bungee cords and duct tape so that her arms were stretched out behind her and around the tree trunk. He did the same with her legs and feet. He then taped her mid-section and head to the tree, covering her mouth as he did. She looked as though she belonged on the front of a ship as the figurehead. The evening clouds had cleared and the moon's luminescence cast an eerie, milky glow across her body.

Lucas was trying to move as quickly as possible because being out in the open made him vulnerable. He knew that people came here at all hours, all the time. Every noise that he heard was his potential downfall. At one point, he was being scrutinized by the knowing scowl of a barn owl. It looked right through him with the glare of the moon reflected in its mirror-like eyes giving Lucas an ominous feeling that found him riddled with shame. He had to continue and be quick about it.

He laid out his arsenal of horror on top of the stump; the relief from merely touching the tools was visceral and he was able to quell his anxious emotions. In his newfound calmness, his mind drifted to Rosa Marie. He felt this absorbing love for her. He was always so appreciative of the love she gave him. It was marked by a desire to always please her, knowing that he would forever smooth over the rough patches she may encounter. If proving his love for her was what she needed, then that was what he would always do.

The tactical knife was selected and Lucas set out to complete the deed. The removal. Yet again. He needed to remove everything that tempted his Rosa Marie. This could never happen again. Not to her. Not to anyone. He would see to it.

He began slicing off her right breast. It wasn't as easy as he thought. Her breasts were not round and full like his love's. They were long and more cylinder-shaped. There was an excessive amount of blood, which made it very slippery and turned a difficult situation even more difficult. To add another layer of misery to this night, the woman began to come to. She moaned and looked at him with terror in her eyes and then they rolled up into the back of her head and she was out again. With another round of relief, he continued the dissection. Left breast removed, he moved down and sliced away her clitoris. He quickly realized that he should have started there. Navigating through all the blood that was running down her body was getting more and more arduous. He had planned to remove the labia as well but decided against the trouble. The point was made. She would never seduce anyone again. He wasn't sure if she would bleed to death as a result of his handiwork. He didn't know if he should cut an artery like with the other one. Erring on the side of caution, he decided to be safe and cut the carotid artery in her neck.

Packing up his equipment, he was ready to leave. The only problem was what to do with the body parts. With the man, he buried it, which seemed to work well. Tonight, he decided to do the same. He knew that serial killers kept trophies of their victims and he didn't want to be categorized like that. He was different. He was doing his love and his community a service by ridding them of such vile people. The trees dancing in the gusty night air seemed to applaud his decision.

TWENTY

Paige

Back at the school, Paige changed out of her cheerleading uniform and left to meet her friends in the parking lot.

Brooke offered, "Great job, Paige! I can't believe you enjoy being thrown around like that. I think I'd barf!"

The others laughed and congratulated her as well. She thanked them as they dispersed and went to their respective cars, excited to meet later.

The invigorating autumn air filled her lungs with a renewed purpose, yet she couldn't help feeling apprehensive. She wrote it off as nerves about tonight's party. She was dreading how difficult it will be to keep the peace. As she got to her car, she felt a vibration from her backpack and pulled out her phone. It was a text from her mom:

> **Hey kiddo. Aunty hurt her back again and I need to go by and see her. I need u 2 watch Tim 4 a while. I know u r sleeping at Jenna's 2nite, promise it won't be long.**

Paige felt so badly for her aunt. She had been in a terrible car accident years ago and had never been the same. She didn't mind going home for a bit. She wanted to freshen up anyway. She felt guilty for lying to her mother about her plans. Then she thought that this would be a good time to score some points with James. Maybe she would have him come over so they could chill out before the night's events.

Sure Mom. No prob.

♥

She sent a group text and told the *mean girls* that she'd meet them later when she was picked up. She then sent James a text telling him that she was stopping at the house to watch Tim for a while before the party. She told him that he should come by. She worried about his introspection. He was alone most of the time and now when they did get together it took forever for her to draw him out. That was one of the main reasons she didn't end their friendship altogether. She felt like it shouldn't be that hard to be someone's friend, but she knew his past had shaped the person he was now and she would feel terrible if he became more solitary and withdrawn. She couldn't be that cruel.

When Paige arrived home, she went into the living room. Timothy was using the area below the massive marble coffee table as some far-away planet. He had a robot and was pretending that they were somewhere that had no air and was full of aliens. She thought that she would have some fun and regale him with a story that would put some hair on his chest—sooner rather than later.

"You know, Tim, when I was your age, some aliens really did come to earth."

"Yeah, sure."

"No, really. Two of them came into my room one night. They were very tall and very thin. They had very long arms and really long hands with only four fingers. They wore no clothes and didn't have any familiar body parts. Their heads were flat and had no nose or mouth—just three large round eyes with no lids or lashes. The eyes stuck out of their heads and looked like Jell-O. Where our chest is, they had something that resembled fangs that were covered in long fur. As tall as they were, they had extremely long torsos and very short legs. Where their feet should be were pointed masses that resembled arrowheads."

"Oh really? Why didn't they take you up to their flying saucer and do experiments on you? Like prooobing you?"

Pretending to be more interested in something on her phone, she said, "Well, they didn't know that there were two different kinds of humans. They saw the family picture on my nightstand and wanted to know what you and dad were. It was so weird, they didn't speak, but I heard them in my head. I told them you were boys. They talked together for a while and decided that because they already had a female specimen from some other family, they wanted to get a male." She glanced down, ever so slightly, at Tim to gauge his emotions and saw that she was getting to him.

Paige continued, "If you remember, there was that little girl from school who went missing and then turned up in her house the next day; well, she was abducted. Her parents and the police all searched that house from top to bottom and she was definitely not there—and then poof!" She paused for effect.

She added, "They promised to spare me since I was a girl, but only if I would help them get a boy. They said that dad was too old and that you were too young. They said they would wait until you were the perfect age and then return." Now was her chance to see if it worked.

"Hey, I'm going to make a snack. Do you want anything?"

Timothy quickly answered, "Wait, I'll come too." His voice was higher, and his beautiful dark brown eyes were bugging out of his head. Success!

"You don't have to come; I'll be right back."

"No, I want to pick out my own snack. You pick gross stuff."

She smirked and ruffled his fluffy milk chocolate hair. "Come on, let's see what there is."

"Paige?"

"Yeah, squirt."

"If that was a real story, how would the boy be able to not get abducted?"

"Well, it is a real story, and the answer is simple.

You would have to get some paprika from mom's spice rack and put it on your forehead in the shape of an X. When they were talking to each other in my head, I heard them say that, but I don't think they realized that I could hear."

Timothy whispered the word "paprika" under his breath. It took all her strength for her not to burst out laughing.

Paige received a text. She looked and it was from James.

Hey. Can't come by. At the clinic c u later.

Hmm. She thought that was weird. He never mentioned having to work today because he was so psyched to be able to be with her for the whole day. She shrugged it off and began to freshen up for the party.

TWENTY-ONE
James

After the rally, James knew that he needed to have a plan B. It was getting harder and harder to keep the *Red* away. The harder he pushed it back, the angrier he became which would bring it right to the forefront again. He thought that he had found true love. He saw his future with Paige—the family they would have, the whole package, and now he wondered what's wrong with me? Why was she obsessing over Bryce when she had always had the undying love she needed right here? It didn't make any sense to him.

He went to the clinic to see if he could formulate his next moves. He felt at peace the most among the animals. He was able to calm the *Red* and come up with a plan for tonight if and when things became too unbearable. He knew those creeps would taunt him and if he thought they were crossing a line, with Paige or with him, at any time, he'd initiate his plan.

He caught a glimpse of himself in the observation room window and realized that his hair was covering his dark green eyes again and becoming entangled with his lashes. He knew he needed a haircut but also knew that he didn't have enough time. He wished that he took better care of the way he looked—maybe then, Paige would think of him the way she thinks of *him*. James hated the greasy, pale face staring back at him. In his reflection, he could see the dark *Red* of his mind within his bloodshot eyes.

His phone vibrated with a return text from Paige that read:

Meeting at Jenna's house 8:30. Once Sade & Karol pick me up wl swing by n get u.

He replied:

K

He left to set up everything needed for his plan B.

TWENTY-TWO
Paige

Sloane came home a little after seven o'clock and started her nightly ritual of getting Timothy ready for bed. He was acting very peculiar and she couldn't seem to get him settled. She went into Paige's room. "You look nice. Any idea why your brother is acting so weird? He made a red X on his forehead and refused to wash it off in the tub."

"Thanks. Uh, no idea what goes through that boy's mind. Don't forget, I'm staying at Jenna's tonight."

"I remember. And somehow I think there's more to this situation with your brother than what you're letting on."

Paige gave her mom a smirk and finished getting the final touches applied. She wanted everything perfect for tonight. She kept thinking about possible scenarios and how she would act or react in each one. She knew that Bryce and the guys were going to bring the alcohol and hoped that they didn't go overboard—especially with James there. He was so overprotective of her. She knew that if anyone did anything that he construed to be negative or offensive toward her, he would overreact. She was very anxious over the whole situation and began to second-guess inviting him.

Her phone buzzed alerting her that her ride was there. She grabbed her things, yelled to her mother, "Ride's here. I'll see you tomorrow," and flew out the door.

She threw her bag into the trunk and then jumped into the back seat and greeted her friends. "So, everyone covered for tonight?" They all said yes.

They weren't going to be without adult supervision the whole night, she thought to herself, as a way to assuage her guilt that reared its ugly head. Jenna's sister was working late and knew about the party. She'd join them once she was finished with her shift at a local restaurant. She was cool, sometimes.

They arrived at the Lowden house and she sent James a text that they were outside then quickly reminded her friends to be nice to him. As he came out of the house, he looked like he made an effort to be more put-together. Usually, it appeared that he didn't care much about what he looked like.

When they arrived at Jenna's, Amber and Brooke were already there, but there was no sign of Bryce or the guys.

Amber could read the disappointment on Paige's face, as she scanned the basement and said, "Don't forget they had to go to the packie and try to get someone to buy the stuff for them. They'll be here any minute."

Paige tried to shrug it off. "I know, it's no big

deal."

"Suuuure."

The basement room at the bottom of the stairs was set up for the night's festivities. There was a folding card table set off to the left corner of the room with an old, stained tablecloth covering it. The girls had set out pretzels, nacho chips, potato chips, and dip, and cut vegetables. A faux crystal bowl held the contents of a raspberry punch concoction sans alcohol. The obligatory red Dixie cups were lined up waiting to be filled. The teens milled around the bare concrete-walled room buzzing with the electricity of what was to come once the jocks arrived. There was a narrow concrete column in the center of the room. It was covered in the same orange, green, and brown patterned indoor/outdoor carpeting that covered the floor of the room. The seams where it came together were frayed and Paige was nervously picking away at some of the loose fibers.

They were all listening to music and fighting over who's playlist was the best. They finally agreed on a song, grabbed some snacks, and played a game of Never Have I Ever. That was fun for all of a hot minute. James had never played and wasn't very good at it. It felt like hours had passed and Paige was going out of her mind.

There was a loud bang when the outside door was flung open and hit the house. It sounded and felt as though there was a stampede of elephants moving through, when all of a sudden, six burly teenagers ran down the stairs and into the basement with triumphant looks on their faces. They were laden with paper bags. Bryce and his friends came booming into the room with the booze they conned someone into buying for them.

Sade asked James to help her finish the punch. He was stunned and didn't know what to say. Paige elbowed him and he snapped to and went over to the table. Paige caught her eye and mouthed, "Thank you." Unknown to her, her friends decided to keep him occupied throughout the night so that she could spend time with Bryce. They knew that they could keep him talking if they brought up animals or trucks—as shy as he was, he could talk forever if it was a topic that interested him.

Paige made her way over to Bryce and his friends. With a teasing smirk she asked, "So what are we drinking tonight? I hope it's not that golden sludge you brought to the last party."

Bryce leaned against Paige, resting his elbow on her shoulder. "Um, that was Goldschläger, which is the choice drink of champions. And, yes. There is more for celebratory shots once we get loosened up with the beer and the punch the girls are making!"

James heard the laughter and looked up to see the jocks looking his way and laughing. One Neanderthal was pointing at him. Brooke quickly tried to get his attention by bringing something up about the clinic. Seeing them laughing at his expense, along with Paige, who had Bryce's arm on her, incited his biggest fear coming to fruition. He had to work extra hard to keep the *Red* at bay.

James saw that the tallest behemoth squirted beer out his nose while he laughed.

Paige pushed Bryce's elbow off her shoulder and stepped on the giant's foot as he wiped the beer from his upper lip. "Knock it off guys," she said. "I won't have anyone ruin tonight. You will all be civilized or you leave!"

One of the jocks apologized, "Sorry, M 'lady. I was just trying to lighten the mood. Didn't mean to disrespect."

Bryce smacked his friend on the shoulder then looked her in the eyes and she almost melted. She smiled and went over to the punch table to see how they were doing.

They erected another table and a few of the teens began a game of beer pong. The jocks turned up the music even louder and turned off some of the lights. It made the room look and feel much better. Paige thought that she couldn't be sure of her feelings because, with Bryce around, she was not herself.

James and the girls filled 12 cups of the now spiked punch and set them out on the table. Paige grabbed them and passed them around. She grabbed her cup of punch and tried it.

"Go slow," said Jenna. "The taste is deceiving. Goes down smooth but you'll be staggering before you know it."

Of course, with that roundabout dare, Paige downed it and slammed the cup on the table. "Hit me, barkeep!"

James refilled her cup and they all drank and

laughed—*mean girls*, jocks, and James alike. She felt a sense of accomplishment and pride in seeing everyone getting along.

Then it all felt wrong. It felt as if there was a gravitational force pulling the room inward. Everyone's faces became elongated—as if she was seeing them through a funhouse mirror. She was losing control of herself and her surroundings. Then it was all a void.

TWENTY-THREE
Sloane

Sloane had finally gotten to sleep and was stuck in that threadlike foggy layer between slumber and consciousness. She began having a nightmare. Her hands were clenched with fistfuls of sheets. She dreamed that she was hugging Paige for an exaggeratedly long time when a woman nearby said that it was so nice to see a mother and daughter so close. Sloane looked at the woman and said, "You would never know that I buried her three days ago."

Sloane bolted up, drenched in sweat, and screamed, "Paige!"

Mitch tried to turn on the bedside lamp, but it would not go on. He grabbed his cellphone, used the flashlight, and asked her if she was all right.

She described her nightmare and he told her not to worry, that it was just a bad dream.

"I know it was a bad dream, but I think there's more to it. I think there's something wrong with Paige. You know that I can tell when she's in trouble; I know when something's wrong with her. It's stronger than intuition; I can't explain it."

"Yes, but do you feel that way because of the dream, or did you dream that because of an unsettling feeling? I think it's because of the dream, Sloane. Let's try to go back to sleep."

She grabbed the mini flashlight from her nightstand and got up to get a glass of water and to check on Timothy who was finally asleep. He insisted on keeping every light on in his room when she finally got him into bed. He also kept a baseball bat in bed with him. Now, she noticed that he had also set up boobytraps underneath his windows and elsewhere, and she had to be careful not to trip on any of the noisy items he had arranged in his room.

Sloane flashed the light around and found pots and pans, different types of utensils, old electronic toys, and other items that when touched, would alert the sleeping boy. Her heart broke a little at seeing this. She made a mental note to grill Paige deeper about what had transpired between the two of them.

Tim's bedroom was baseball-themed. It was adorned in blues and greys after his grandfather's favorite baseball team, the NY Yankees. His grandfather had died just before the family was to redecorate his room and make it "less babyish." She could see the faces of his favorite players looking over him while he sleeps beneath them. He displayed his grandfather's autographed jersey in a case on the wall among other sentimental team memorabilia that was left to him. Sloane quietly crept over to him and kissed his forehead atop his baseball pillowcase. She had to avoid the red X that was still displayed on his forehead.

Sloane went back into bed but still couldn't shake

the feeling that something was wrong with Paige. She grabbed her e-reader and started to read, hoping it would lull her back to sleep. Not long after, her cellphone rang, startling both her and Mitch. She knew it was bad before she answered—and she knew it was about Paige. She grabbed the phone and saw that it was from her brother.

"Sloane, it's Will. I'm working at the hospital. They just brought in a bunch of teens and Paige is one of them. She'll be okay, but you need to get down here."

"What happened, Will?"

"I'll explain everything when you get here. We're still running tests. We don't know exactly what happened yet, but it looks like they were drinking and took some drugs."

TWENTY-FOUR
Paige

Paige partially came to several times before she was fully conscious. Each time she did, she was confused and knew that it would be better to drift back into peaceful oblivion. Once she fully awoke, she was met with a searing pain in her throat, an incredible pounding in her head, and terrible nauseating spasms in her abdomen, roiling within her like a tempest out at sea. The rough texture of the sheets covering her had a pungent smell of industrial-grade disinfectant that was unfamiliar to her. She was trying to figure out why she felt so horrible, and where she was, but nothing would come to mind. She tried to remember the last memory she had, and it was as if it was locked away in an unreachable cabinet drawer—absolutely nothing would come to her.

"Hi there. Welcome back."

She looked up. "Uncle Will? What? Where am I? What are you doing here?" Paige tried to sit up and noticed that she was somewhere very unfamiliar. The sights and smells were all wrong. The fog in her mind was clearing a little and she realized that she must be in the hospital where her uncle worked. She was too weak to sit up. Her uncle pushed a button to raise her bed a bit for her.

"Paige, you have just had a gastric lavage. You might feel some discomfort in your throat and abdomen. I have an important question to ask you and you must answer me with total honesty. What did you and your friends take tonight?"

"Take?" Paige didn't understand the question. It started to come back to her in waves. The party. The punch. All her friends on the floor. "Um, we had the guys get us some booze. We drank some punch. I don't understand. Was it bad? Where are my friends? How did I get here? And what's a gastric lavage?" She became very upset and started to cry. It hurt her everywhere, which made her cry harder and then it hurt even more.

"Take it easy, Paige. A gastric lavage means that we had to pump your stomach. That usually leaves your throat sore and you will most likely have some stomach cramping for a while. I need you to tell me what else you all took. Some of your friends are pretty sick. If I don't know what they took, I can't treat them."

"I don't know. If some of them took something, they didn't tell me. Honest, Uncle Will. I would tell you. I didn't see anyone take anything."

"Paige, I'm not judging you. You won't get into trouble, but you all took something. Even you. You didn't end up in here because of alcohol. When Jenna's sister came home, you were all unconscious on the floor in the basement. Alcohol didn't do that.

Experimentation is a part of being . . ."

"No! We were NOT experimenting! We had some beer and punch with vodka and then we were gonna do shots. I didn't take anything. You have to believe me. Isn't there some kind of test you can run to see what it is?" Her throat was so raw that talking made her feel like she was on fire.

"We are running them, but they take a long time and two of your friends went into anaphylactic shock. We're not sure how long everyone was out. They're stable now, but it would help to know exactly what they need. The eleven of you are very lucky you were found before it was too late."

Paige tried to voice an objection but could only bring her hand to her throat as it protested.

"Let me get you some ice chips for your throat." Will signaled to a young man in the room to get them.

"I've called your mom. She's on her way. I want you to think very hard about what was said and what was done. Ah, here's the ice." The man set the bucket on the tray next to her.

"Wait! You mean twelve. There were twelve of us there." Paige was racking her brain to remember who was there with her. "There was Sade, Amber, Karol, Jenna, James, Bryce, and his five friends—I can never get their names straight. With me, that's twelve."

"I'll check again, I may be mistaken."

Sloane arrived at the hospital and was disoriented by the twists and turns of the corridors and the glare of the harsh fluorescent lighting. She found the right room, 702, and went in. "Paige! Oh, my gosh. Are you all right? Will. How is she? What the hell happened?"

"Sloane, let's step outside and I'll fill you in."

"Wait, Mom! I want you to know I didn't take anything! You have to believe me! They did a gastric lavage." Paige began to cry and then she cringed because of the pain.

Sloane was very confused, saying, "What? Didn't take anything? You had your stomach pumped? Will . . ."

He led her by the shoulder, "Come on. Let's talk."

They went out into the hall as the other parents were beginning to arrive. Carl and Arabella arrived as well.

Will made his way over to them, "Hello. I'm Dr. Will Gildan. I'm the physician on call tonight. I'm also Paige's uncle, Sloane's brother."

Carl and Arabella introduced themselves then told Will that they would like to address the parents. Will decided to direct them all into a private waiting room so that they could both update them at once. He informed them all of what he knew and asked them to see if anyone could find out exactly what was taken. Before they left to be with their children, Carl took over the conversation.

"I know a lot of you here because our kids go to school together. For those of you who don't know me, I'm Carl Lowden, a sergeant at the Cumberland police department. This is my partner, detective Arabella Luthor. There are many unanswered questions here. Because they're under 18, we'll need to meet with everyone whose parents are already here. Head to their rooms and we will make our rounds to question them with you present. Do any of them know who bought the alcohol? How did they get drugs? This is crazy. They're good kids. I can't believe they got messed up in this."

Will told Carl that he might have to wait to see James because he was the last to come to, and it was only a few minutes ago. He thought that it might be because he ingested more drugs than the rest of the kids.

Carl was shocked at this news. While he admitted that they were far from close these past years, he knew enough about his son to know that James would never indulge in illicit drugs. He thought James had chosen his friends well. Paige seemed to have her head together. He wanted to understand exactly how and why this happened.

Carl tried to get in touch with Lydia before he began the interviews, but she didn't answer. He left a message for her to call him. Carl told Arabella that he would check in on James and then interview everyone in even-numbered rooms and that she should take the odd-numbered ones. They split up and got to business. He went into James's room and was stopped in his tracks. His son was lying helpless in the bed before him, almost unrecognizable. The once buoyant, jovial, and fun-loving young man was replaced with a pale, clammy, shell of what he usually was. He cleared his throat and James opened his eyes.

"Dad."

"Son, how are you feeling?"

"I've been better." His voice was gravelly and it looked like it pained him to speak. "Look, Dad, I'm sorry I got into this mess. I know it won't look good for you at the police station. We were just having some fun. I don't know what happened. How is Paige? Can I see her? Have you seen her?"

"Don't worry about that right now. Everyone is okay. I'll go to see her when I leave here. I need to get to the bottom of what happened, James. First of all, why were you there? You don't even like most of those kids."

"They're mostly Paige's friends. It was just a small party after the pep rally and the big game. She wanted to have all her friends there, so I went. The jocks brought the booze. It was just a bunch of beer and then vodka poured into the punch. We didn't even do any of the shots they brought."

"Were they the ones who brought the drugs?"

"Dad, there were no drugs. Well, I didn't see any anyway."

"James now is not the time to cover up what happened. You all had your stomachs pumped—that wasn't because you drank a little vodka in some punch! I need the names of the ones who brought in the alcohol."

"Okay. It was Bryce Walker and his buddies. Henry Loft, Trevor Belmont, Thomas Turk, Mikael Swan, and Aaron King." James took a drink of water and the pain showed even more on his face.

"Which one of them brought the drugs—and what were they? Dr. Gildan says that the tests haven't come back yet, and they can't identify what you all took."

"Dad. I told you, we didn't take any drugs. I would tell you. At this point, why would I lie?"

"Do you think the boys brought them? They could have put them in the punch when no one was watching."

"I don't remember anyone doing anything like that—but I didn't think I'd need to pay attention and remember every detail. Besides, things are still pretty foggy."

"Okay. Well, when you get clarity, try to piece it together. If you remember anything about what could have happened, write it down and let me know. I need details like what time the party started."

"The girls picked me up at eight forty and we were at the house for a bit before the guys showed up. They probably showed up a little after nine or so."

"Okay, how long do you think you were there before you blacked out?"

"We all had a few beers and one or two cups of punch. We just hung out listening to music and stuff for a couple of hours. I don't remember much after that."

Carl flipped through some notes and said, "It says here that you were all discovered around midnight by . . ."

"Wait. Midnight? What time is it now?"

"It's almost four o'clock in the morning. I need to interview the others. I've left a message for your mom and Arabella is trying to locate her also. I'm hoping that she'll be here soon."

Carl finished getting reports from the kids on his side of the corridor and then met Arabella in the hall. They needed to compare notes before they met the parents in the waiting room. All teens reported the same information. As he combined the list of names from Arabella's with his, he noticed they were one short. No one had interviewed Bryce Walker. She confirmed that she hadn't so they walked over to the nurse's station and asked which room he was in. The nurse checked her computer and stated that they didn't have a Bryce Walker on the floor. Carl had her page Will. He came to the station and updated them on the substances that were found in the toxicology screen.

Will told them, "These kids were dosed with Ketamine and hydrochloride which is similar to being given GHB or Rohypnol. It's sometimes used as a date-rape drug. It acts as a form of anesthesia. They were given four times the amount they would be given normally, which explains why they were out for so long. I say 'given' the drugs because I just got off the phone with someone in your forensic lab and the punch tested positive for the same drugs. Whoever did this could have permanently damaged these kids. Luckily, the sister found them when she did. We'll need to keep them here for 48-hours because there are possible residual effects they could suffer."

Normally, Carl took cases involving kids and teens more to heart than any other cases. With his son lying helpless in a hospital bed, it hit him harder than any other case he could remember. The fact that they were most likely drugged unwittingly was very disturbing. He desperately needed to speak to Bryce Walker to get a better understanding of what took place. He seemed to be the ringleader.

"Will, is there any reason Bryce Walker is not with the others? Is he on a different floor?"

"I don't remember seeing anyone by that name, but I wasn't the only physician tending to them. You should double-check with the nursing staff."

"I did. They said that there is no record of him being on this floor. How can I find out if he's somewhere else?"

"Let me see what I can find out. I'll meet you in the waiting room."

Will came back a few minutes later. Carl, Arabella, and Dr. Gildan gathered the parents and updated them. Carl wanted to make sure that they knew the basics and wanted them to push hard to get answers from these kids.

"This is what we know so far. The teens were having a party at 58 Mandarin Street, as no parents were present or expected home. An adult sibling arrived home after work at approximately midnight to find eleven teens unresponsive in the basement.

EMS arrived on scene approximately four minutes later and called for additional rescue assistance. They arrived here and were immediately treated for an unknown substance ingestion. This is still an active investigation and more information will be released soon. I'll let Dr. Gildan take it from there."

"We now know what made the kids so sick. They were given a form of an anesthetic medication. The substance is frequently known as a date rape drug. We know it was put in the punch that they all drank."

Carl interjected that it was unclear at this point if everyone agreed to take it or if it was done maliciously.

Will motioned to Carl and Arabella to step out. They met in the hall and Will told them that there was no Bryce Walker admitted with the other teens. Carl didn't know what to make of that news, but he did think that it was very suspicious. Carl went back into the room and asked the parents if anyone had contact information for Bryce Walker's parents and was quickly given the info.

Just as Carl was about to call the Walker family, Lydia came running out of the elevator, clearly shaken. He told her what was said to the other parents and showed her to James's room. He called the Walkers and after apologizing to them for the untimely phone call, requested that they bring their son, Bryce, and meet him at the station as soon as possible. Mr. Walker said that it would not be possible because Bryce was sleeping at a friend's house. Carl asked which friend and was told, Mikael Swan. Carl gave him a quick synopsis of what happened over the last few hours and said that Mikael Swan and his parents were at the hospital and that there was no sign of Bryce. Bryce was missing.

TWENTY-FIVE
Carl

Carl and Arabella were at the station and had just updated the other officers. They were printing pictures of Bryce to distribute. Captain White came in and Carl noticed he looked rather pale.

Carl asked, "What's going on, Cap?"

"Everyone. They've found a body," Captain White explained.

Arabella asked, "Oh no. Is it Bryce?"

"No. It's a female. She was found bound to a tree in Diamond Hill State Park. Some hikers called it in. They're pretty shaken up. From what they're saying, it's very gruesome."

Carl asked, "Who can we spare, Cap?"

"We can't spare anyone. Blackmore, take Chung with you and let me know what's going on. Hopefully, it's an exaggeration and we can have all hands-on-deck for the Bryce case."

"Wilson, you and Elan head to the liquor store where they bought the alcohol. Check the CCTV to see if you can tell who it was that bought it for them. I also want to see if the purchaser did anything to the stuff before it was given to them—so track them as much as possible. Could have been some sicko who dosed the stuff thinking it was funny. If not, my money is on Bryce—that might be why he ran. The rest of you, we need to find him. Start with the contacts his parents gave us."

Now, with their assignments, they all exited the station. Carl and Arabella were left to contemplate their next move. Carl was pacing back and forth and she knew better than to disturb him when he was in the zone. A vein on his forehead always protruded like a fat squiggly blue worm whenever he was upset and needed to think. It was bulging right now. This was how he processed best. Personally, Arabella thought, it's better to make notes and then connect them all for the big picture to appear. That was how she got her mojo flowing. She was trying to enter notes into her phone, but she was getting frustrated because the table was wobbling. She stood up and found a napkin. She folded it and placed it under the culprit's leg, making it level. She wished she could make the world level.

"I just don't understand it."

"What's that, Sarge?"

"Why put drugs in the booze? To what end? What was his goal?"

"You're assuming it was him, Carl. We still don't know for sure. No one was assaulted, or harmed when they were unconscious. It doesn't add up."

"I know. That's exactly why I don't understand it." Carl's phone rang. "What's going on there? Oh, shit. Okay, we'll be right there." Carl put his phone back in his pocket, "That was Blackmore. He said the scene is worse than we thought—something out of a horror movie. We need to get there."

Arabella headed toward the cruiser when Carl said, "Let's take the SUV, we don't know how far in they are." They climbed in and he headed to the park with full regalia of lights and sound.

The ride was silent so Arabella tried to bait Carl into talking. She asked him if he remembered when people could ski on the mountain at Diamond Hill.

"I remember. I was a teenager when they shut down. My friends and I went there a lot. I can't remember exactly when it closed or why, but we were pretty bummed."

She informed him, "It was called Ski Valley and it was shut down in 1981. It went under when larger ski slopes opened up in New England. The land, over 300 acres I think, was then acquired by the town."

"It's like working with a walking encyclopedia." Carl gave her side eyes and a slight smile.

Mission accomplished.

They arrived at the park to find markers and crime-scene tape, which led them to their destination. They were met with grown men and women, hard men and women, pale and shaken. These women and men were trained for the worst scenes imaginable. What they saw was beyond anything they could have ever imagined or comprehended. For as long as Carl had been a cop, he had never witnessed such perverse insanity. He tried to get Arabella to wait in the car, but she refused. He wished someone had offered the same escape plan to him.

Carl overheard some of his fellow officers saying things like, "This is Cumberland. Things like this don't happen in Cumberland." Others wished to remain solitary and try to process what they had just witnessed. He walked over to the scene and was taken back by the juxtaposition between the beauty of nature and the horrific sight in its midst.

The Chief brought him up to date. "Looks like the perp sliced off both breasts and part of the vaginal area then buried the body parts." This rang some bells with Carl. This had to be connected to Paul's death.

Carl sought out Blackmore and found him downhill, away from the scene. He thought that he left the area to be sick in private, so he didn't ask why he was there.

When he saw Carl, he said, "I know what you're gonna ask—what do we know? I'll tell you what we know, Carl. We know that there is one sick monster out there. In all my years, I've never . . ."

Arabella found them and shared her observations. "This killer likes them to suffer. This is a very personal killing. The amount of blood at the site indicates she was alive and suffering for a while."

Blackmore asked her how she could be sure about that.

She answered, "Once the heart stops beating, the evacuation of blood from the body stops. The rest of the blood in the body pools to the lower-most regions in situ as gravity takes effect. There is a lot of blood present."

It didn't seem right that there was such a vile and horrific scene at such a beautiful and normally serene place. People came here for the beauty and majesty of the region. He hoped they would find the perpetrator soon so this evil carnage would stop.

Captain White came over to them, "The FBI has just arrived. They think there may be a connection between this case and the one on 146."

Blackmore stated, "Really? No shit. I didn't see that crime scene, so I can't say. What do you think, Carl? I know you were privy to that crime and now this one."

"There are definite similarities. We should bring in Natalie Frazee who is point on that case." Captain White agreed and said that he would take care of that.

Carl was trying to process the events of the last few days. "The cases are similar but different. One a male, one a female. Both had sex organs removed. North Smithfield may know something we don't. I wasn't privy to the reports from the first murder. They only called me in as a courtesy because of my connection to the victim, Paul. I'm going to get Arabella and head back to the station to check on the search for Bryce. Blackmore, you stay here and keep me updated."

The ME arrived on scene along with the crime scene investigators. There were numerous amounts of photographs taken, along with measurements and plaster casts of footprints and tire tracks. Sometimes the most innocuous piece of evidence could be the missing puzzle piece that made everything come together to solve the case.

Once they accomplished all they could, they began the onerous task of taking the woman down from the tree.

TWENTY-SIX
Paige

Release day from the hospital found the group with mixed emotions. They were very relieved to be getting home, but they were also very apprehensive about what was to come. After they exhausted every possibility as to what could have happened that night, they realized that they were no closer to uncovering the truth than they were when they first awoke. The underlying thought that no one would voice was that it had to be Bryce. They had no idea why he would do such a thing, but it all pointed to him. Why else would he have left them like that?

Paige certainly took it the worst. She felt so betrayed and foolish. How could she have been so wrong about someone? She thought that she was in love with him. Her friends let it be and gave it their best shot to take her mind off him.

James was even more protective of Paige than ever. He acted as if he thought Bryce would show up at any minute to finish the job. He had the nurses change the private rooms that they were in for a double room that they both could share. She surprisingly found it comforting to have him with her. Even though his father made sure there was always a police officer there to roam the halls, she didn't feel as safe as having him in the same room. She couldn't shake the feeling that if she were out of there and at home, she would be better able to piece together what had happened that night and she couldn't wait to leave.

Eventually, everyone's parents arrived at the hospital to take them home. Lydia made arrangements for James to go home with Paige. She had to work, and Carl was too busy with the case to look after him. She didn't want him to be alone and knew that he would be well taken care of with them.

"Paige, are you sure you don't mind me going to your place? I wouldn't hold it against you if you've had enough of me. I'm sure you'd like to be alone."

"No, not at all, James. I think it will be a good idea if we both put our heads together and see if we can't fill in some of the missing pieces about what happened that night. You are the last person I remember seeing before everything went black. You gave me my drinks and that's all I can remember."

"Yeah, that's pretty much all I remember, too. I don't know if we'll ever remember it all. Did they say how long it would be before everyone's memory would return?"

"No one mentioned a timeframe. They said that it could be a while though."

Although Paige and the others felt much better, they were still very lethargic and only able to be active for limited amounts of time. She was ready to close her eyes and nap a bit when her mother walked in.

"Hey, you two. Ready to blow this clambake?" She was always so proud of the corny, old-fashioned sayings she used. At times, Paige thought she did it to embarrass her or to get her to laugh. She really couldn't tell anymore.

She grabbed the two overnight bags she brought and set to packing each with the belongings for Paige and James. "James, I'll take you by your house so you can get what you'll need to stay with us for a few days."

"Okay, Mrs. Vale. I really appreciate everything."

"It's no problem at all." She finished packing everything away and put out some clean clothes for Paige. "You both should get changed; sorry I didn't think to grab some fresh things for you, James. I'll go out to the desk and see if your release papers are ready."

Paige changed and sat on the bed. Sloane came back in and let them know that they were ready to go.

Two friendly orderlies came in with wheelchairs. One asked, "Did someone order a manual taxi?" and began to laugh at his own joke with a little too much vigor, which made the lame joke a lot funnier.

"I don't need one of those," said James. He was standing up beside his bed in the clothes he had worn to the party. He was standing up straighter than normal and his chest was puffed out much more than usual.

"Well, my good sir, it is standard procedure to

escort all patients by these two-wheeled chariots. I can assure you that it is the policy for every man, woman, and child." He could see James pondering this. He waited a beat and James gave a slight nod of approval. They were both loaded into the chairs and wheeled into the elevator with Sloane right behind them. Once outside and free, they filed into the SUV.

They took an unexpected exit on their way home. Once Paige realized where they were, she was very hopeful she knew why they were there in the southern part of town. In just a few minutes, she knew that her suspicion was correct. She was elated. They were stopping to get some Portuguese food to take home. They had a favorite little spot that had the best food ever. "Pork, potatoes, and littlenecks for me, please!"

"There are five orders ready and waiting. James, I can't remember, have you had that dish before?"

"I don't think so, but I'm sure I'll like it."

Sloane ran in and came out with two large bags that she put into the back before driving away once again.

The next stop was to let James gather his things to take back with them. James quickly collected what he thought he would need, took care of the dogs, and returned to the vehicle.

Once they reached their final destination, they were greeted by an overzealous canine and a lanky boy who was all feet and tripping over them at the moment. Mitch came out and helped with the bags.

While they ate, Timothy asked numerous

questions based on what he had heard on the news and repeated by the grownups. Paige and James left it to Sloane and Mitch to answer them because they knew it was a delicate balance between a partial truth and protecting him from the whole truth. There was a halt to the television program that Tim was watching to announce that the FBI was considering the murder of the tortured woman found at Diamond Hill State Park to be the work of the same individual who had murdered the man in North Smithfield. The announcer was eager to share that there was another breaking development. "Bryce Walker, a Cumberland high school student, is missing. He is wanted for questioning regarding a party where underaged teenagers took a dark turn. All of the participants were found unconscious and were rushed to the hospital. All are alleged victims of someone drugging their alcohol. There is a reward for information regarding his whereabouts."

"Hey, isn't he your bo-yyy-fr-ie-nnnd?" Tim asked in a singsong manner, very proud of himself for embarrassing his sister.

"Tim, shut it!" Paige immediately looked over at James who had stopped chewing and stared at Tim.

Mitch got up from the table and turned off the television. He made eye contact with Sloane, cleared his throat, and tried to liven the mood. "Why don't we all play a board game once we've finished with dinner?"

James got up from the table, scraped off his plate, and placed it in the dishwasher. "I'm still very tired. I think I'll head upstairs." He flashed a brief, sad smile and left the family.

It was silent for a few seconds and then they could hear his footfalls ascending the stairs to one of the spare bedrooms.

"Why did you say that, you jerk?" She crumpled her napkin and threw it at her brother.

"I heard you talking to your friends. What's the big deal?"

"Ugh! Mom, can you go and talk to James?" Paige felt so terrible for James but was still extremely weak and was not ready to have this discussion with him.

"While I think it should be you that has this conversation, you look like you need to lie down as well. You head up to your room and I'll handle everything."

Paige did as she was told, and began to head to her room when Sloane said, "Oh, and Paige, my dear, you owe me one. We *will* have this discussion about the red X Tim insists on putting on his forehead every night."

Paige laughed, "You got it, Mom." She retreated to her room as well. As soon as she changed and got into bed, she received a group text message from the *mean girls*. It was yet another text message to see if anyone remembered anything further about what had happened the night of the party or if anyone had heard about where Bryce could be. As usual, no one had any new information. This was getting very tiring for Paige. She was constantly trying to remember and became extremely frustrated that she could not see through the veil in her mind surrounding that night.

Sloane went to the guest room and knocked on the door. She opened it a crack to look in and saw James sitting on the bed. She entered. "James, don't pay any attention to what Tim said. He is always trying to get a rise out of his sister." She walked closer to him and saw that he was off somewhere retreated deep within himself. He didn't even hear what she said. She became very concerned, "James? James?" She touched his shoulder and still nothing. She nudged him gently while again calling to him.

All at once, he met her gaze. What she saw behind his eyes sent a shiver down her spine.

"Mrs. Vale? What is it?"

"Oh, nothing, James. I was just telling you not to pay attention to anything that Tim says because he is always trying to get under his sister's skin."

"I know. Don't worry about me." When he spoke, it sounded very robotic; not at all like him.

Sloane wanted nothing more than to run out of the room. She composed herself, "James, get some rest. Come on down when you're ready and we'll all play that board game."

He looked up at her and smiled, nodding in compliance, looking more like himself.

She left the room not knowing exactly what had just taken place.

+++++++++++++

A few days passed and the group was excited to get on with the normalcy of every-day-life, which meant going back to school. They wanted to stay together as much as possible, for support, so it was decided that they would carpool; Sade volunteered to be the chauffeur. The group also agreed to spend every study and lunch together. They even arranged to get a pass from their physical education classes and instead meet with either Ms. Little, Ms. Pastor, Ms. Butcher, or Ms. Zenun in a counseling session. James was surprisingly agreeable to this; Paige knew it was so he could keep an eye on her. Her friends also liked having him around because he made them feel safe, although they would never admit to it.

Sade's parents took her to Jenna's where she had left her car on that fateful night. Jenna jumped in the passenger seat and Sade got behind the wheel. She adjusted the seat and mirrors and began the pick-ups. She brought everyone to school safe and sound.

During the day, Paige noticed James hovered over her between every class. As soon as someone would attempt to ask her what had happened, he would whisk her away. This even happened when the assistant principal approached her. At first, it was a little embarrassing, but she grew to be thankful for not having to answer everyone.

During the last class, which was a study period for her, Paige made her way to the advising wing. It was located on the ground floor. She descended the cold cracking gray concrete stairs, with worn black treads, and could not stop the icy feeling from seeping into her bones. She meandered down a long concrete corridor. The building was very old and there was nowhere that displayed its age more than the cracking foundation of the ground floor. Sporadic dark water spots could be seen on the cork portion of the drop ceiling above. An unwelcome musty stench also assaulted her nostrils. She found the conference room and entered to see the welcoming faces eagerly waiting to greet her and her friends. She was set at ease the moment she entered the room and saw Ms. Little, Ms. Zenun, Ms. Pastor, and Ms. Butcher. They offered much inspiration and healing.

Only Karol and Sade had this period free and they soon arrived to join Paige. Every time Ms. Little would try to help the three of them, she would turn into a blubbering mush. She felt their pain. When that would happen, Ms. Pastor's green eyes would pierce through them directly into their souls. She always knew the right words to speak. It didn't hurt that Ms. Butcher and Ms. Zenun had tea and sweets for the group. They never intruded on their experience, only offered hope and guidance.

At the end of the school day, Paige met up with everyone at Sade's car. She and James were dropped off at her house.

They were having a snack in the kitchen when Sloane came in. "I need to run out for a bit. Tim should be home soon. Please help him with his homework and I might just bring home something special for dinner."

"Sure thing, Mom."

"No problem, Mrs. Vale."

"Thanks. Be back soon."

The pair was searching for a movie to watch when Paige heard the bus. She opened the front door and noticed a strange, unpleasant smell. Tim came running up the front walk and up onto the porch. He barreled his way by Paige and told her she smelled bad. He ran into the living room and began wrestling with James. Jasper took this as a sign that it was a free-for-all, barking his approval and joining in, wagging his fluffy gray tail.

Paige attempted to put an end to the roughhousing and gave James a look that said she meant business. "That's enough. Time for homework. Once you finish, we'll let you watch a movie with us. There's a snack for you to eat while you get to work. As soon as you're done, I want to check it to make sure you did it all. James, keep me company while I unload the dishwasher."

Tim stood up, mockingly saluted his sister, and then ran away from her, snickering. James followed suit and deflected a punch from Paige as he laughed his way into the kitchen behind her. Tim opened his backpack and got busy with what he had to complete for the next day's lessons.

Paige straightened up the kitchen a bit and told James that they needed to talk. She wanted to know if being out of the hospital had brought any memories of the party to the surface. He told her that he was so frustrated because nothing after them having a drink around the table was obtainable. She concurred and voiced how frustrating it was; especially feeling like there was something just behind a shroud that she could not see.

They decided that Tim should be about finished with his homework, so they went to see what he was doing. When they entered the living room, they were greeted with a very bizarre sight. Tim had arranged a good amount of his toys and other household objects directly in front of the front door and windows in the living room facing the farmer's porch at the front of the house.

"What the hell, Timmy? What are you doing?"

While they were trying to figure out what was going on, Sloane arrived home and parked in the garage. She came in through the kitchen, placed the take-out on the table, walked through the foyer, and met the kids in the living room with a perplexed look on her face.

"What's all this?"

Tim answered by saying he was guarding the family against the aliens. He told them that he knew they were on the porch. Paige looked up at the ceiling and began to say something to her mother when she was cut off.

"Paige, I have a feeling this is a continuation of the other night's escapades. I want to know what is going on right now!" She knew that there was information she wasn't given by Paige's earlier laconic answers to her questions.

She started to pick up the toys and Tim began to

scream and cry, "No, Mom. Stop! We need to know if they are trying to get in. There's one out there now!" Sloane cleared the way to the door and proceeded to open it. Tim grabbed onto her leg. "I'm going to show you that there are no aliens here, Timothy. Calm down."

"It's in the scarecrow, Mom. Don't go near it."

Sloane went over to the scarecrow with Tim still attached to her leg, and Paige and James followed them. She noticed something odd. There was a foul smell emanating from it and the clothing was stained with tinges of red and brown ooze. She gingerly touched the shoulder and backed up in a panic. She quickly rounded everyone up and made them go into the house.

"James, can you please give your dad a call and have him come over? ASAP. Please."

Paige felt a terrible feeling of nausea roll in the pit of her stomach. "What's going on, Mom?"

"I'm not sure, Paige. I'd just like him to come and check on things to make us feel more comfortable. Can you take Tim and James into the kitchen? I brought home some tikka masala. Get everything set up and I'll be in soon."

Paige was very concerned—she could see that her mom was trembling. She did as her mom asked and corralled everyone together in the kitchen.

James looked very worried and even a bit pale. He began pacing and moving his lips as if he was talking to himself, but the words were imperceptible.

"James, can you help me?" He looked at her as

if he saw her for the first time. He helped Paige set the table and began to take the containers out of the bags. They could hear talking from the other room and guessed that Carl had arrived.

Sloane came into the kitchen and told them that they were leaving.

"Is it cuz of the aliens, Mom?"

"No, Tim. No aliens. Let's pack up the food again and we'll take it to Cookie's. I've called dad and he is going to meet us there. I want you all in the garage. I'm going to pack a few things to bring and grab Jasper."

"Pack? What the hell, Mom? What's going on?"

Sloane gave Paige a look that made her stop asking questions. She rinsed off the dishes they used while James re-packed everything. Tim sat on his chair hugging his knees to his chest and rocked back and forth while he watched them. Once everything was sorted, they grabbed Jasper, went through to the garage, and waited in the SUV.

Sloane stopped to speak to Carl and Arabella before heading into the garage. "I'm taking James with me to Mitch's mothers. Mitch will meet us there. I'll text Lydia—I know you have your hands full."

"Thanks for that. I feel like I'm in the middle of a horror movie. Who could have done something like this? I hate to ask you, but can you look and see if you know who this is?"

With trepidation in her voice she answered, "I'll look." Sloane braced herself and looked. "That's Bryce. I'm almost certain."

"Are you sure it's him, Sloane?"

"Yes, I'm pretty sure it's him. Whoever did this is not human."

"Okay, thanks for keeping James. I have to get back to this."

As Sloane was going to leave, flashing lights and sirens blaring alerted the neighborhood that four squad cars, an ambulance, and a fire truck were approaching. Neighbors began to peer through windows and came out onto their porches and front lawns to try to steal a glimpse of what was going on. Sloane knew this was going to change everything and everyone for a long time.

TWENTY-SEVEN
Carl

Captain White got out of the cruiser, lifted the police caution tape to crouch under, and approached Carl and Arabella.

"We need to stop meeting like this." It was meant to lighten the mood, but the delivery failed. He looked like he hadn't slept for days. His long, oval face was pallid and unshaven. His greyish-blue eyes were bloodshot and Carl believed that he was wearing the same clothes that he had worn for days now. He was a good man. A hard-working man. It was evident that he cared about his job and more importantly, the people in his town.

"We have reinforcements coming in from all over the state. This is getting out of hand. We stopped a local news truck from trying to enter the plat. Before long, this will get out and we'll have all of New England panicking."

"Cap, do the feds still think this is the work of one person?"

"There's been too many bodies and scenes to evaluate. It will take time to assess it all, but my best guess is that it is the same perp. The feds are bringing in more people and setting up a temporary base at the old Ski Lodge at Diamond Hill."

Captain White also injected, "We need to re-interview the kids from the party. See if any of them remember anything else from that night. I know it's a longshot, but it needs to be done."

Carl went quiet and stared at his shoes. "That could have been James. I know I'm on the job, and I should be professional, but I can't help think what I'd do if it were him on that porch." He thought back to his life with James. He regretted how much he missed since he left. He had always felt terrible about leaving his family. He never meant for it to happen. He knew what people thought of cops and their promiscuity, but that wasn't the case with him.

It all began when he and his first partner were called to a domestic violence situation. It was a very bad call. When he came upon the scene, he realized that it was his wife's friend, Tara. She was in and out of consciousness. Her face was bruised and swollen beyond recognition. If it wasn't for her identification, he never would have been able to tell it was her. Her boyfriend hit her repeatedly with a steel pipe he was using to fix some gas lines in the kitchen. He didn't stop at her face. Her ribs were shattered and he had punctured one of her lungs. She was wheezing and stammering for breath. Both shins were also shattered.

His partner stayed with the perp and Carl stayed with Tara until the rescue arrived. It was touch-and-go for a couple of days. The doctors weren't sure she would regain her normal functions due to the severe head trauma and lack of oxygen she suffered.

Carl had met her a few times previously. Lydia took it very hard and asked him to monitor Tara's progress. He kept his word and went by the hospital as often as he could. She was so strong; such a fighter. His admiration for her slowly turned into more. He didn't see exactly when it turned into more, but it did. Then, all at once, he loved them both, probably always would.

The worst part was how it affected James. He felt like a lurch because he betrayed Lydia, but he knew she would eventually be all right. He worried about James the most. He began to act out in strange, scary ways. He would get himself worked up and then just retreat into some deep area within himself to the point that he became unreachable. When it was over, James would say that he couldn't remember anything and didn't know what happened. The doctors didn't know what it was. The best they could offer was that it was a form of oppositional defiant disorder or a dissociative fugue. He and Lydia realized that after dragging James to every doctor suggested in Rhode Island and Boston, no one knew what was happening and that they probably never would. The older he became, the less frequent the episodes happened—much to their relief.

Captain White put his hand on Carl's shoulder and told him that he understood. "You know the homeowners well?"

"Yes. I've known them for a long time. Our kids grew up together."

"Okay. Make sure they get to the station for an interview. I know it's just perfunctory, but we need to follow procedure amid this chaos. Also, the feds want us to set up three separate minor task forces— one for each case and then we will convene and communicate our findings to the entire group. The chief is coming back early from her honeymoon in Greece—I'm sure her husband is ecstatic. I'll be catching her up as soon as she gets in."

The crime scene team worked for hours collecting their samples and photographing the warped scene on the porch. When the ME approached, he said that they would be able to inspect the body soon. He told them that the victim had been dead for approximately 72 to 84 hours.

"That would mean he was murdered the night of the party or the day after." The realization that Bryce was on the porch that long, made his insides churn in disgust.

Shortly after, the techs left the area and Carl and Arabella went up the wide, sturdy steps of the wrap-around. They still could not believe what they were looking at.

When they first arrived, they saw a dead body dressed in a mishmash of jeans, a plaid shirt, and a tuxedo jacket seated on the Vales' front porch. He had a welder's helmet covering his face. Now that the CSI team removed most of the mismatched clothing and coverings, Carl and Arabella could view the torturous destruction of a promising young man's life. Donned in their hairnets, gloves, and shoe coverings, the pair saw that Bryce Walker was brutally murdered. There was so much carnage; they didn't know where to begin.

As always, Arabella reined him in and injected her practicality into the situation. "Let's start at the top, shall we?"

She noticed that the skin pallor was a stark contrast to the dried blood on his cheeks. Both eyeballs were removed which left a bloody trail that had run down his face, neck, and onto his chest. She added, "Removal of the eyes means this was very personal. Usually, it is done to send a message."

Carl nodded in agreement. "What kind of sick message could this be?"

Arabella looked up at him and used her hand as a visor against the large portable klieg lights in her line of vision. "Probably one that coincides with the reason for opening his chest and removing his heart so crudely. This is some next-level slaughter. A professional definitely did not do it. The whole doctor line we were investigating can be ruled out now."

Carl agreed with her assessments. Every wound was rudimentary and haphazard.

She continued, "Both hands are also removed. This is usually done when someone doesn't want the body to be identified by fingerprints. They had to know that this family would know who he was. They also knew we were looking for him."

Arabella had that look on her face that told Carl to let her be and formulate what she was putting together. She reluctantly unzipped and pushed down the waist portion of the jeans he was wearing. The three major wounds they uncovered were the only ones inflicted upon him. "It's odd that he left his penis."

"He could have run out of time. This is clearly not where the murder took place."

"Could be, but it doesn't feel like that's the case. We will need to get the reports from the officers who had canvassed the neighbors and see if anyone knows anything."

Carl agreed and decided to look around the entirety of the porch. He did not find anything, but he did notice that there were two cameras set up.

He called Sloane to ask her about them.

She answered right away. "Hi, Carl." In a very hushed voice, she asked, "What is going on? Is it definitely Bryce?"

"It hasn't been released yet, but yes. It's him. We're waiting for dental records, but it's safe to say many of us recognize him. I'm sorry Sloane, I don't have a lot of time and I need to ask you about the cameras you have on your porch. Do you keep the video?"

"Yes. I can access footage for 30 days from the cloud."

"Okay, we need to take a look at the footage from the night before the kid's party and beyond."

"Sure. I'll get it right to you. Oh, wait. The power was out for a while in the whole neighborhood the night of the party. When I left for the hospital, the electric company was working on the line."

"All right, we'll contact them directly. Thank you. One other thing and it's just a formality. You and Mitch need to get to the station as soon as you can to give us a statement. They'll need to ask you questions and may need you to provide proof of your whereabouts on certain dates."

"I understand. We can have the kids stay with Cookie and head over as soon as Mitch gets home."

"Great, thanks." Carl ended the call and went over to a uniformed officer whom he put in charge of finding out the details for the power outage that night.

The night was quickly ending and the sun was rising over the pergola that stood covered in vines that in the spring and summer displayed a beautiful array of multicolored flowers. It was located on the east side of the backyard. The sun was painting the sky in beautiful hues of yellow, orange, and pink. If it were under different circumstances, it would make a picture-perfect print with the tree limbs devoid of their leaves at the forefront of the scene. With the circumstances being what they were, it cast an ominous mood instead.

Captain White walked back to Carl and Arabella. He took one look at what used to be the active, muscled body of Bryce and shook his head in disbelief. Carl met his gaze and said, "This is the biggest thing to ever hit this town, Cap. We can't mess this up. We need to catch this bastard."

"I have every intention of pulling out all the stops

to find him. We are getting help from the feds, and every department in the state and Massachusetts has offered their assistance as well."

To most of the world, it was just any other day. The sunlight was trickling through the oaks and weeping willows while the dahlias, marigolds, and sunflowers danced in the breeze. People were heading to work and walking their dogs while trying to steal a glimpse of what was happening at the Vales' residence. What little was left in his stomach undulated with the thought of what was to come.

When the news got out about the horrific scene on this family's front porch, life would never be the same. How could they have had it so wrong? They thought that Bryce drugged his friends for some nefarious reason. This would go down in the history of Rhode Island as the worst killing spree ever. They had to find who was committing these gruesome murders—and find them fast.

Arabella finally revealed the angle she was forming. "I'm thinking that the perp could be the one who purchased the alcohol for the teens. He could have doctored the booze, followed them, and then grabbed Bryce once everyone was unconscious."

Carl and Samuel exchanged a look that said her revelation was noteworthy. The captain left to talk to the FBI who had just arrived at the scene.

Arabella received an alert on her phone. "Carl, there were no unidentified prints anywhere on the porch. The hits came back for the family, James, and a few that have been recognized on file as delivery personnel. Not surprising, but it would have been nice to have even a small lead."

"Yeah, I'm not surprised. This guy is too malevolent for a rookie move like not wearing gloves."

"Carl, you should head over to the Walker's and tell them we found their son. I'll go to the high school to talk to the teens from the party."

TWENTY-EIGHT

Rosa Marie

Rosa Marie was late again. She hated having to open up The Walk-In Closet store at the mall. It cut into her "extracurricular activities." There were already two moms there with their daughters impatiently looking through the gates. They were so annoying. She hated the runny-nosed spoiled brats yanking their mother's chains and always getting their way. They always wanted the tackiest crap on the racks. Rosa Marie prided herself on wearing nothing but the best, classiest clothing available—she was worth every penny. She would tell this to anyone who would listen, not knowing that people who were classy and wore classy clothing would never have to broadcast it.

Rosa Marie announced that she was going on break shortly after she arrived. The other two sales associates looked at one another with disdain. She knew they disliked her. They were just jealous. She went into the breakroom, grabbed her purse, and headed to the donut shop on the outskirts of the food court. Walking past the store windows, she caught a glimpse of herself. She looked damn good. She was wearing everything from the best-looking mannequin at her favorite "high-end" shop. She added the classiest pair of pumps she could find and bam! She liked the way her blonde wig, which she usually wore for work, framed her long face with piercing dark brown eyes and a wide, seductive mouth. The dress showed her curves exactly the way she liked. She was confident that at any moment, she could have anyone she wanted. She was so lucky to have Lucas. He understood her like no one ever had. She had to remember to do something special for him tonight.

TWENTY-NINE

Arabella

Arabella went to the high school as busses were arriving with teenagers filing out of them en masse, and parents dropped off sleepy, cantankerous teens to fill their brains with knowledge. She would need to meet with the party group again. She felt a little anxious meeting with them at the school. It brought back memories of the uncaring malice of the bullying classmates that she had to endure when she was young. There were three or four bullies whose mere existence was an exercise in sociopathy. They did nothing but plan and scheme to make every insecure student quake in their wake.

She was buzzed in and met with the secretary, Ms. Butcher, who rounded up all of the students involved. She was so helpful—whenever anyone needed help navigating the school campus, they sought her expertise. She also suggested that even though Arabella said she still had permission from all of the parents, they bring in some of the teachers to join the students, just to be safe. Arabella agreed and they brought in Ms. Little, Ms. Zenun, and Ms. Pastor because they were the teachers that most students were already meeting with and felt comfortable around. They treated the students like equals and never spoke down to them.

The eleven waited outside of the conference room while they were called in, one-by-one. They started with James and ended with Sade. No one had remembered anything worth repeating, just jumbled pictures and sounds. Arabella assured the group that it was a start and that she was sure more would come back to them in time.

Arabella told the women that she was finished with the group of students. Ms. Butcher, Little, Zenun, and Pastor decided that they would give the group a pass and had them head to the gymnasium a little early as there was a scheduled assembly beginning shortly about joining the armed forces.

Carl called to ask how the interviews had gone. She said that it went about as they expected with no new developments. He told her that the dental records had confirmed that the body found was definitely Bryce. He said that the Walkers were inconsolable, as was expected, and that they needed to get ahead of the news before it spread like wildfire.

Arabella had an idea. "The students are heading to an assembly right now. I will talk to the principal and have her make the announcement." Carl agreed that it was a good idea.

Arabella made her way to the assembly and spoke to the principal. She was clearly nervous and was willing to comply with changing the topic of the gathering. She spoke to one of the service personnel who looked like they were in charge. With a downcast look on his face, he walked over to the microphone and put a hand on the recruiter's shoulder. This stopped her in her tracks and she conceded the mic to the principal.

"Thank you to all the representatives from the varied military outfits. I'm sure your messages have been received. Now, unfortunately, we have some very sad news to convey to you all. Detective Luthor will fill you in." The short, pixie-like woman turned to Arabella who was clearly not expecting to be put on the spot like that.

She made her way up to the microphone and tapped it. "Thank you, Principal Newman," she spoke with a quiver in her voice. "Hello everyone. I am here to announce some terrible news. Earlier today, it was confirmed that the body of Bryce Walker was found. It is an ongoing investigation, and as we learn new information, ah, we will, um, let the public know." She began to walk off the stage and then went back to the mic, "Thank you."

Principal Newman went over to the microphone. The students were shocked by the news. There were tears and sniffling and many lost looks on the faces of the students. "I want you all to know that there will be counselors available to help you in any way you need. If you would like to go to the counseling wing, they are there and ready to assist."

Paige was running toward the exit and ran into two of the football players that were at the party.

The tall one with the red hair and freckles hugged

her, "Paige, we're wicked sorry. This is so awful."

Tears clouded her eyes once again. "I know. I can't understand why this happened."

At that moment, James came up to Paige and put his arms around her. He gave a very disapproving look to the two football players and they were on their way.

"James, this is so terrible. Do you think it was Bryce on my porch? Can you ask your dad? I can't take all the disturbing things going around in my mind. I have to know for sure."

"Of course. Let's find the others—I'll text him right now." He sent the text while the others were meeting at Sade's car. Their worst fears were confirmed—it was Bryce. Someone had murdered him and set him in place of the family scarecrow. Paige was devastated. James had to help her to Sade's car.

THIRTY

Paige

Once school ended, Sade dropped everyone off at their house and James was taken to the animal clinic. Paige asked Sade to drive by her house. She didn't think that she could ever step foot in there again but had an obscene need to see it. As they entered the cul-de-sac, everything she saw looked different—but in essence, she was only looking at everything through very different eyes. The houses, decorated for Halloween, once looked joyful and entertaining, but now looked macabre and chilling. This was her neighborhood. This was where she had grown up. She didn't know if she would ever feel the same about anything ever again.

Paige was inconsolable after the discovery that Bryce's murdered body had been on her porch. Whoever killed him had set him at *her* home, which added an extra layer of evil to the sick, perverted act.

The car radio announced an update on the killing spree. The news announcer stated that all of the murder victims had been dismembered. Unconfirmed sources stated that it was the work of an alleged serial killer and that the murderer took body parts as trophies.

It was just too much. How could anyone wrap their head around three murders in these small towns? Paige began to feel the horrible guilt and overwhelming sadness creep back into her subconscious. She couldn't believe that she and everyone else had originally blamed Bryce for drugging the group and then fleeing. She should have known better. Especially her.

Sade could sense the difference wash over Paige. "Hey, get out of that dark space." Sade looked over at Paige and saw a tear roll down her cheek. "Remember, everyone thought the same way. You've done nothing wrong." She searched the center console for a tissue and offered one to her. "Even if you shouted from the rooftops that you didn't think it was him, the outcome would still be the same. If anything, you should be upset with the police."

Paige looked at her with a quizzical expression and one eyebrow raised.

Sade finished with, "If they didn't keep the fact that some weirdo serial killer was out there a secret, this might have been figured out sooner."

They parked as close as they could get to the caution tape in front of the house. The pair sat in silence, Sade turning off the radio in respect. The silence was broken by a knock on the window that made the pair jump out of their skins.

Sade rolled down the window when she saw a uniformed police officer. "Nothing to see here. Better move on, you two."

"She lives here, officer." He peered into the car

and saw Paige.

"Well, this is still a crime scene, and no one is allowed in or out."

Paige said, "I know. We're sorry. I just felt like I needed to be here to take it all in."

The officer nodded and walked back to his post but kept his eye on them.

Paige then received a text from her mom asking her when she'd be getting back to her grandmother's. She told her that she was on her way.

THIRTY-ONE
Carl

Carl and Arabella met up with Captain White and the other teams at the Diamond Hill Ski Lodge home base to be brought up to date and to share what they had uncovered. All the teams had converged and were now relaying the newfound information to Allan De Luca, the Assistant Special Agent-in-Charge, ASAC, and to the Chief of Police, Anika Haverhill. They both took command of the investigations.

The old ski lodge was set up quickly and it showed. There were mismatched tables and chairs cordoned off in sections. The floor was stacked with dozens of boxes containing supplies, and files were everywhere. They were making the best of the space and trying not to encroach on one another.

Carl felt bad that Anika had to return prematurely from her honeymoon. She worked hard and never took any time off. She didn't seem to be fazed by it at all. She remained incredibly focused. Her sun-kissed cheeks and even lighter blonde hair were the only proof of a recent Grecian getaway. Wilson and Elan came into the building ready to share some news but stopped when they saw what was unfolding. The chief signaled him to speak.

Wilson spoke, "We located the liquor store where the teens purchased their liquor. I've just come back from reviewing the video footage. It was a group of four young men in their late-twenties that went in for them. The video from inside the store shows they looked at their phones, which must have had a text listing what the teens wanted. They picked out a few things and went right to the register. Nothing fishy happened inside. Once they left the building, they handed the bags to the teens and left. If the alcohol was drugged, it had to happen in the car or at the house."

The Chief thanked the officer and said, "Okay, so there doesn't seem to be a link to the drugs at the liquor store. Now we need to look in another direction." She wheeled over a very large white case board that was divided into two sections by dry erase marker lines, and she wrote similarities and differences at the top of each section. She then asked the officers to list the similarities of the cases. She wrote them in the similarities section as they were called out. When they were finished, she went over the most important ones. "We know that all victims were drugged, they were all tortured, and they all had body parts removed."

As if in a perfectly choreographed dance, ASAC chimed in asking for the differences between the cases. Once again, people would shout out information for him to add to the other side of the board. "We also know that the types of drugs used to render the latest victim unconscious changed with the last kill, and also the conspicuousness of the locations of the bodies changed—he's getting more brazen. Another variance is that the sex and age of the victims differ, and also that there is no apparent connection between any of them." This information was given with complete aplomb. Everyone was on their top game trying to impress the feds.

While the information was being combined, there was a draft seeping in from the numerous windows aligning two sides of the building's hall. The decrepit state of the building was no match for the chilly drop in temperature outside. The building was old and in need of renovation. However, those who were calling this place home were grateful that there was a full kitchen in the back of the structure. Many of the officers' family members used the kitchen to take turns making sure that they were all fed home-cooked meals instead of ordering out all the time.

Another case board was presented and divided into thirds. Each victim's name was listed at the top. All pertinent information about each person was applied including photos and the major bullet points about their murder. This was so abnormal for the small town; the law enforcement officers were grateful for all of the aid they were receiving to end this killing spree.

Captain White stepped up to the front with the Chief and ASAC. He looked at them and asked what everyone was dying to ask, "Are we looking at one killer for all three murders?"

The Chief began to answer when ASAC cut her off and took over.

"It's too soon to know with any certainty, but we are assuming that it is the work of the same person. The varying of the way the bodies are being displayed and the type of drugs he is using might be nothing but accessibility and the fact that he is escalating with every kill."

Lieutenant Frazee entered the building and updated the group that all of the Vales' whereabouts checked out for the times of all three murders and that the electric company had indeed repaired a frayed wire on the night of the party. "When I asked if it was manually cut, they couldn't say for sure. They said sometimes animals damage wires. There was no way to be certain." She was thanked for the update.

When the brief was over, Carl and Arabella went out to their patrol car. He got behind the wheel and waited for her to say something. When she didn't, he glanced at her. "Hey, what's on your mind?" He could tell by the way her deep-set, dark eyes had begun to squint that she was in deep thought. In addition, her chestnut skin began to crease at the bridge of her nose and her jaw was locked tight— another dead giveaway.

She shook her head and made a dismissive noise. If he pursued this line of inquiry, it would only anger her. Although she had a slight frame and was not very tall, he would not want to cross her when she was angry. "I'm just processing everything. If I come up with anything significant, I'll let you know. I know that having the expertise of the FBI is like having snow on Christmas day, but I think their cookie-cutter assessments are antiquated and they might not be going in the right direction. You know, with all the testosterone floating around the task force, it feels like if we follow their lead, we'll catch him by the end of the day. This isn't a TV show where they'll figure out who the bad guy is right before the end of the hour. There's gonna be a lot more carnage before we figure it out. Especially because they are so narrow-minded."

They left the temporary headquarters and headed south. He was biding his time before he spoke so that he wouldn't disrupt her train of thought. As they drove past a popular apple farm and marketplace, it conjured up memories of when James was a young boy. He and Lydia would take him there to go apple picking. He would put him on his shoulders and let him pick from the tops of the trees. He would be so happy. The three of them would go on hayrides and James would never leave without a candied apple and a pumpkin. He would draw the design that would bring life to it and transform it from a pumpkin to a jack-o-lantern. He would participate in the entire ritual sans removing the pumpkin seeds because he hated getting the *gook* on his hands. Thinking back to those times, he could actually conjure the smells of the fresh-baked pumpkin pie straight from the oven and the cinnamon spice candle burning each fall season.

"Look Luthor, even if they're sniffing in the wrong direction, it doesn't mean we can't follow our own leads to see what we uncover. We need to follow directives, but the rest is subjective. If you feel that strongly about it, we'll be more open-minded. You've never steered me wrong yet. Once we get back to the station where we can think on our own, we'll go over all the clues from the crime scenes, and look for something common between them."

THIRTY-TWO
Lucas

Lucas read the text from Rosa Marie and bile rose to the back of his throat. He checked his phone for the local news alerts and was floored at what he read. They found the bodies. They were beginning to put the information together. He felt his pulse begin to quicken. He knew this would happen eventually; he also knew he would never be ready for it. He balled his fists and pounded at his temples letting out a primal scream.

Once he regained his composure, he called her. She answered, "The news is out all over town. I can't believe you are so weak that you let them find the bodies that easily," and quickly hung up on him.

"Rosa Marie, hello? Hello? Damn!" He tried her cell again—no answer. Lucas knew he needed to find her and soon. He attempted to track her cell phone, but the location app had been turned off. He knew that she was supposed to be working today so he headed to the mall.

When he arrived at The Walk-In Closet, he learned that Rosa Marie said she wasn't feeling well and had left for the day. He expected as much. He decided to drive by the apartment but had no real expectations that she would be there. The late afternoon sun was dazzling in the vivid, cloudless, sky. Although it was warmer than usual, the nights were beginning to get very cool which was indicative of the winter to come. The beautiful scene before him was quite the contrast to the storm that was brewing inside him.

He was correct. She was not there. He drove past some of the bars he knew she liked and did not spot her car. He passed by a few other places with the same outcome. He didn't know what to do with himself. Every shadow he saw played tricks on his mind getting him to think she was around every corner.

He knew what was to come. He couldn't be unprepared this time. He stopped to procure the tools he would need, went home, and made a kill kit—this time he'd be ready. No more adrenalin-fueled encounters where mistakes were inevitable. He had heard his hunting friends talk about getting all of the tools and supplies that they could possibly need and keeping them in a kit so that there would never be any surprises come hunting day—he did the very same thing for his next hunt.

Lucas felt the dread creep under the very skin that held him together. He couldn't fail her again. He needed to get her back; to find her and make things right again. He needed to prove he could be a better man for her and always defend her honor.

THIRTY-THREE
Paige

Sade delivered Paige to her grandmother's house. She was saying her goodbyes when they both heard the text alert on their phones. There was going to be a vigil for Bryce at Tucker Field, across from the high school, on Saturday night. Sade looked at her friend with deep concern. "Paige, everyone would understand if you aren't up to going."

"I can't miss it. I owe him that much." Paige knew that this would be one of the hardest things she would ever do, but she had to be there. She would take this hurt and regret with her to the grave. She vowed to make it as special and memorable as she could. "We need everyone to show their support. I can't even imagine what his family is going through right now. We need to get the gang together tomorrow and brainstorm about how we can help."

Sade had an idea, "I can have my mom reach out to Mrs. Walker. They go to yoga together. I'll have her find out what they have planned so we can take it from there."

As they sat outside the beautiful English Tudor, they made plans to honor Bryce and attempted to erase all their misgivings that had been forged against his name. Paige always loved the sight of the massive white stucco and dark brown timberwork that reminded her of a gingerbread house. She would eat her lunch on the front lawn and gaze upon it trying to see how many different patterns she could discover. The most prominent feature of the house was the massive and ornate chimney. It was made of a perfect balance of different-sized stones and seemed to reach the clouds. She would look at it and relive the story of *Hansel and Gretel*, believing that if she were to enter through the front door, she would see the bottom of the witches' shoes as she was being stuffed into the fiery mouth of the fireplace.

"Great." Paige hugged Sade and got out of the car. Her heart and soul were so heavy that it felt as though even her shadow was weighing her down as she entered her grandmother's house.

If she thought that her somber mood would improve once she arrived, she was mistaken. As soon as she walked through the side door, she could sense the apprehension and desperation in the air on behalf of everyone in the kitchen. James, Tim, her mom and dad, and her grandmother, all sat at the table and looked up at her as she entered. Cookie had made her famous spaghetti and meatballs. If that couldn't liven up this bunch, nothing could.

James immediately went to Paige and threw his arms around her. "You okay?"

"I'm good. You don't need to worry about me."

"That's my job. Forever." James had a forced smile on his face that told her he was really trying.

She felt bad for James at that moment. She knew that his feelings for her went deeper than hers did for him, but there was nothing she could do. At this moment in time, she felt that her heart would always belong to Bryce—no matter what.

"Is there any left for me?" Paige said trying to sound cheery.

Cookie jumped up and quickly got her a steaming plate. "Here you go, sweety. Eat up."

Paige thanked her grandmother. Her light brown eyes searched Paige, through her fashionable frames, to truly see her and assess her well-being. She was so worried about her granddaughter.

"They're planning a vigil for Bryce this weekend."

Everyone stopped eating and talking, and looked at Paige.

"I think it will be a good thing for everyone. Sade's mom is going to find out what we can do to help."

Sloane spoke and said that she thought it was a terrific idea. "Let me know if there is anything I can do to help."

"Thanks, Mom."

"What's a vizzle?" asked Tim.

All eyes were on Paige. She wasn't sure what she was going to do and then she burst out laughing. Everyone joined in. It was just what was needed to relieve the awkward tension in the room.

Sloane said, "Tim, honey, a v-i-g-i-l is a gathering to celebrate the life of someone who has died. It is held somewhere special so that all the person's family and friends can come together to remember the person and mourn together."

Paige told them that they would be meeting at Tucker Field and then would have a candlelight procession to the field at the high school. "It's the perfect place. He loved it there. That will be very hard on the team, but I can't think of a better place. Mrs. Walker said that if the weather is bad, it will be held inside the high school."

Paige drew her mind back to a day when she had met up with Bryce right after practice. He had showered in the locker room and his shiny black hair was still damp. He wore his favorite NFL football team's sweatshirt and she could see the muscled definition of his upper arms and chest. He didn't overdo the weight lifting. She didn't like that. He was just right. He erupted into a wide smile when he caught sight of her. It made her heart skip a beat— no—two beats. She loved the way his face changed just for her. She loved how his piercing dark brown eyes could see all the way into her very soul. They walked out onto the football field and sat at the entrance to a grove nearby. They talked about the dreams they had and what they hoped the future would hold after high school. Bryce wanted to make it to the NFL. She said that she knew he could make it if he wanted it, but she said that he should always have a plan B. He laughed and told her that he wouldn't mind being an architect if it didn't work out and teased her for being so practical all the time.

"Paige, are you there?"

Paige stopped ruminating. "Sorry, Mom. What did you say?"

"I said to let me know what supplies you need for the vigil. Check with the girls and decide on what you will make for decorations and then I'll make a list and take a run to the craft store. You look a little run down. Why don't you go upstairs and rest for a bit first?"

"I think I might. I'm not sleeping at all. I'll text the girls and have them meet here tomorrow if that's okay."

"Already cleared it with Cookie."

"Yes, I'm excited to see the girls."

Paige and Cookie went upstairs while Sloane and Mitch cleaned up.

James watched this unfold with great unease. He knew she was thinking about *him*. He didn't stand a fighting chance against a ghost. He felt as if Bryce's malediction still had a hold on her. He told Paige that he would help her with the vigil and began planning exactly how he would help her.

James went up to the room he shared with Tim. At the same time, Cookie came out of her room, with her jade velour tracksuit and perfectly coiffed hair, and almost bumped into him.

"Ooh, honey I'm sorry. You were miles away there. Everything okay?" she said startled.

"Yes, of course. Do you need help with anything, Mrs. Vale?"

"I do as a matter of fact. Come down with me and let an old lady tell you a story."

James smiled at her and went downstairs.

She led him to the kitchen, pulled out a chair for him, and put her owl cookie jar in the center of the table. "There are two different kinds in there. Help yourself."

James dug in and grabbed one of each, macadamia and chocolate chips and peanut butter and butterscotch chips. He took a bite from each and moaned with pleasure. Jasper came barreling into the room hoping to get a treat as well. He ran the litany of tricks he knew and performed them one after the other.

"Yes, they came out pretty good! Do you know why the kids call me Cookie?"

Holding up the cookies he said, "Well, I can sure guess."

She sat down and took a cookie for herself. "When our Paige was just a little one, her parents were very strict about what she could eat. They didn't let her have sweets or junk food. So, every time she came to my house, I would sneak her cookies. The jig was up when it was one of her first words!" She laughed, very pleased with herself. "Soon, every time she would see me, she would say 'cookie' and it stuck!"

James loved being with this family. Every one of them. He wanted to be a part of them so badly he could taste it.

Sloane came into the kitchen and announced that she would be leaving to go shopping for the girls. "Do you need anything while I'm out?"

Cookie shook her head no because her mouth was

stuffed with food.

"I won't be long."

Sloane was given carte blanche over the supplies and types of decorations to make. She needed to attack this project the way she attacked everything—plan, make lists, and be ready for anything. It was the only way for her to feel as if she was in control and right now, she needed that feeling. She came back from the craft store and had really outdone herself.

The next day came and Sloane was glad there would be a large craft project to occupy the kids. Everyone was getting a little stir crazy. Paige's friends arrived and Paige and James directed them to Cookie's dining room where there were materials to create beautiful Chinese lanterns and shining luminary bags. There were also two large white sheets to use as banners for display on both the north and south sides of the catwalk crossing over Mendon Road between the high school and Tucker field.

They made 100 lanterns—all in the school colors of blue, white, and yellow gold. They inserted battery-operated tea lights and would hang them from the trees at Tucker Field, at the high school, and from either side of the catwalk.

The dining room began to fill with so many lanterns it looked like they were in the middle of a Dr. Seuss story. They were hanging from everything that protruded from the walls and were piled up in every corner. James was able to reach the highest points without a ladder or chair which came in very handy.

"Karol, can you find a spot for the last of these?" asked Amber. "I think that some of us should probably take some home, it will be less of an inconvenience for Cookie."

Paige thought and said, "Let's see what we have when we are finished. Thanks, that's a nice offer."

The group began to work on the luminary bags next. The bags were the same colors as the lanterns. Sloane bought several hand-held football-shaped paper punches and several football player-shaped punches. They punched the designs into 300 bags. Those were much easier to store. Once they were punched, they added a tea light and folded them flat.

"Bryce would've really like these," Jenna said while she was packing them up. She looked up at the group stunned. She hadn't meant to say it out loud.

Amber elbowed her and gave her a look.

Jenna apologized, "Sorry."

Paige said, "Don't worry. You don't have to tiptoe around me. I'm fine. I agree. He would love these."

They put the first of the two sheets on the large table. Sloane had purchased royal blue glitter paint and brushes. They painted: *RIP Bryce—We Miss You!*, in the blue glitter paint. The letters were large enough to fill the center. They repeated this on both sheets. They decided that they would bring both banners and some markers to school the next day for everyone to sign messages to Bryce in the empty spaces.

Mitch came into the room and saw their

creations. The sheets were laid out to dry on the table. "Nice work everyone. What do you plan to do with these?"

Paige said, "We're gonna hang them on the catwalk at the high school."

Mitch had a pensive look on his face. "I can put some grommets at the corners. It will be easier to hang that way."

"That would be great, Dad. Thanks!"

Sade leaned in toward Paige's ear, "Your father has every tool ever invented!"

The following day at school, Paige went to speak to Ms. Butcher to ask if she would announce that the banners were there for anyone who would like to sign messages for Bryce. She said that she was happy to help. She told Paige to leave the sheets with her and that she would take care of everything. She announced details about the vigil and notified everyone that there would be sheets to sign in the gymnasium.

THIRTY-FOUR

Lucas

He received another dreaded text:

In Lincoln. Come quick. 126 Racer Blvd.

Lucas felt a burning rush enter the back of his throat from the deep hollow of his stomach. His pulse quickened and he flew into action. Changing quickly, he ran to his car and checked that his kill kit was safely where he had hidden it. It was. The sun was beginning to set low on the horizon and another day was coming to an end. He wondered how long he could keep this up and thought about what his life had become. Looking up at the beautifully colored sky he laughed to himself over the stark difference of black and gloom residing within him.

When he arrived, Rosa Marie was standing on the front porch in his favorite red wig, smoking a cigarette—she didn't smoke. She spotted him and a look of utter disdain clouded her face. She did not even try to feign her fury.

He took his bag from the trunk and walked up the steps. When he attempted to speak, she quickly turned and went into the house after flicking her cigarette in the bushes. She led him to a bedroom with a couple asleep in each other's arms.

The room was very large and bright; decorated in a pleasant shade of steel blue. The wall to the right faced a lake and was made up entirely of sliding glass doors. The louvers were open highlighting a beautifully lit patio and stone walkway leading down a slight incline to the reed-strewn lake at the edge of their property.

The wall directly in front of him displayed the largest bed he had ever seen. Behind the bed and on the wall all the way up to the ceiling were what looked like steel blue upholstered panels made of soft leather. The same blue leather was what covered the base of the bed. Everything was crisp and modern.

Lucas was at a loss for words. He had no idea what he was looking at but became overwrought with disgust. He decided that he didn't want to know about the torrid mess she had gotten herself in this time. He swore to himself that this was going to be the last time. He could not keep doing this. He noticed that Rosa Marie was standing in a corner of the room up against the wall and had her phone out. This lit a fuse in him that he could not extinguish.

"Rosa Marie, what are you doing?" Not knowing how much time he had, he knew it was better to ignore her and get to work. He thought that he knew what she was doing and it made him more enraged. She was always chatting with coworkers and friends to get her supply of drugs and getting herself into debasing situations. Who knew what she was getting into now?

Lucas, assured that the two were out cold, began to hogtie and gag the male, and then did the same to the female. Because the property extended from one side of the block to the next, he decided to move his car around the block to the back of the property. He went back into the house and carried out the man then returned for the woman. When he went inside the second time, Rosa Marie was nowhere in sight. He looked outside and her car was gone. He went about the house trying to imagine any surface they may have touched and wiped everything down. He noticed three wine glasses and an empty bottle of Lambrusco. He grabbed it all thinking that was where she must have added the drugs. He performed his normal sanitizing ritual and, on his way out, he retrieved her discarded cigarette.

He drove around for a while waiting for the sun to set completely and for some inspiration. Once darkness had won its battle over light, he found himself at Lincoln Woods State Park and turned in. He drove up and down the winding path amidst the looming trees, passing several numbered picnic sites, and pulled into the parking lot of the boathouse where they rented canoes. There was a pile of them, stored upside-down in a roped-off section behind the boathouse. He took one and brought it to the car.

Looking at the canoe brought back memories of his childhood and vacationing in Maine with his family. Every year his parents would rent one of four cabins—the others would be for his aunts, uncles, and cousins.

Lucas heard a moan coming from the trunk and knew that he needed to get back to business. He grabbed his heavy-duty flashlight, opened the trunk, and presented the man with a hard blow to the side of his head. That silenced him, but he knew he needed to make haste before they both came to from their drug-induced stupor.

He carried the man and placed him into the canoe. He cut the bindings and released his hands and feet. He then removed his clothing and placed the man onto the floor of the boat facing the front of the craft. He taped his body so that he would remain sitting up with his legs apart and his hands on each edge of the canoe. This act brought back a memory of his cousin Neil trying to tape the oars to the canoe so he wouldn't lose them and face ridicule from his cousins. This made him laugh as he removed the man's genitals and sliced his femoral artery.

The man awoke with a wild look of confusion and agony. There was a brutal white-hot pain emanating from his groin area. He was naked and couldn't understand why. The man. Right. There was a man. His breathing came in rapid gasps, which made him lightheaded. As he looked toward the source of the pain, he saw that he was sitting in a pool of blood. That made him feel even more lightheaded. He tried to free his hands but to no avail. Whether from exhaustion or the loss of blood, he was losing the battle of consciousness. He began to shake and convulse. He was so cold. He fought to stay alert. The white pain won out and he faded away into the abyss.

When Lucas went back to the car, he saw that the woman was awake. Her eyes opened wide as she tried to scream. Again, he used the flashlight to hit her on the side of her head and she became quiet once more.

He repeated the same process as with her partner, silently cursing Rosa Marie for making him work twice as hard. He sat the woman with her back to the man's and taped them together. He taped their heads together. Once the woman was taped in a sitting position, and facing the back of the canoe, he sliced off her right breast. Her eyes, which were facing down, flew up toward the star-laden sky. They were bulging out of their sockets. She heaved and tried to scream, but only a rattled breath escaped. Lucas wasted no time and began slicing through her left breast. She blacked out; no doubt from the immense pain. He opened the carotid artery in her neck. He thought that would do nicely enough. He didn't want to become too repetitive. He watched a bit while the blood pooled at the bottom of the canoe and experienced a euphoria like never before.

Lucas pushed the boat into the pond and watched it float away. With the moon's beams shining down upon the water, it looked like the couple had their own spotlight guiding their way to nothingness. The canoe slowly floated away. Once the boat drifted far enough to his satisfaction, he grabbed the discarded clothing from the couple, carved out a spot, heaped everything in a pile, and placed the dismembered body parts on top. He set everything ablaze.

Lucas got back into his car, drove to the road, parked the car, and got out. He took off his shoes, walked through the tire tracks, and kicked the sand around so that the tread marks were not visible. He did the same to the shoe prints near the scene then shuffled back to his car and left.

Adrenalin was pumping through his veins. He was surprised by how alive he felt. He would never admit it, but he was beginning to enjoy this.

THIRTY-FIVE
Paige

When Paige and her friends arrived at Cookie's after school, she updated her mother about how helpful the school staff had been. Sloane revealed that she had called Bryce's mom to give her condolences and told her what their plans were for the vigil. Mrs. Walker told the girls that she was very happy with the idea of having banners, lanterns, and luminary bags. "Mrs. Walker is getting candles from her church for everyone to hold during the procession from Tucker Field to the high school. It will look beautiful with all the lights."

They went to the garage with all of the items for the vigil. Paige wondered how long the family would remain here because they still couldn't bring themselves to move back into their house. Cookie came into the garage with cans of soda, candy bars, and chips. Tim was right at her heels. He wanted to stay and help them. When Cookie gave Paige "the look," she knew he would be staying.

Jenna was the first to give Paige an eye-roll. She quickly engaged the group in a secret language that they had made up so that Tim wouldn't understand what they were saying.

"Dathago yathago thethagink hethage withagill bethage methagessuthged uthagup athagafathagertatheger whathagut hethage suthagaw?" (*"Do you think he will be messed up after what he saw?"*)

Paige answered her by saying, "Nathago. Mathaguy mothagagotherger ithagis muthagakuthagakuthaging uthagall uthgov uthagus suthagee uthaga thuthageruthagaputhagathuthagist." (*"No. My mother is making all of us see a therapist."*)

They all looked at Tim with sorrowful faces and he stopped eating and asked what they were looking at.

Paige biffed the top of his head playfully and helped him sign messages on the two banners. Once that was done, they folded up the banners, and started packing up the lanterns and bags. She knew that he was strong but was still deeply worried about what he witnessed at their home. She especially felt horrible about the story she had told him and how he interpreted what he had seen the way he did because of it.

After a few hours of getting everything just right, they were done. Everyone decided to meet at the high school early the next day to set up.

Paige had said goodbye to her friends and felt a vibration from her cell.

Sorry I couldn't help – had to help with a puppy who ate a shoe. I'll be there tomorrow. Send me the details.

**No prob. Meeting at Tucker
Field/HS at 5:30 to help
Mrs. Walker
set up. See you @ Cookie's.**

K

That night was extra hard for Paige to sleep. She was very apprehensive about seeing the Walker family. She couldn't imagine what they thought about their son being killed, but for the killer to place his dead body on her porch must be unfathomable to them. She wished she could figure out why. She felt as if she were being stalked; that someone out there was watching her.

She tried to force herself to think of happy memories instead. She thought back to the summer when she first knew they were more than friends. They both had brothers that played for the Lil' Kickers town soccer team. They were getting food when the snack bar attendant announced that two hot dogs, fries, and soda were ready, and they both grabbed for it. They locked eyes and laughed at what had happened. They had both placed the same exact order. Being that he was a chivalrous person, he let Paige take the first one. They walked together to their families and promised to meet back at the snack bar the following week.

The next week came. Paige arrived at the meeting time to have her order ready and waiting for her. They took the food, walked across the street to the high school, and found a spot on their own. They talked for a while and she realized how easy it was to be with him. He was funny, intelligent, and kind. She had gone to school with him since they were in kindergarten. She had always had a secret crush on him but never acted on it. Bryce said that he had to get back to his family and asked if they could get together after football and cheerleading practice the following night. They met afterward and from then on, they had deep feelings for one another.

This wasn't working. She needed to employ some relaxation techniques that the therapist had recommended. Paige began relaxing every part of her body, beginning with her toes. She was asleep by the time she reached her hips.

+++++++++++++

At five-thirty on a crisp fall evening, everyone intending to help the Walker family prepare for the vigil gathered at Tucker Field to set up. You could catch the smell of burning leaves in the air whenever the wind blew from the east. Bryce's teammates came wearing their football jerseys and got right to work.

Paige and the *mean girls* were on the catwalk. They were having difficulty reaching the top of the safety fence when two long arms grabbed the banner and brought it up where it needed to go. Paige looked over her shoulder and saw James. They could all say what they wanted, but he was always there for her when she needed him. As he held up the banner, Paige and the girls used the wire Mitch provided to fasten through the grommets to the fence. He had even made two slices on each banner so that the wind could easily pass through without bowing the fabric.

They hung both banners and then spaced out the luminary bags so that both the north-facing and south-facing traffic could see them. When they were on the ground, the sight was spectacular. She was confident the homage to Bryce would be greatly appreciated by the Walker family. They then went to the field, placed the luminary bags around the perimeter, and hung the lanterns at the top of the fence that surrounded Tucker Field.

Once they were finished there, they went across to the high school, leaving bags and lanterns on the catwalk. They deposited the luminary bags from the beginning of the entrance, around back to the parking lot, straight onto the athletic field. They placed the remaining lanterns hanging from the bleachers and the trees at the back of the field. Once the area was properly lit up, they made their way back across the street to the field.

Hundreds of supporters began entering Tucker Field—they filled both sides of the bleachers and circled the field four rows deep—all took a candle as they entered. The Walker family lit theirs and then they lit the supporters near them. In a domino effect, everyone turned to light their neighbor's candle until they were all glowing. Together with the shine from the luminaries, the entire field was alight. Once finished, Paige, along with James and her friends, found their families who were saving seats for them on the bleachers. Mrs. Romano asked Paige where Karol was. It struck Paige just then that she hadn't been with them to help. She had just assumed that she was helping elsewhere and said as much.

Mrs. Romano got up from her spot on the bleachers and made her way down to a police officer. Paige watched as she began plucking at her cell phone. She assumed that she was calling or texting Karol. Paige took out her phone and texted her also. She was searching the vast crowd to see if maybe she was sitting with someone else but could not spot her.

There was a tapping repetition heard over the speakers from Mr. Walker hitting the top of the microphone. That quieted the crowd and brought their attention to him. Looking at him was like seeing an older version of Bryce. They shared the same hefty frame and strong, chiseled jawline. He and his wife wore t-shirts displaying a photo of Bryce in his football uniform. It was just so sad. He thanked everyone for coming to honor Bryce, especially his teammates, and said that he would have loved the turnout. Many people wanted to say something about Bryce and were standing with them awaiting their turn. He handed the microphone to Mrs. Walker. The grief was evident in the sallow tone to her skin, and the lines on her face that seemed to have deepened over the last few days.

"Tonight, is about the beginning of closure, about family and friends coming together to share memories and help each other get through their grief.

As hard as it is to fathom who has done this horrible thing to our family, or why, we must stay strong and support one another. There are a lot of people that I need to thank tonight. Bryce's friends worked tirelessly to make tonight the beautiful glowing memorial that it is, thank you all. To our neighbors, thank you for all the meals—I don't think I'll need to cook ever again." She began to lose her composure, turned to the side, and wiped her eyes. "I'd like to turn the mic over to Father Bernard before some others speak."

"Good evening and God Bless. This is not an easy occasion. But through coming together as a community we can heal together and help the Walker family." He lowered his eyes and said, "Though this is a terrible tragedy, Lord, we feel very blessed to have known Bryce. His family and friends should have had him longer. Please, pray for the family and help them find peace. Let us bow our heads for a moment of silence."

Every person bowed their head in silence, candles held high. Once heads were raised, the coach of the football team held the microphone. His pale Irish skin gave away the fact that he had been crying recently. His face was mottled with red patches and his eyes were rimmed in red.

With a pure Rhode Island accent he began, "Hello, everyone. I am hea tonight to honna Bryce—I'd like to have his teammates come up hea with me." They all went to stand with the coach, a sea of blue and white. The coach held up a large frame with Bryce's jersey, #19. The coach said, "We will be foreva honoring Bryce by displayin' his jersey in the gymnasium"—and then a blood-curdling scream was heard from somewhere across the road. The coach stopped talking and everyone was silent until another scream was heard. Carl and Arabella who were next to speak ran toward the scream.

THIRTY-SIX
Carl

Carl and Arabella ran across the street to find four teens huddled together near the D.A.R.E. crash car. They approached the teens and asked what was wrong. They pointed to the car and Arabella looked inside.

Arabella said, "Oh, my God. Oh, my God. We have another DB. I'll call it in." A roll of nausea overcame her and she fought against the excessive amount of saliva filling her mouth. She became clammy and lightheaded. She wanted to scream but knew she had to get a grip on the situation.

Carl looked inside and couldn't believe what he was seeing. Another dead body? And it was clearly murder. What was happening in his town? He thought things couldn't get worse, and then BAM!

The clear night sky was lit by a sparkling roadmap to the moon that brightly lit the way for the weary. And weary they were. What was left of the leaves on the trees cast menacing shadows around the car. The shadows seemed to beckon some of the curious people that began to leave the vigil and make their way across the street. Carl couldn't believe what was right in front of his eyes. His insides were twisted in knots. He felt responsible for this death. They had to find this monster.

Carl said, "Arabella, I'll keep the crowds away. You get the information from the group."

While Carl was busy keeping the area preserved, Arabella learned that four teens—three female and one male, found the body. The teens were still hanging on to their awkward phase. Their limbs were not under their full control and their faces were spattered with angry red spots. They were on their way to the vigil and stopped behind the high school to "smoke." On their way to the catwalk, they heard a phone ringing from inside the crashed car on display. When they looked inside, they saw what they had assumed was a dummy to enhance the effect of the crash. Every year, the police force and the D. A. R. E. program placed a demolished car on the school grounds by the main road, for all to see, and be reminded that anything could happen when you were under the influence and got behind the wheel. One of the teens realized what they were seeing and she began to scream.

The sight was horrific. The body was that of a young woman in her late teens to early twenties. The body was wedged behind the mangled steering wheel. She was devoid of her eyes and lips and several teeth were missing. A deep laceration to the neck pointed to what was most likely the cause of death. To Arabella, it seemed probable that because there was not much blood in the car, the victim was killed elsewhere and then placed there, leading her to believe what she had been mulling over since Bryce was found — that this was the work of a pair of killers working in tandem and not just one single killer.

The law enforcement officials that were already present at the vigil descended on the scene in record time. Sirens could be heard from additional units approaching. Carl sent James a text telling him to go with Paige and her family to her grandmother's house and to tell the others to go home and stay there. He told Arabella he was going across to the field to end the vigil and have the remaining people go home. The murderer could very well still be in the area. Once she finished with the witness statements, Arabella sent them home and guarded the scene. There was always an abundance of traffic on this busy street and tonight was no exception. She watched the officers maintain control over the area as a breeze made the fallen leaves dance around the main road as if they were offering a private show for those who needed it most.

A show of red and blue lights preceded the first of the squad cars as she flagged them over to the crime scene. Two more squad cars arrived, as did a news van.

Carl walked back to the scene, "That didn't take long. We'll need to keep them as far away as possible."

Arabella nodded and went to two of the tall, burly patrol officers with strict instructions to cordon off the area, especially from the press. As soon as she finished giving her instructions, a helicopter could be heard above.

Captain White appeared and looked up, "Is that ours?"

Carl shook his head. "This will not go over well. His lips were a flat line of fury that felt wrong on his patrician-looking face. The Chief's gonna blow a fuse."

Carl put on some gloves and protective gear and walked back over to the demolished car. He reached in and picked up the handbag that was left on the side of the body. "Someone, bring me an evidence bag."

Arabella provided one. He opened the handbag and reached around until he found the victim's wallet. He opened it to find a driver's permit issued to a Karol Romano. His heart stopped and all color drained from his face.

Arabella asked, "Sarge, you okay?"

"No. I'm not. We know this girl. She was at the party with Bryce and the rest. You interviewed her."

"What? Shit. You have to be kidding. Who is she?"

"Karol Romano."

Arabella recalled seeing a frail, scared young woman with dark brown hair that had beautiful, subtle tones of red interwoven throughout the thick mass. The contrast of her hair to the stark white of the hospital bed left an impression on Arabella. Karol was very meek when she was being interviewed. She refused to have her parents present during her conference. Arabella thought it was because she had not wanted her parents to hear what she was about to say to the police, but after   Karol warmed up to Arabella, she told her that she was worried because they always seemed to make problems—especially with authority—wherever they went. When she met with Karol the second time at the high school, she remembered that she felt as if she were meeting a different person altogether. Karol had a more confident, beautiful smile that showcased her pearly whites and when she smiled, the spark lit all the way up to her dark brown eyes. She now felt such an overwhelming wave of sadness that the world would never see her potential because she had been taken much too soon.

She turned and shouted, "Let's get the patrols to section off a grid of five hundred feet around the car, and get this center area tented. The dwindling leaves on the trees won't stop an aerial crime scene photo from being shot."

Carl thought he detected a waiver in her voice but said nothing. As he walked away, he saw her wipe at her left eye, but it wasn't before he could see the tear on her nimble brown cheek glistening in the moonlight. He approached the reinforcements and told them what else needed to be done.

A black SUV arrived on the scene. The vehicle was carrying Chief Haverhill and some of the FBI. Carl approached them. "We've instructed the patrol officers to cordon off a grid around the car and to get a tent erected over the area. We have eyes in the sky.

The fall trees don't provide much cover."

The Chief questioned how the media could know what was going on so soon.

Carl said, "There were some news vans already present at the vigil for Bryce Walker across the street at Tucker Field."

"Keep them at bay," she instructed and then asked, "Have we ID'd the victim?"

"Yes, Chief. It's Karol Romano. She was one of the group of teens drugged at the party with Bryce Walker."

"What? What the hell is going on here? How was she found?"

Carl explained, "Some teens were on their way to the vigil and they heard a phone ringing from inside the car. Her handbag was in there with her. I searched for the wallet and found her driving permit. I bagged everything."

The chief continued, "We need to put protection units on all the teens who were at that party. Someone is after them for some reason. Do you have the phone? Did you see who the last call was from? It's a longshot, but it could have been from the killer trying to mess with us. Also, have traffic rerouted in this area. I don't want anyone coming near the scene. The medical examiner and the crime scene investigators should be here any minute. Is there anything they should pay special attention to?"

"No, Chief. Unfortunately, it's a gruesome scene but pretty clear cut."

"Okay, I want you back at headquarters. A lot of

new information has arrived from the other three cases, and we need all eyes to sort through everything."

"Okay, we'll see you there." Carl took Karol's bagged cell phone and headed back to headquarters with Arabella.

+++++++++++++

Carl and Arabella arrived at the temporary headquarters and were shocked to see the number of people there. A lot had been done since their absence. Carl noticed that they now made efficient use of the cramped space. Each victim had a designated team and area where all the pertinent information was showcased. He solemnly thought that now they'd need to make room for one more.

Once the pair's presence was known, a silence spread through the facility. People couldn't make eye contact. If they didn't look, it didn't happen yet again.

They had to pull some people off the other cases to create a team for the new Romano case. They cordoned off a vacant area and posted a picture of Karol centered on top of a new case board. Victim #4. The team consisted of Carl, Arabella, a patrol officer from Pawtucket who was Carl's friend from the academy, and Natalie Frazee, since the first crime scene had been fully detailed and all pertinent information had been written up. Carl announced, "There are three Cumberland residents and one

Lincoln resident butchered. Gone. How is this possible?" Everyone in the facility felt the same way, but it was very personal for Carl.

Carl gave Karol's cell phone to the officer on his task force to see who made the call to her phone when she was in the D. A. R. E. car.

"Sarge, when we took a statement from her mother, she said that she was calling her at that time to see why she wasn't sitting with them during the vigil. I'll still check, but that's probably the case."

Carl agreed and sent him on his way.

Carl began by asking the group how she fit in with the other victims. Detective Heart, a squat man with a pear-shaped body who looked as if he lived a hard life, was the first to speak up. "There is just no rhyme or reason, Sarge. I was looking over the information for all the victims. Aside from the two school kids, there are no connections. They're all different ages. The only similarities are in the brutal way each was murdered, but even that changes." When he spoke, one could not help but notice his bulbous nose that tended to move every time he opened his mouth. It was clear by the veins that resembled red lightning bolts covering it that he liked his drink. "I know that his MO is to remove body parts and have them bleed out."

Arabella spoke up, "He also adds slight deviations here and there. Karol's throat was slashed—almost to the point of decapitation. And yes, he took her eyes, lips, and her teeth from what we could see."

Detective Heart added, "Eyes, lips, and teeth? Usually, when teeth are removed it's so the victim can't be ID'd, but he didn't care about the others. What made him not want her identified?"

Arabella replied, "Identification wasn't the reason. He left her handbag in the car with her. It had her wallet and her phone and other forms of ID. There has to be a different reason. It's a misconception that MOs remain the same—they can change with serial killers. Their signature or trademark always remains consistent. It is the driving force behind their need to kill the way they do and the process or ritual that is performed before, during, and after. It is deeply rooted in their psychosis. That's why I think . . . "

Carl put his hand on her shoulder and stopped her before she went overboard. She tended to go on with her ideas that went against the majority's beliefs. He could feel her leering and knew that if he made eye contact, he might turn to stone. He would have to deal with her later.

She said, "We need to find why and how *he* is choosing his victims. That's the only way we stand a chance at stopping *him*." She looked at Carl with a satisfied, cunning, grin; the others were left wondering what that was all about.

The teams converged to plan what important steps needed to be taken next. There was much to be done. The town police departments wanted to be the ones to solve these cases; for their families, their friends, and their fellow townspeople. They also wanted to make a good impression on the FBI and prove to them that they were not just some small, insignificant town with a bumbling police department that couldn't effectively catch a serial killer. However, they were grateful for all of the state-of-the-art equipment and the quick turnaround they received for lab results.

Carl shared the one thought that came to him. "He certainly wants us to know who his victims are. He doesn't try to hide their identity or the bodies themselves once he's completed his horrifying deed. Let's look into where they were found as a possible connection. We know some of the crime scenes are where he actually did the killing and then left the bodies in whatever bizarre, macabre display he wanted for us to find. Then there are some crime scenes where the victims were killed somewhere else and moved to a specific location. This has to mean something. These are very odd choices—usually, serial killers want their victims hidden so that they can keep their work undetected and continue killing. Except for the old ice cream place, these are very public places frequented by plenty of people." They all jotted down this information to follow and were eager to help sort it out.

He then asked, "Where are we on the door-to-door canvassing of the crime scenes for each victim?"

Someone from the North Smithfield PD spoke up, "We've made a second pass at any home or business that are close to each site where a victim was found. We viewed surveillance footage but found no common thread between any of them. We are still waiting for the footage from Ocean State. Hopefully, that will give us something."

Carl looked at a text message he had just received. "The higher-ups have scheduled a press conference for late tomorrow afternoon. The FBI will take the lead. We will be given talking points to follow in case we are asked any follow-up questions—they'll be sent to everyone's phones. The best response will be '*no comment*,' but we all know that the press can be pushy and manipulative. It's better to be prepared. They also want us to set up a hotline for civilians to call in with tips. We will set this up in the basement here because space is limited. We will need volunteers round-the-clock from everyone, North Smithfield, Cumberland, Lincoln, especially. Other towns and counties have volunteered their services as well—we'll have to take advantage of their generosity."

Captain White walked through the door of the Diamond Hill building and spoke with Carl. They each brought one another up to date with what they knew about what was going on. Captain White then told him that Cumberland and the surrounding areas were planning to impose a curfew. They didn't want to take any chances because it seemed like CHS students were now being targeted by the killer.

He clapped his hands together as he addressed everyone in the room, "Okay, Carl already informed you about the moves the superiors have planned next. They want to have the press conference outside the Cumberland Town Hall tomorrow. They will be choosing their words very carefully. They are trying to instill enough fear for everyone to take this very seriously but not enough to cause a panic. We'll see what the experts decide. I know that these cases are taking a lot out of everyone, but we must remain vigilant and watch the crowd for anyone that peaks our suspicions. We'll have it taped so we can review it later. Serial killers love to be present to hear about their work and the fear it has brought upon the citizens."

They began to discuss their thoughts among themselves. Arabella was the most emphatic so Captain White asked her to share what she thought.

"I think that most people will surprise you. They can take in large quantities of important information and compartmentalize it without overreacting. I think we should individualize all pertinent information so that the public will want to help."

The room, overall, was split half and half about the issue.

++++++++++++

When Arabella and Carl arrived at the town hall the next afternoon, they weren't expecting the circus they saw before them. Every news station in Rhode Island and the surrounding states was present. They all had huge lights, large cameras, and boom microphones set up around the portable stage. Reporters were checking sound and lighting and everyone was abuzz. The town hall was located in the historic district at the southern end of town. It was a beautiful brick colonial revival that was built in the late 1800s.

Media vans filled the small parking lot located on the side of the old picturesque building. Many people who wanted to attend the press conference had to park across the street in various empty lots. A large black SUV stopped at the entrance to the town hall parking lot and the FBI, along with some other officials exited the vehicle and made their way to the front of the crowd. They went up on stage all lined up behind the podium. The journalists were shouting out questions before they even began.

A burly man approached the podium with his hand raised to signal the questions should stop. His presence commanded attention. He wore a black trench coat and a black fedora. He screamed FBI. He blew into the microphone before he spoke. "Good afternoon, everyone. My name is Allan De Luca and I am the Assistant Special Agent-in-Charge of the recent occurrences in the surrounding areas. Because they are all still open cases, there is very little we can divulge at this time. It is too early to speculate how or if these victims are connected. The causes of death are varied. Law enforcement agents are still gathering evidence and sorting through numerous leads. It may take several days to come to any definitive conclusions. These events are tragic and we offer our sincerest condolences to the families and friends of the victims. That being said, we do want to share some important information with everyone.

Right now, I will turn it over to the Cumberland Chief of Police, Anika Haverhill." He signaled for her to replace him at the podium.

She moved from behind him, stood in his place, and lowered the microphone. "Good afternoon, everyone. First, let me say how deeply sorry we all are over the tragic losses of our fellow residents. These are people we all knew and interacted with. They are irreplaceable. Rest assured; we are doing our very best to get to the bottom of this. We are receiving assistance, not only from the FBI but also from surrounding cities and towns, as well as the state troopers. We have all convened and feel the best course of action to take, is to impose a curfew in the following cities and towns: Cumberland, Lincoln, Smithfield, and North Smithfield, Woonsocket, Central Falls, and Pawtucket. Anyone under the age of 18 living in any of these named regions, must be home or accompanied by a guardian from six o'clock pm to six o'clock am beginning tomorrow. Anyone over 18 must be indoors after nine o'clock pm until six o'clock am. If you work and must travel during the curfew hours, you must be ready to show proof of that fact."

This caused quite the reaction from the crowd. Everyone began shouting at once. People were vehemently either for or against the idea of implementing a curfew. When Carl looked out among the crowd, he could see people trying to calm those who opposed the idea.

Trying to take command of the situation once

more, the Chief said, "Please, calm down. We are only doing what we feel is best to keep you and your families safe. We don't want any other fatalities."

A local TV news reporter shouted, "Does this mean you have no idea who the serial killer is and have no way to stop him?"

Chief Haverhill tried to regain control of the situation, "That is not what this is about. We have a duty to maintain law and order—if we didn't try everything within our power, you would be the first to report that we didn't use every tool available to keep everyone safe."

This seemed to quiet everyone. As she was looking over her notes, Anika added, "We will also be setting up an anonymous hotline for anyone to call and leave any information they may have about this killing spree. Once it is up and running, we will alert all those in the area via the Emergency Alert System. Any information we need to share with everyone will be delivered this way. You will receive an alert on your smartphone and other smart devices."

As she began to bring up another point, she was interrupted by a uniformed officer. She covered the microphone and tilted her shiny blonde head toward the officer. All the blood drained from her face. "Thank you, everyone. This concludes the press conference for this afternoon." She quickly made her way over to ASAC and whispered something to him. They all hurriedly filled into the SUV and departed, leaving the reporters and journalists thinking the worst as they were promised a Q & A session at the end.

Carl and Arabella quickly retreated to their vehicle and headed to the temporary headquarters while they awaited word on what just happened. They had traveled only a few minutes when both cell phones went off. An ominous feeling passed between them both. Carl put the call on speaker.

"We have two DBs at Lincoln Woods. Head there and we'll brief you both."

"Roger that—our ETA is 10 minutes."

Carl turned the SUV around and headed in the opposite direction. "Two more bodies. What's going on?" They sat in silence trying to gather their thoughts about what was happening around them. This was so difficult to comprehend. Carl asked aloud, to no one in particular, "What are we missing?" He glanced over at his partner who looked as devastated and confused as he felt. "How far are you on your theory of there being two killers working together?"

Arabella was feeling exhausted and depleted in a way she could ever remember. She rested her cheek on the cool glass of the passenger window and gathered her thoughts. "I'm not very far, but I feel like I will take it to Haverhill to see what she thinks. I'm working on the best way to shape my ideas into words that will make sense with the evidence as I see it. This case is just all over the place. There are several different drugs used, there are both male and female victims, some are brought to the crime scene and killed there, while others are killed somewhere else and then brought to the crime scene. Generally speaking, there are four different motivations for serial killers—this one has elements of all four motives, which usually doesn't happen. This leads me to believe it is the work of a pair of killers."

"I get what you're saying, but couldn't it just be the work of one very disturbed individual?"

"Sure, anything is possible, but I really don't see it that way."

++++++++++++

Carl and Arabella entered Lincoln Woods from the Great Road entrance and followed the instructions that were texted to them. The state park had many turns and trails. If you didn't know exactly where you were going, it was easy to get lost. They arrived at the horrific scene. A man and a woman were staged in a canoe. They were taped together sitting up, back-to-back. Her naked body was covered in blood. She was devoid of both breasts. The man's left arm was taped to the side of the watercraft, but his right had come free, so they were slumped in a precarious position. After surveying her wounds, they could surmise what had killed him without assessing the body.

One of the officers came over to them. "The park ranger was making his rounds and saw the canoe stuck on some brush in a little alcove on the pond. He went out in a lifeguard rowboat and pulled them ashore."

Arabella asked, "Where is he now? We'd like to speak to him."

The officer told them that he went with another officer to the part of the state park where canoes were stored to see if there was anything else awry or of note. He said that there were also two patrol cars sent to both the Great Road and Twin River Road entrances to ensure that only police personnel would be allowed access.

Arabella concluded with, "Okay, let us know as soon as he gets back here."

Arabella went to talk to the ME while Carl went to talk with the FBI, Anika, and Samuel. They realized there wasn't much new information to share at this stage. The officer brought the park ranger over to them. Once he returned, he was still shaking and he was sweating profusely even though the air was quickly becoming more indicative of the winter to come.

Carl said, "Hello, Mr.. . ."

"Tomlin, Noah Tomlin."

"Okay, Mr. Tomlin. Can you tell us exactly what happened earlier this afternoon when you saw the canoe in the pond?"

"I already told those officers." He pointed to a group of uniformed officers combing the area for clues.

Arabella answered, "You will probably need to tell the same story many times before the night is over. This helps you to remember anything that you may have originally thought was insignificant. The more you think about what happened and verbally recall it, the more will come to mind. And it could help us in ways you wouldn't understand."

"Sure. No problem. I was making my rounds before the end of my shift."

"What time was that, exactly?" she asked.

Noah was thoughtful and then added, "It was four thirty. My normal shift ends at three thirty, but I was asked to stay an extra hour because my relief was going to be late. I was in the Jeep, making my rounds when I saw the canoe stuck in some brush in a spot where the pond feeds into a small pool. Luckily, it was well hidden from the reduced number of visitors we get this time of year. I went back to the office and grabbed a truck with a rowboat in it. I put the boat in the water and rowed it over to the canoe. As I got close, I could see there was something inside. When I got even closer, it looked like bodies. At first, I thought maybe it was a prank, you know? But, when I looked around, there was no one there watching me. I tied ropes to the canoe and rowed it in. When I saw what I was really dealing with, I called you guys."

Trying to pull additional information, she asked, "When you were at the canoe rental site did you notice anything out of place?"

"Yes. You can see where he put the canoe in the water because the slide marks in the sand at the edge of the parking lot are leading into the pond. There was also a pile of ashes there in the sand. The other officers thought he burned their clothes."

The tree frogs' melodies along with the conk-la-ree songs from the blackbirds gave an eerie feeling to the desperately sad scene.

Carl asked, "Mr. Tomlin, will you bring us there please?"

He retrieved his cell phone and looked up at him nervously. "I'll take you there, but if that's it, can I go right after? I have to pick up my son. He's at drum practice."

Carl said, "Okay, just make sure those officers over there have all of your contact information."

They followed him to the canoe rental site so that he could leave and tend to his family. Carl looked around in the ashes while Arabella looked over at the multi-colored canoes stacked up on top of each other.

As the park ranger said, there was a small hole filled with ashes. Carl took a stick and poked around in the ashes. "He burned the clothes all right, but he also burned the body parts he removed."

Arabella went in for a closer look and was utterly revolted.

THIRTY-SEVEN
Paige

The following day at Cumberland High School was like no other. When the students and teachers arrived, they were welcomed by the presence of a dozen uniformed police officers. They were outside on the school grounds as well as in the building patrolling the halls.

This did not serve to suppress the despair and anxiety among all who belonged there. Paige and her friends decided to go to school while many others chose to stay home. Many parents called the school to say that their children would be kept home until the murderer was caught. Her parents gave her the choice. She needed some semblance of normalcy in her life so she decided to go. Everything else was so topsy-turvy at the moment, she felt that being in school would ground her.

Paige went to her homeroom and took her seat. There was a substitute teacher in place of her normal teacher. She wondered if it was due to the afternoon's press conference. The sub was taking attendance when an announcement was heard over the loudspeaker:

"Good morning, everyone. Today, there will be a

special assembly directly after homeroom period. Please report to the auditorium. Thank you."

She could barely hear the words spoken above all the chatter among her classmates. There was talk of serial killers and curfews. While every nerve in her body was frayed, her schoolmates discussed the events that had taken place with excitement in their voices.

Once in the auditorium, they were informed that there would be counseling sessions, which was a regular occurrence at this point, right here in the auditorium to accommodate the number of students that had signed up. They could not house such high volumes in the offices on the ground floor.

THIRTY-EIGHT
Lucas

That's it. I'm not going to be her henchman ever again. She can do her own dirty work from now on. Lucas didn't know what was worse, the things he had done, or believing that he could stop. He had an itch now that nothing else could scratch.

With the moon directly above him and nearly full, the bare branches in his immediate line of sight cast an ominous mood that easily matched his emotion. Seeing a young man walking to his car alone made his salivary glands react. He felt his kill kit beckoning him. His pulse quickened and he began to shake. If another customer hadn't pulled into the parking lot just then, he wouldn't have been able to stop his impulse to grab him and kill him.

++++++++++++

Troy woke up to a paralyzing headache and was extremely disorientated. He was about to open his eyes when he heard voices. Something deep within told him to stay as he was and not move a muscle. He heard a man and a woman. Her voice sounded familiar. What was happening? He tried to recall the events leading up to this moment and couldn't. He remembered meeting a woman, Rose something or other, at the bar he usually frequented on payday. She offered to come back to his place. They were talking and drinking. He tried to get things to move to the bedroom, but she must have been scared because she kept prolonging it. He got his way and then everything became a vast nothingness. The man and woman in his house continued to argue. It sounded like he was going to kill her; oh no, he's choking her. He could hear her gasping. He was so conflicted. Should he help her? No. He would stay right here and pretend that he was still unconscious. He stayed motionless, unable to move even if he wanted to. The fear was paralyzing.

He knew that this was a mistake for so many reasons. He had a girlfriend going on four years now. They were so good together. She was out of town at a pharmaceutical sales convention. He thought, why not, it would just be this once, she'll never know—karma sure is a bitch.

They were still arguing when he heard a thud and then a loud scream emanate from the woman. It was a different kind of scream than the others. It was primal and came from deep within. There were many more thuds and more screams that turned to a whimper and then to silence.

Lucas snapped. He went to Rosa Marie with both hands around her neck and slammed her into the wall. His need to kill her was visceral. He went to his kill bag while she crouched down trying to breathe, and retrieved one of his Japanese hunting knives. She was trying to stay conscious as she gasped for breath. He grabbed her by the neck once more, threw her against the wall, stretched her left arm up, and stuck the knife into the palm of her hand. She screamed and her eyes revealed the sheer terror she felt as she realized what was happening to her. Then he did the same to her right. She continued to scream and attempted to escape. She was using her feet to try to push herself off the wall. When Lucas saw this, he spread her legs out and staked her feet to the floor. This was not as easy. He had to try a few times until he found the exact spot that the knife would go through and remain stuck in the floor. He didn't want to have her bleed out. He wanted this to be a slow and painful death; after all, she had caused their love to die a slow and painful death. It was only right. After everything that happened, he couldn't stand by and watch this unfurl. He looked into her eyes and with the last of his knives, drove it into the center of her heart. The very heart that she could never give completely to him.

Troy was not sure what he should do. It was quiet in the room now. Aside from a few crickets chirping outside, only heavy breathing from the man was audible. When he opened his eyes ever so slightly, the only view he had was of his bedroom window where shafts of sunlight filtered through the blinds to his own personal show of dancing dust motes. Troy could hear the man pacing frantically in the next room. "What did I do? Shit!

What did I do? All those people I killed for you and this is how you repay me?" The man sobbed. He then said in a hushed tone, "I'll make it look like he did it."

Troy realized with terror that he meant him. He couldn't believe that this was happening. He thought that maybe he was still under the influence of whatever drug she slipped him. He had taken enough in his day. That was the main reason he started going out with his girl—a pharmaceutical rep would have lots of connections and be able to score whatever he wanted. Little did he know that she would be the one to finally get him on the way to being clean. But, no, this was really happening.

He realized that he had the element of surprise. If this guy thought he was still out, he'd have a rude awakening—literally! Troy's heart was hammering so hard it felt like it was trying to escape his body. He made a mental picture of everything around him that was within reach that could be used as a weapon. He had a shelf on the side of his bed that held a tissue box, a lamp, the empty wine glasses from the night before, and an empty water glass. He wished that the empty wine bottle was there. Not much in the way of options. His best hope was to grab the glass and hit him with it.

Lucas walked over to the bed where the unconscious man was awaiting his fate. He stopped and turned around to grab his kill kit. When he did, Troy grabbed the glass and put it under him, then returned to his original pose.

Lucas climbed onto the bed. The sun shining in from the window glistened off his bloodied hands and face. He plopped the bag next to him and kneeled at Troy's side. He was rummaging through his bag when all of a sudden, he felt a sharp pain at the back of his neck. When he touched the spot, it felt warm and wet. His vision began to blur. He was taken completely off guard and couldn't figure out exactly what was happening. Dazed, he toppled onto Troy. Troy began to wriggle out from under Lucas, wishing that he had knocked him out completely. He was now close enough to reach for the lamp. He grabbed it and went to hit Lucas over the head once more but, as he did, Lucas saw what was about to happen and deflected the blow with his forearm.

The two struggled to take control of the lamp. Troy decided to go in a different direction. He tugged the cord out of the wall outlet and used it to wrap around Lucas's neck. He straddled the man from behind and pulled tightly as Lucas tried to escape the suffocating hold Troy had over him.

Lucas could feel his lungs burning as he fought for air. Everything in the room turned grey and then pitch-dark.

As Troy was pulling the cord tighter, he felt Lucas go slack and then felt the life exit his body. There was a loud bang at his front door and then two police officers entered his room.

"Let him go—now!"

The police officers now had their guns drawn. One was a woman with dirty-blonde hair tied back and sticking out of the cap she wore. The man next to her was short and stocky. He had a mustache that looked comical—very contradictory for an officer.

He focused on the situation and realized that he needed to explain himself. Troy cried, "Wait, you don't understand. This is *my* house. He broke in to kill me. It was self-defense. He killed the woman in the other room over there!" He pointed in the direction where he heard the scuffle earlier.

The first officer turned to her partner, and told him to check on the woman and said that she'd cuff Troy. While she was cuffing him, she asked, "Who are they?"

"I have no idea. I was at Gill's Pub last night and met the woman, um, Rose something. We came back here and she must have slipped me something because we were laughing and drinking here in my bedroom and then I woke up hearing them arguing, and it was already light outside. He told her he wasn't going to do her dirty work anymore. I heard these weird thumps then screams coming from her. I don't think he meant to kill her at first. He couldn't help himself. He was in a full-blown rage. He was pretty torn up afterward. The guy said, 'This is because your heart was never mine!' And then I heard him say that he was going to pin it on me."

"How did he end up with a lamp cord around his neck?"

Her partner shouted, "What a mess!"   He walked to the doorway of Troy's bedroom and said, "I've never seen anything like that. He put a knife through each hand going into the wall and then through her feet too. She looks like a human X. He stuck a knife in her chest for good measure. That will be listed as the COD."

The female officer shook her head. "Okay, continue with what happened to this man."

"I pretended to still be unconscious and grabbed the water glass from the shelf. When he came onto the bed, I hit him with it. It just stunned him. So, I grabbed the lamp." Troy became choked up. "You saw the rest."

"All right, we need to get you to the station to sort this out and have a forensics team go through the house."

"Um, one other thing." The first officer looked at him. "He said that he killed other people for her. I don't know if it was true, but again, they thought I was out cold so they didn't know I heard it."

She looked at her partner and something passed between them. They needed to call Sergeant Lowden to fill him in on what just happened.

They moved into the other room with Troy in cuffs, and the sight before them sent shivers down their spines. There before them was a woman with several knives through her extremities attaching her to a wall. Her head hung slack. There was blood dripping down the wall in thin trickles, resembling arteries running into each other, making it look like the very wall where she perished was now nourished by her death.

THIRTY-NINE
Carl

Carl got everyone's attention at the makeshift base. All the *bigwigs* were at a meeting with the higher-ups at the Attorney General's office to deliver a status report on the investigations. "There's been two murders at a duplex off Diamond Hill near Interstate 295. One male and one female. Neighbors called 9-1-1 to report a domestic. Suspect en route to CPD right now. Said it was self-defense. Here's the thing, he said the male victim said he had killed other people for the female."

A collective buzz spread through the small headquarters. People looked at one another with disbelief. If anything, this news sent a shockwave through the task force that gave them the smallest glimmer of hope. Could this be their guy?

"Okay, Arabella and I will go to the CPD after this briefing and interview the suspect and see exactly what he knows. He could be telling the truth. If so, this vic could be linked to our murders. If not, he could be trying to shine the spotlight away from himself and onto someone else—someone who we can't interview. For now, I think each team should brief us as a whole so that we can go in there with full knowledge of all six victims, not including the two new cases. Team #1—what do we know?"

The leader of team #1, Natalie Frazee, stood before them. "Paul Cooper, 41, resided at 826 Green Boulevard, Cumberland, COD—exsanguination. His penis was removed and the femoral artery in the right leg was cut. The appendage was buried outside of the old milk can on Rt. 146. Tox screen showed that he had over four times the approved dose of both Xanax and Gabapentin in his system, and his alcohol level was slightly higher than the legal limit. The vic was taken from his apartment and killed at the Milk Can, crime scene #1. Apartment was cleaned well—no traces left behind. Vic's car was still in the driveway. Killer must have taken him in his. No witnesses or CCTV footage at or near the residence or crime scene. We have CCTV footage from the casino and have a clear pic of him and the woman he left with." She pointed to the photo on the Victim #1 whiteboard. "We have not been able to ID her. No viable connection to any other vics. We did get a DNA hit on the vic's shoulder. The perp must have touched his sweaty forehead with his gloved hand when he was doing the deed and left some skin cells. No hit in CODIS."

Carl said, "Okay, thanks, Nat. What about victim #2?"

The case board for victim #2 quickly came to the front of the room displaying all the gathered information. A rookie Carl had seen a few times at the CPD brought it. He rarely made eye contact and seemed to be too shy to be a police officer. If these cases didn't break him of that, nothing would.

The short, bald, rookie, whose shirt buttons were straining against their threads and threatening to burst, gave the next report. "Victim #2 is Ruby Shea, 38, of 702 Garden Avenue, Lincoln, COD—also exsanguination. She was drugged with high doses of Xanax, Vicodin, and Gabapentin, and had a blood-alcohol level two times the legal limit." He took a deep breath and continued. "Um, her breasts and clitoris were surgically removed and her carotid was sliced on her neck." He exhaled and it was evident that he was glad to have that part of the briefing over. He looked up sheepishly. "No witnesses. Lived alone—trying to trace her movements leading up to her death. Vic was also taken from her apartment and killed at the crime scene. He transported her body as well. No relation to any other vics. Her body parts were also buried near where she was strapped to the tree in the state park on Diamond Hill, crime scene #2. No DNA at the scene, but we were able to get a good tire print to match if—um, when the time comes."

When he wheeled back his whiteboard, Victim #3's team gathered materials and their case board and moved to the front of the room. One of the techs from the FBI said, "Bryce Walker, 17, 219 Jewelers Way, Cumberland, COD—the removal of his heart. His eyes and hands were removed post-mortem. Large quantities of Acepromazine, Gabapentin, and Ketamine was found in his blood. This is the same combination found in all of the partygoers the night he went missing. His blood-alcohol level was slightly higher than the legal limit. Vic was abducted from the Angeli home at 56 Mandarin Street, killed at another location, and placed at the Vale home, crime scene #3. His original clothing was removed and the clothing of the family's scarecrow was replaced on the DB. We have not located his original clothing. Folks in the Vale family's neighborhood said they saw no strangers in the area during that time. The power was out briefly the night of the party, which seems like when he was killed. He had a connection to victim #4 as they went to school together and were at the same party where he vanished. His body parts were never recovered. DNA was recovered at the scene, but it doesn't match with the DNA from victim #1. Because the body was taken from the Angeli house, killed at another location, and placed at the Vales' house, the lab is still ruling out DNA from members of both families.

Carl spoke, "Right, so if we locate the kill site, I imagine we'll find the body parts, most likely buried. Any leads on where he could have taken him?"

The FBI tech added, "The lab uncovered some soil and debris ground into Bryce's shoulders and back. They are trying to narrow down a specific area where it could be from as we speak."

"Okay, thanks. Team 4 what have you got for us?"

Once the board was moved away the next presentation began. Shandra Neely, from the Pawtucket PD, stepped up with the information that team #4 put together. Her sloping nose, between two round piercing dark eyes, was her leading feature. Carl went through the academy with her. She graduated top of her class. She cleared her throat and said, "Karol Romano, 17, residence 403 Songbird Lane, Cumberland, is victim #4. COD is a very deep laceration to the throat. She was nearly decapitated. Her eyes were removed, her lips removed, and several teeth were knocked out with a blunt instrument. These body parts were removed preceding her death. Acepromazine, Gabapentin, and Ketamine were found in her bloodstream. No alcohol was ingested. There was a puncture mark located on her neck below her right ear—as if someone came from behind and injected it. The car she was found in was placed there by the D.A.R.E. team ten days prior. She was expected at the vigil for victim #3 but never showed. Friends and family said the last time she was seen was when she was helping her mother with groceries before the vigil. Mother knew she was waiting for friends to get her to help set up at the vigil. She heard a beep and assumed that she was picked up by friends. The commonality is her connection to vic #3 and the fact that she was at the same party he was when he was abducted."

Carl commended her and asked for the next team.

A very tired-looking pair of officers from the Lincoln Police Department brought up the boards for victims 5 and 6. The first was a tall redheaded man who had deeply lined and tanned skin like that of someone who enjoyed the great outdoor life offered in the state. He said, "Vics were a married couple, Burt and Jolie Stand, from 127 Cowboy Lane, in Lincoln. Their daughter said they went to Ocean State casino the night before they were found. Daughter stayed with a friend so she can't confirm if they came home. The house looked as if it were wiped clean. A long red hair was found inside a bathroom—synthetic, probably from a wig. Wife had no wigs in the house and the daughter said she never saw her wear one. Lab is testing that strand. Victims were taken from the home—both cars are still there, and they were brought to crime scene #5, Lincoln Woods, and killed there. Neighbors said they saw nothing out of the ordinary but that the couple was not "ordinary." It was rumored that they were swingers. They approached several of their neighbors at one time or another to ask if they'd like to try out the lifestyle—none were willing, they were all very emphatic about that. Um, the pair were naked when found. The clothes and body parts were burned in the sand near the boat rentals."

An officer with salt and pepper hair continued, "Victim # 5 is Burt Stand, 42, who was killed before his wife was in the same manner as vic #1, but it was a full castration with the removal of the testes as well. This and the fact that they were at Ocean State Casino link them to the first vic. His, ah, penis, and testicles were removed and there was a cut to the femoral artery on the right leg. Died of exsanguination. Both vics had excessive amounts of Flunitrazepam, Gabapentin, and Xanax, along with a very high blood alcohol level; his was almost three times the legal limit. He was taped into a canoe. The lab is testing the tape for prints. Hair and fibers were found in the boat, but because of the large volume of renters there, we're not too hopeful."

"Victim #6 is Jolie Stand, 40. COD is similar to victim #2. Her breasts were cut off and he cut her carotid artery—but he did not cut anything in the, ah, vaginal area. Her blood-alcohol level was slightly higher than the legal limit. She was also taped to her seat in the canoe on the opposite side and taped to her husband. They were seated back-to-back. Based on the amount of blood in the canoe, that is where they were killed."

Carl looked around the room at all of his colleagues' hard work and was very impressed. "Great work, everyone. I know the labs are backed up, they've never dealt with anything like this before, but we all need to stay on top of them. Team #2—check with the footage we now have from Ocean State and see if she can be spotted there the night she died. It's a long shot, but worth a try. Everyone, please have these reports ready for me when I get back. I need to update ASAC, Haverhill, and White." After he said that, he looked at Arabella and sensed that she was puzzled about something. "Okay, we're off to interview our suspect."

FORTY
Paige

"Paige, honey, we want you to let us know when you feel you are ready to go back to the house. We're not rushing you, but we want you to think about it."

"I love being here at Cookie's, but I miss my bed and my shower. I'm sorry everyone had to be uprooted for so long. I'm ready to go back any time."

"We were all upset, Paige, it's fine. No one wanted to go back right away. I hired a cleaning service to clean everything outside and in, top-to-bottom, so everything should be back to normal when we get home. I'll go find Cookie and tell her she'll have her house back."

Paige went to find James and Timmy to tell them the news. They were playing video games in the family room. Seeing them together, you would think they were brothers. That thought instantly gave light to a feeling she had tucked away. She loves James in her own way, more like a brother. Seeing them together solidified that very fact.

"Hey, guys, who's winning?" she asked.

"Me! I'm whipping his butt," laughed Timmy.

"Oh, yeah, take that!" shouted James. A loud explosion emanated from the television screen, and they both laughed.

"Well, sorry to be the bearer of bad news, but you need to pack up your things. We're going back home. Mom's telling Cookie right now."

They paused the game and looked at her. Once she finished talking, they went right back to the game.

"Hey! Move it, you two!"

They both sighed and placed the controls on the table, turned the game and television off, and looked up at her. "Okay, okay." They stood up. Timmy ran up to the room he was sharing with James.

James remained. He stood up, stretched, and said, "My mom has been bugging me to come home too. She doesn't like being home alone with everything going on. I told her that I'd be home today or tomorrow. I'll go pack up now."

Cookie came in and hugged Paige. "You don't really have to leave, do you?"

"Aw, it's time to go. We'll visit again soon."

They said their goodbyes and dropped James at his house. They pulled into the cul-de-sac and Paige's pulse began to quicken. She began to feel sweat beads develop on her upper lip and her forehead. Her breathing became more rapid. She tried to steady herself so that no one would notice. She could tell her mother was trying to catch a glimpse of her in the rearview mirror. When they drove up to the front of the house, there was no scarecrow. No chair for him. No evidence that a scarecrow had ever existed. They pulled into the garage and went into the kitchen. The familiar, clean scent of Pine-Sol and bleach was what finally eased her jitters. It made her feel like she was home and safe.

Paige went to her room to collect herself and unpack. As she sat on her bed, she looked at the photographs that she had affixed to her bureau mirror. Her heart shattered when she saw the ones with Bryce and Karol. She couldn't believe that they were gone. She stood up and moved to the mirror. With each picture, she relived the memories they all shared. A tear fell onto her jewelry box. When she got to the picture of Karol sliding down the laundry chute, she couldn't help but laugh. They had so many good times. The pain of losing Bryce was insurmountable. She felt so bad that the vigil was ruined and was angered that this maniacal killer would torture the family in that way. She was longing for the days when she was younger and everything was easy. She recalled that most times in her past when she felt free and calm were times with James. She called him, but it went to voicemail. She lay down on her bed and fell asleep.

FORTY-ONE

Carl

Troy Andrews was moved from his cell and sat waiting in Interrogation Room B at the Cumberland Police Department. Carl and Arabella came in and were stopped by the arresting officers who had updated them about what had transpired at the Andrews residence. "He's really upset. He keeps saying that he can't believe he killed someone. Before I asked him, he revealed that he had kept some illegal drugs in his bathroom medicine cabinet. Carl, the guy is a wreck. His bloodwork came back with high amounts of Xanax, Vicodin, and Gabapentin. We couldn't find any traces of those drugs at his residence. He is claiming that he was drugged. I think that if he didn't wake up when he did, he would be another victim and the killer would be on the loose again. I spoke to a doctor at the forensic lab who said that because he was a regular drug user, the effect was minimal for him. That's why he woke up early and was able to defend himself. Once you finish talking to him, I think you'll both agree."

Carl said, "Thanks. We're heading in now to question him. Let us know if any new developments come up."

Arabella opened the door and she and Carl went in and sat at the table.

Carl sized him up. He seemed to be tired and scared. "Troy, tell us everything that happened in your apartment over the last two days."

"Like I told the other officers, there's a lot I can't remember. I decided to go to Gill's Pub after work on Thursday. I didn't expect to stay long but then this woman sat near me at the bar. We had a drink and started talking. After a few more drinks, I invited her to my place and she said yes. I remember getting to the apartment, having more to drink, and then moving to the bedroom, but nothing more until I came to and heard them arguing."

"Who was arguing?" Arabella asked.

"I don't know. I'm pretty sure that it was the woman from the bar but I have no idea who the guy was. He was very angry. He kept saying that he was tired of her, that he wouldn't clean up her messes anymore. When I woke up, I was scared and trying to figure out what was going on so I just pretended to be out cold. He kept punching something—I thought it was her, and saying, 'No more.' Then it sounded like he was strangling her, then I heard a bunch of thuds and screams and it got quiet."

Carl said, "Explain what you mean by you were pretty sure it was her. Was it?"

"Well, as I said, I tried to pretend that I was out, but when I looked at her through the doorway and saw her up on my wall, she was a blonde. When I met her at the bar, she had black hair."

Carl and Arabella looked at one another and then he said, "Okay, continue with what happened."

"He was saying stuff like, `All those people I killed for you' and I heard him say that he was going to make it look like I killed her. I grabbed a water glass off the shelf near my bed, and then got back into the same position, and then when he came near me, I hit him over the head with it. We fought and then I grabbed the lamp and put the cord around his neck. It didn't take long; he went limp and then the cops were there." Troy became upset and started to cry. It took a while for him to regain his composure.

Carl gave Troy a bandanna to wipe his face.

"I've barely ever been in a fight before. I can't believe I killed him. What the hell happened—why was he there—who drugged me?"

Arabella said, "Mr. Andrews, we are still looking into everything. Is there anything else you remember?"

"No. I can't think of anything else. Am I being arrested?"

Arabella knew that this was no killer. Sometimes good people just snapped and became killers, but this was altogether different. The man sitting in front of her was a victim. Nothing more.

She answered, "Hang tight. Someone will be in shortly."

They left the interrogation room and both agreed that the man they just questioned was not the killer. That meant the killer was most likely dead. They went to find the captain in the viewing room to share their findings. Samuel decided to convene the team.

Carl, Arabella, and some other members of the task force met in the conference room. Captain White took command of the meeting once everyone was present.

"Let's focus on what we know about the person in custody."

There was a knock on the door and the tall officer that brought Troy in was waived in. Captain White asked, "What have you got?"

She cleared her throat, "We just verified that victims 5 and 6 were also at the casino. We have footage of them talking to a woman with purple hair at a Blackjack table."

"Good work. That fits with the MO for how he's selecting most of the targets. Do we know if the high school teens were at the casino?"

"Um, Cap, that's not all. The woman who was killed today is the same woman on CCTV with the other victims at Ocean State. She has been identified as one Rosa Marie Hoover. She had different hair colors on each of the CCTV recordings with every vic, but it's definitely her. No ID on the male vic yet." She never witnessed a room fall silent so fast. All eyes were on her, peering through her. She felt like she was in a dream where she was naked on stage— but she was wide-awake. "Um, well, that's it." She stood there not quite knowing what to do next.

The captain asked, "Have we checked her DNA results to any of the victims?"

"The crime scene techs just finished processing

the new crime scene a little while ago. Other labs have volunteered to take some evidence to expedite the findings. I'll have them put a rush on these tests." She left to carry out the rush with the lab.

Carl noticed Arabella twisting her rings. He knew this meant she was stressed. He had seen it several times before. "What's up?"

Arabella said under her breath, "I've been working on that *different angle*. I don't want to say anything until I am absolutely certain. I'll fill you in later."

He knew better than to push her, so he let it go.

The captain stood up and began to address them further, but ASAC cut him off, as usual. "That changes everything. She must be the decoy who baits them for him to kill. I just met with the profilers on these cases and the latest profile came in that there is a high probability that two killers are working in tandem. This all fits. We now know the woman was involved. We need to find out if the dead vic or the live suspect was her accomplice." He looked at Arabella and Carl. "You two interviewed him, what are your thoughts?"

"Arabella and I both feel the suspect is innocent. If Mr. Andrews wasn't a recovering drug user, he would not have woken up when he did and we would most likely have another victim on our hands and the killer on the loose once again. Something went wrong at the scene. We're waiting to retrieve phone records and to get a look at the text messages. Also waiting on a search warrant for her residence."

Captain White finished with, "Okay, as soon as the DNA results are ready, we should know more about who her accomplice was." He displayed the same extreme fatigue and confusion that everyone was feeling because of these senseless murders happening in such a rapid-fire succession.

FORTY-TWO
Paige

Paige awoke with a start. She was not used to napping and her body protested. Her limbs were stiff and her head felt as though it were wedged between boulders. It throbbed with each pulse of her heartbeat and settled behind her eyes. She went into her bathroom and got a drink of water. She looked to see if she had anything for the pain, but there was nothing there. She plodded down the dark cherry stairs, to the main bathroom, and found the remedy she was looking for. She went into the kitchen and found Tim with his head in the refrigerator.

"Hey, squirt, anything good?"

"No. Mom just left to go to the market."

"So why are you staring at nothing?"

"I don't know."

She went over to him, nudged him out of the way, and closed the fridge door. "I'll see if I can find us something in the cupboards." She did and they enjoyed some crackers with peanut butter for a snack.

Paige remembered that she had called James before she dozed off. She checked her phone to see if she had slept through his return call, but there were no missed calls. No texts either. She sent a group text to her friends to see what everyone was doing. It was getting close to the curfew time and she knew that they couldn't get together, but she felt isolated and wanted to commiserate with them. Everyone soon replied and she realized that they were all in the same boat. It was funny because if the curfew hadn't been put in place, they probably wouldn't feel so captive.

Sloane came home and the kids helped her bring in the bags of groceries.

Paige sat down and sent James a text:

Hey. Where are you? I called earlier.

She waited for the magic jumping dots to appear on her phone indicating that he was reading her message and would reply soon, but they never appeared.

Tim asked to go to a friend's house.

"You know you can't go out, squirt. It's not safe."

"Is it because of the aliens, Paige? Tell me the truth."

"Yes, Paige, please, tell us the truth," chastised Sloane.

Paige quickly added, "Timmy, don't be silly. It was just a story I made up to scare you. Nothing more."

"Well, who did that to our scarecrow then?"

Sloane answered, "The police are searching for him. They will find him and put him in jail forever.

He'll never be able to hurt anyone ever again."

"How could a person do that? I still think it was an alien." Jasper came barreling in and found his favorite ball. Tim ran into the living room with him to have a game of fetch.

Paige was afraid to make eye contact with her mother. "I know, I know, Mom. It was just supposed to be a scary story. I had no idea something terrible was really about to happen. Believe me; I'll never do it again."

+++++++++++++

The following day, the family decided to go apple picking in the morning to kick off the weekend. Sloane thought that it would be a good distraction for the whole family. She told Paige to see if James wanted to come along.

"I'll ask him, but I haven't been able to get in touch with him since we left Cookie's."

They waited to hear back and when they didn't, they drove by his house to see if he was there. You couldn't be too careful these days. There was no sign of the truck they teasingly called the Clampett mobile, so they went without him. Paige made a mental note to drive by Dr. Doolittle's when they returned home to see if he was there. She now knew what it was like for James when she was too busy to get back to him. It was intensified a thousand times now because there was a crazed killer on the loose. She would have to remind him of that.

The Vale family brought home everyone's favorite

apples and some extra for Sloane's apple pies. She decided to make two right away—cooking and baking calmed her anxiety. She got all of the ingredients together and turned on the television in the kitchen for an added distraction. She came across *The Silence of the Lambs* and felt like life right now was too much like a horror movie and kept searching. When she came upon *The Pink Panther*, it brought back fond memories of watching it with her father, so she settled for the comedy. She was peeling apples when the network interrupted with breaking news. It was another press conference about the recent murders. Sloane ran to the basement door and yelled for Mitch to come up. Paige and Tim heard and flocked to the kitchen.

A news anchor appeared on the screen with a glimmer in her eye. "This just in. The killing spree that has taken over the sleepy New England area of Rhode Island has finally come to an end. We take you now to a live press conference of the joint task force for the latest information."

Footage flooded the TV screen and there were several groups of official-looking individuals behind a podium in front of the Parks & Rec building at the entrance to Diamond Hill.

A man stepped up to the microphone and began the briefing. His pleasant square face looked through the television screen and imbued utter confidence. She was sure they chose him as the spokesperson because of this.

"Good afternoon, everyone. My name is Captain

Samuel White. I, along with the joint task force you see behind me, have some good news to share with you about the recent murders that have rocked our communities. All of the people you see here have worked tirelessly to bring the *murderers* to justice. My two lead officers, Sergeant Lowden and Detective Luthor, were instrumental in assisting local PDs and the FBI team brought together by Allan De Luca, the Assistant Special Agent-in-Charge." He paused while everyone clapped. "Justice for the victims has been realized. Justice for Paul Cooper, Ruby Shea, Bryce Walker, Karol Romano, and Burt and Jolie Stand. Utilizing DNA and other technology, we are confident we know who was behind these heinous crimes."

There was a pause.

"You may have noticed that I mentioned the *'murderers'* responsible. Yes, two people were working together to commit the torture and murder of these six people. A botched attempted seventh murder led to the identification and subsequent death of the killers. Lucas and Rosa Marie Hoover were a married couple who resided in Cumberland, and they were responsible for the murders. Details are still being collected, but for now, we want our families and friends to sleep better tonight. More details will be forthcoming as we put the full picture together. We will be lifting the curfew and normal life can resume!" Once again, there was a smattering of applause and the news anchor was back filling the screen telling everyone what they just heard.

Sloane turned off the television and asked, "A married couple? I can't believe this. Do their names sound familiar to anyone?"

They all agreed that no one knew them.

"Why would they have involved us in their macabre game?" Mitch said and then added that he was sure as time went by, all of the answers would become clear.

Paige sent James another text:

Your dad was just on TV! Press conf
They caught the murderers! Some
married couple. Call me!

The apprehension Paige felt was surprising. If the killers were targeting her friends, she thought there was a possibility James had been another victim.

Paige pushed the troubling thoughts about the worst-case scenario to the back of her mind as she was asked, "What do you think?"

"Sorry, Mom. What?"

"I am making pies. I can make some turnovers too and we can bring them to the task force. I'm sure they'd like some home-cooked treats."

"Sure, Mom. That's a great idea."

Paige's phone announced that she was getting several texts. Relief spread through her body thinking it was James. There were several. She read through them—mostly about the capture of the two killers, but still nothing from him. She asked everyone if they knew the couple and no one had any idea who they were. She felt like there was a giant chunk of this puzzle still missing. They had to know her and her relationship with Bryce for them to do what they did. It couldn't be a mere coincidence. She decided to do some snooping online.

She pulled her dark hair into a ponytail and settled at her desk. She started by typing their names into a popular search engine. She learned that the woman, Rosa Marie, was 42-years-old. She moved to Rhode Island from a suburb outside of Seattle eight years ago. It listed other cities that she lived in such as Pawtucket and Woonsocket. All of her social media accounts were either secure or had no recent activity. The minimal information available to Paige solidified the fact that nothing about this woman seemed familiar to her at all.

She typed in the same searches for Lucas which resulted in even less information than Rosa Marie. He was 44-years-old and came from Chicago over ten years ago. He had no social media accounts. Nothing but roadblocks at every turn for him. Paige's pale complexion was made paler by the screen's blue glow and she felt the paleness seep into her internally.

Sloane called up to Paige to tell her that the turnovers were ready to go.

"Okay, Mom, I'll be right down."

She went down to the smell of apples, cinnamon, and nutmeg, and she wanted to dive, headfirst, into one of the pies.

"Go get your brother and tell him we are going for a drive. I think he'd get a kick out of seeing all the uniforms."

Paige went into the living room and found him asleep. She called his name and when he didn't respond, she went over to nudge him. His skin felt like it was on fire. She went into the garage where Sloane was loading the turnovers.

"Mom, he's asleep. And when I went to wake him up, he felt really hot."

"Oh, no! Well, your father just left and I can't leave him here alone, especially if he's sick. Why don't you take them over?"

She agreed. She planned to go by and see if she could finally locate James and take him with her.

Paige called James. She left him yet another voicemail message saying she was going by and explained what her plans were. When she arrived, he was nowhere in sight. She racked her brain to try to remember if he said anything about going somewhere or if she could have said anything to upset him. Nothing came to mind. Now she was really starting to worry.

FORTY-THREE
Carl

The mood at the task force headquarters was a drastic change from what it was. Upbeat conversations were happening and people looked happy, well rested, and relaxed. There was still work going on—a lot of connecting the dots and tying up loose ends.

A very muscular woman with a buzz cut came in through the door and got everyone's attention. "My partner and I just got back from the mall where Rosa Marie Hoover worked. She worked at a low-end clothing store called The Walk-In Closet." Everyone could tell that she was making sure her mouth did not outpace her thoughts. She tried to speak slowly and steadily while it was evident that she was very eager to share her news. "Her co-workers, when interviewed separately, each described her as 'white trash' and a 'sexual deviant'. They said that she really thought that she was the next Marilyn Monroe but looked more like a train wreck. She frequently tried to pass knock-off clothing and accessories as designer products. She had a beer belly and wore overly tight clothing. She traded sex for drugs with whoever was willing." The task force members seemed to think that this new information fit with their suspicions. "One last thing. Two of the women she worked with said that she and her husband had a non-conventional relationship. He liked to watch her have sex with other people. She let it slip that he was becoming angry recently with the *men and women* she would parade around in front of him. They said she told them that he would hurt them when it was over."

Natalie Frazee stood and said, "This definitely fits in with the killer desecrating the bodies by removing the sex organs. If he started out hurting them, it is safe to assume he progressed to murder. Once he had a taste for killing, he most likely couldn't stop himself and went after other victims."

Everyone there agreed with her summations. The cheerful conversations began once more.

There was still one member of the task force who was somber and not celebrating with the others. Carl went over to Arabella, "Why the long face?"

Before she could answer, the door opened and Paige came through it.

"Hi, Mr. Lowden. My mom made some apple turnovers for you all to help celebrate solving the murders. She wanted to bring them herself, but Timmy has a fever."

"Wow. That was thoughtful. Tell her thanks from all of us and that we hope he feels better."

Arabella took the containers of turnovers and passed them around to the team members that were still there.

"Okay, I will. Mr. Lowden, have you heard from James? I haven't been able to get in touch with him for days."

"No. The last time I saw him was at the vigil for Bryce. We've sent some texts back and forth; I know he stayed with you at your grandmother's house for a while. Lydia told me he was going back home."

"Yeah, he did. I've called, sent texts, and gone by the house, but there's no sign of him anywhere."

"Let me text him." They waited a while for a reply. When none came, he decided to text Lydia.

Arabella came back over to them with a turnover for Carl. "Oh, my gosh, this is the best thing I've tasted in a long time. Tell your mom she is . . . what's wrong Paige?"

When Carl looked at Paige, all of the blood had drained from her and she was swaying. She was looking at Arabella's case boards. She tried to speak. Carl dragged a chair over and put her in it.

Carl said, "Sorry about all the gore. We usually don't get civilians in here. Arabella, why don't you turn these around so . . . ?"

Paige's shouting interrupted Carl. "No! That's not it. I never heard exactly how they were murdered. I knew they dismembered people, but now that I see it, it feels . . . familiar." She took a long, educated look at the case boards, surveying them intently. She turned to them, "Why is Mrs. Hansen there? Is she dead too?"

Carl answered, "No. She's just missing. Arabella was going with a different theory from what the FBI thought about the killers before the case broke. Now, Mrs. Hansen is just classified as a silver alert. She has dementia. The family doesn't know exactly when she left the nursing home, but it was after the Hoovers were found deceased. She will be removed from the case board."

Carl's phone rang. "It's Lydia. I'll be right back." He stepped outside to the gravel-strewn grounds. He moved away from the door where people were constantly coming and going. The crunching sound of his feet hitting the stones sent vibrations through his arms and into the phone so he stopped walking. "Hey, Lyd. How are things?"

"Okay, I'm on my way home right now. I was thinking of going by and kidnapping my own son to bring him home. It's safe now, right?"

"Wait. He hasn't been home? Paige said they left her grandmother's two days ago."

"What? No way. I've been home. He came by to get his truck. I thought he was using it to go back and forth to work from Cookie's, but he hasn't been home. What's going on Carl? Where is he?"

"I'm not sure. He hasn't been answering texts or calls from me or Paige."

"I'm almost home. I'll call you once I'm there. Maybe something happened to his phone."

"Okay. Let me know ASAP."

Carl went back into the building to quite a scene. Arabella was trying to calm Paige down. She was crying, shaking, and yelling incoherently. Nothing was making much sense.

"Hey, hey, calm down Paige." He was bewildered. "What are you trying to say?"

Arabella told her to take some deep breaths and counted with her. Once she was calm, she was able to speak in coherent sentences. As she paced back and forth, glancing at the boards, she remembered, "The body parts. I know why they're missing. It's from my journal." Surprise, confusion, and heartbreak flooded her emotions, each trying to take control of her.

"What journal, Paige? What are you talking about?" Arabella asked.

Pushing the competing emotions aside, Paige regained command of herself. "Okay, listen. When I was a kid, I kept a journal about the people I loved and why I loved them." She stood up and went over to one of Arabella's boards. While Arabella was working out her own theory, she had the victims separated on two boards. On one board were Paul Cooper, Ruby Shea, and Burt and Jovi Stand. On the other board were Bryce, Karol, and Fiona Hansen.

With a shaking hand, Paige pointed and said, "See. Right here—with Bryce. I loved the way he looked at me, how big his heart was, and the feel of his rough, calloused hands. And, here, with Karol, I loved her smile. Oh, my gosh! Someone did this using my journal!"

"I'm sure it's just a coincidence. Where is your journal?" asked Carl.

"Um, I'm not sure. I haven't seen it in . . . oh, wait. It's in the hideout. Oh, no. James. He's the only one who could have . . ."

"What hideout, Paige?"

"It's over by the Reservoir near my house, but it's underground and hidden. I'll have to take you there."

"Who knows about the hideout?"

"Just me and James. We've never told anyone else."

The look of terror on Carl's face was palpable. It seemed he was realizing what the gravity of her words meant. He looked at Arabella who returned his gaze with the most somber look he had ever seen.

"It's too risky to bring you, Paige. Just tell me where it is."

"No way. I'm going. You're stuck with me. You'll never find the hideout. It'll waste too much time. Let's go!"

They could tell by her stance, her balled-up fists, and her stone-cold stare, that she wouldn't budge on the matter.

"Okay, let's go."

The three exited the makeshift task force office and headed to the SUV. Arabella asked if she should call it in and Carl told her to wait until they knew what they were dealing with.

Arabella was disconsolate, "Carl, do you know what this means? My hunch. If I had just shared it with you earlier, this all . . ." She wouldn't allow herself to finish the statement.

"Arabella, don't. I know how you operate. If you knew for sure, you would have said something. It's not your fault."

Carl read the text from Lydia aloud saying that James had not been home at all.

"Paige. Could anyone else have found this hideaway?"

"It's pretty secluded, but sure. I guess so. I haven't been there in a while. James has asked me to meet him there a few times over the last few months, but I've been too busy."

The women could see how Carl was grappling with the misery playing through his mind. He now believed that these murders were the work of not two but three killers. His brain wrestled with the realization that one could be James. There had to be some other explanation.

"Um, pull over here," Paige instructed.

They stopped and followed Paige when they got out. They walked through the woods that encased the reservoir. She led them over a slippery, decaying, leaf-strewn forest floor where the sunlight streaming in through the tops of the trees acted as a searchlight to their destination.

She added, "It's been a while. Let me get my bearings. I usually just followed James."

She stopped and looked up at the sky through the tops of the trees. They looked different devoid of leaves, but all at once, she knew where she was.

"This way!"

They followed Paige trying not to trip over exposed roots and vines that spread out like the lifelines of the forest.

Carl's phone rang. "Lowden. What? Repeat that.

Shit! Okay. Who's there. Good. Okay, I'm with Arabella following a lead. We'll connect soon. What? No, there's no time. I'll fill you in soon."

Arabella asked, "What was that about?"

"Some women were walking at the Monastery and found another DB. It's Fiona Hansen. She is dismembered too."

Arabella looked crestfallen. "Oh, shit. I can't believe this."

"Mr. Lowden, were her arms removed?"

"Yes, they were."

"It's definitely my journal!"

Paige led them through the woods and down a path of secrets and betrayal. The smell of decaying leaves grew stronger as the air became cooler. They picked up the pace and followed her another 500 yards or so until she stopped and ran over to what looked like an ancient campfire. There were remnants of charred logs and large stones and boulders all placed in a circular pattern. "Here! Here it is." She pulled the scorched wood away that was fixed to a circular disk, and opened the trapdoor. Paige knew instantly that something was wrong. Instead of the stale earthy, wormy smell she was used to, she was hit with a stench that brought her back to biology class and the dissection of frogs. Carl and Arabella smelled it too.

Carl said, "Formaldehyde. Shit. Okay. Paige, you wait up here."

Before she could protest, the two were climbing down the large stone steps. After everything that she had seen earlier, she didn't want to see any more carnage anyway.

She yelled down to them and told them where her journal should be. She waited for what seemed like forever and called down, "Did you find it? Are you guys okay?"

He shouted up, "We'll be up in a minute. Don't come down here." Carl looked around and couldn't believe what he was seeing. They appeared to be in an old storage bunker. The kids had set it up with lights, seats, and tables. A large table was covered in blood and gore. There was straw in small piles on the ground along with bloodied garbage bags and rags.

Carl found the bin where Paige said the journal would be. There were a few there along with toys and books, but none that fit the description she gave him. They took photos of everything and called in for a forensic team to get there.

They came up and Carl told Paige that the journal was missing.

"It was there. I'm sure of it."

"Okay. Look, Arabella is going to wait here for the forensics team to work the scene. You come with me so that we can guide the team to the right place and then I need to get you home and head to the new crime scene to see if we can figure out exactly what is going on."

Arabella stayed at the hideout while Carl and Paige went to meet the other officers and directed them to the right location. They arrived quickly, placing markers along the way for easy access to and from the scene. Once the forensics team set to work, Carl, Arabella, and Paige left.

The three filed into the SUV. The ride was an incredibly awkward one. The same thing was going through their minds, but no one wanted to admit it. There was a conspicuous lack of discussion.

Finally, Paige broke the silence, "Mr. Lowden, you know there must be another explanation. Maybe someone followed him there. James could never do those things. I've known him for a long time. He is kind and he takes such good care of everyone. And, the animals. He loves animals. With all the true crime I've read, I know that serial killers hurt and kill animals before they kill people, and . . ."

"Paige, Paige, I know. I'm sure we'll get to the bottom of it. Thanks. Here we are." They were almost at her house when he received a call from Lydia.

"Carl!" Lydia's voice sounded frantic and shaky through the interior speakers.

"What's happened? Is James there?"

"No. He's not here, but I know where he is. Listen, this is crazy, but I just saw him on the news."

"The news? What the hell, Lydia? What do you mean?"

"You know how they have those cameras that show how backed up highway traffic is? Well, I wasn't even really watching the news, but I looked up and I saw his truck—clear as day. There is no mistaking it, Carl. It was him!"

"Okay, what direction was he headed?"

"He was going north on I-95. Where could he be

going?"

"I'm not sure, but if I had to guess, I'd say he was heading to the old cabin. Listen, there's been a lot going on today that I need to tell you. I don't have all the answers right now, but trust me. I'm going to bring him home."

"Carl, I don't like this. Tell me what's happening."

"There's no time. I have to go. I'll call you when I can."

He hung up and looked at the women riding with him. Even though his large frame was menacing, there was always a warmth emanating from his kind eyes. The warmth in Carl's eyes was now gone as he peered into Paige's soul through the rearview mirror. "We need to get you home Paige. Then the two of us will go to the cabin in New Hampshire; if he was traveling north on Interstate 95, I'm sure that's where he's headed."

"No way. I'm going with you. I'm the only person he trusts. Whenever he had one of his *episodes*, no one could get through to him like me. Besides, I already told my mom I was looking for him with you. I'm staying."

Arabella gave Carl a look that told him he was outnumbered. "If you stay, you need to do everything we say. No questions asked."

"Sure. Of course." Paige turned her head, her chin held high, and her blue eyes determined, signaling the end of the conversation. Carl shifted into drive and floored the gas, tires screeching.

+++++++++++++

Most of the FBI agents had packed up and headed back to headquarters. The other officers on loan from nearby departments had cleared out hours ago. Everyone still at the task force headquarters was now at a loss regarding the scope and scale of the new information that had been unfolding before them.

Officers Raya Lang and Julian Lazar, who were pulling out of a gas station near the Monastery, heading back to the Lincoln PD, accepted the call when it came in. When they arrived, they were led to the body of a large woman with very dark hair. They recognized her from the recent silver alert. It was Fiona Hansen. She was missing both arms. It was evident that they were removed crudely. It was very hard to look at the scene before them. She was partially covered in leaves and other debris. Her large feet were protruding out from her body that was haphazardly concealed. It was visible from about 30 yards away on the popular walking path; the stark contrast to the normal earth tones was easily detected.

The forensic team was just arriving so Raya and Julian moved to let them do their work. They went to interview the witnesses. There were three—Miranda Savon and her daughter Jillian, and Jillian's friend, Jordan Whitfield. They were all walking along the trail. Miranda told them that the girls ran ahead of her and then she heard them scream. She ran to them and saw what upset them. There was a body just off the path. It was partially buried and the grave was very shallow. Whoever put her there did a poor job of covering her up. She wrangled the girls away and called 9-1-1.

Officers Lang and Lazar spoke with the girls next. They said that they were walking and looking for objects that they could use in art projects. The woman's daughter wore a wide floral headband and hoop earrings that made her look like a mini fortuneteller. She told them, "Yeah, like, we wanted things from nature that we could make designs with." They both spotted the body but weren't sure what they were looking at. They walked over to it and when they realized what it was, they screamed.

The officers took their contact information and sent the very upset trio home. They walked back over to the scene. Once the debris was cleared away from the body, they could see that her throat had also been cut. They asked the other officers for an approximate time of death and what they were told did not make sense. She was killed after the murdering couple was found dead.

The pair stayed behind to help seal off the area to the public. They decided to allow entrance to the library that was on the premises. There was also a children's playground on the same grounds but closed it because there was access to the trail from there.

Officer Lazar asked, "You know what really sucks?"

"Shoot," answered his partner.

"My kids had her as a teacher. They loved her. My wife and I found her a little weird and passive-aggressive, but I still wouldn't wish that on anyone."

+++++++++++++

Carl tried James on the phone again with no luck. He tried to think back to when the last time the whole family used the cabin. When he remembered, he was racked with guilt and shame. It was the night that he had come clean to Lydia about his affair with Tara. He couldn't keep it a secret any longer. It had been eating away at him. Tara had wanted him to wait, but he felt that the time was right. What they were doing was ruining two separate families, not one, and he couldn't let it go on.

He let everyone down. His wife, his father, James; it was the worst time of his life. It was the catalyst to James having the episodes that left him being evaluated by neurologist after neurologist. Those were truly difficult days. He could never shake the feeling that it was because of his actions that his son suffered the consequences. Could he have suffered some lasting damage that no one had previously found? No. Paige was right; James could never do this. There had to be another explanation.

How could his sweet, caring son be responsible for this? He thought back to the night he saw him recovering in the hospital with the other teens. He was so helpless and—wait! That's right. James couldn't have done this. He was drugged with the rest of them. He was about to share his thoughts when Arabella received a call.

"What do you have for me?" She listened for a long time and then ended the call telling the caller to call again with any new information. From the passenger seat, she looked at Carl with an unfamiliar expression. Even though they were partners now for four years, this was a look that worried him.

"It's not good, Carl. The only prints in the hideout were from Paige and James. His prints were all over the jars with the body parts, and they were confirmed to be from Bryce, Karol, and Fiona Hansen. I had it right, Carl. There were two different killers; Lucas Hoover and whoever else killed these three. I think Rosa Marie was used to lure the victims for Lucas only. She didn't do any killing. The second killer had nothing to do with Lucas. At first, I thought he might have been a copycat, but he had his own disturbing reasons for killing and doing what he did. As far as the displaying of the bodies, I think that was very deliberate also and very separate from the other killer."

They rode in silence for a bit, watching the outside view change to a more mountainous region with tall pines towering along both sides of the road. The air felt cleaner and thinner. She could feel the incline and ascension into a higher altitude. Their destination couldn't be too far now.

Then Arabella spoke again. "When Bryce was taken, James was unconscious at the party with the rest of the teens. That doesn't fit with it being James. There must be something we aren't seeing."

In unison, Carl and Paige said, "That's right!"

He shared how that very thought had been what he was trying to work out. They realized that she was absolutely correct. James was a victim just like the others. They needed to find a connection between Lucas and the teens and figure out how he knew about the party and drugged the alcohol.

Carl began to feel a calmness wash over him. In part because of the discrepancy in the timeline that made James's guilt an impossibility, and in part because of the fond memories rising to the surface this particular ride evoked. This was the best time of year to make the drive into the Lakes Region. It was past peak but there were still some beautifully mottled shades of gold, rust, and maroon to be seen heading up into the clouds. Most visitors had come and gone, all congregating during the peak times for the best photo opportunities.

Paige disturbed his revelry. "My mom checked my room. The journal isn't there Mr. Lowden. I'm sure it was in the hideout. Could you ask Mrs., um, Ms. Lowden to check in James's room?"

"That's a good idea, and please call me Carl."

"Okay, I will."

While they drove over the Kancamagus Highway taking in the sights, they could tell that the further north they drove, the more leaves were missing from the trees and the colors of the leaves daring to hang on for their lives were an even deeper version of the ones they saw when they first entered the state.

When they arrived at the cabin in the unsympathetic light of day, everything looked sadder than he remembered. He made it so. He set off this chain of events; he was sure of it.

The truck was there. Carl was right. Paige could feel James's presence. Her heart was swelling to the point she thought it would tear right out of her chest. She realized that it was a combination of fear and sadness. She still couldn't work out how he was involved in all this, but she had an inkling that he was. She was running over several scenarios of how he could have been with them at the hospital and still had something to do with this but came up blank. She vowed to let the professionals work out the details.

They parked near the truck, got out, and headed toward the open door. Arabella readied her gun.

When Carl saw this, he motioned for her to holster it. "I'll go in first. Stay behind me and if anything goes wrong, leave immediately." The women nodded. They stood near the door and waited for his signal.

Carl entered and called for James. There was no answer. He searched from room to room and then went up to the loft area where James stayed as a little boy. He was there. He was sitting on the edge of the bed with an absent look on his face. Carl called to him, but he didn't answer. "Buddy, what are you doing? Why did you come here?" He grabbed the chair from under the small child-sized oak desk and placed it near him. He put his hand on the top of James's thigh and gave it a little nudge. There was no reaction. "James, I have some questions for you, you need to look at me." James sat there with the same blank expression and did not make eye contact. Carl left to bring Arabella and Paige inside.

Arabella searched the place while Carl showed Paige up the stairs. She fell in behind Carl. The fine hairs on the back of her neck and arms stood at attention, sending her senses into high gear. Once at the top, she couldn't believe how empty and vacant James looked.

She signaled for Carl to leave them alone.

"Hey, James, it's me, Paige." He didn't stir. Seeing him like this made her extremely nervous. This was much more than any "episode" she had previously experienced, but she wouldn't give up; she knew he was in there.

"James, look at me. We have to talk. You have to snap out of it." Still nothing. "James, they are saying that you did some pretty terrible things. Please, talk to me so I can help you straighten this out."

While Paige was trying to get through to James, Arabella was looking for anything to help with the case.

Carl decided to check the truck. When he came back inside the cabin, he looked like he was going to be ill. He was holding a bright pink journal with a large black heart drawn on it and the word "LOVE" printed inside of it.

"It's him, Arabella. Oh, God, it's him."

She looked inside the journal. She turned two pages and came to the section with Bryce Walker's name printed in block letters. There were pictures of him glued on the open pages to the left and right. There were word bubbles saying that he was kind, strong, fun and that she loved the way he looked at her. That part was X'd out in thick red paint. There were also X's over comments that she loved his large, rough hands. She turned more pages and came to one with Karol Romano. It followed the same format. Again, bright red X's were painted over her white teeth and bright smile that "reached her eyes" which were also crossed out with red X's. When she came to the page with Fiona Hansen, she knew what she'd see. There were photos of many of her teachers and beneath Mrs. Hansen's picture was written that she loved getting a morning hug from her. After further inspection, Arabella concluded that the X's were most likely made from blood. She'd have to get this journal to the lab for testing right away.

Paige was still trying to get through to James. "Do you remember when we were kids and we'd play in the neighborhood pretending that we were detectives? We'd walk around taking pictures of imaginary clues that we'd make up and write down the numbers and letters of all the license plates we could find. Once we were done, we would pretend that we would take them to your dad at the police station. You loved that he was a cop. You need to let him help you now."

She saw James blink and move slightly so she kept

269

going. Her heartbeat pulsated rapidly as she continued. "I've been thinking. We should finish that song we started writing a while ago. The one we thought would be funny to play in the background of all those spoofy videos we made. I promise I'll spend more time with you. I know that I've been a terrible friend lately."

To that, he slowly and silently turned his head to face her. She didn't know if she should stay there or run. Everything in her body screamed the latter. This person before her did not look like the James she knew. His eyes were black and soulless, and there was no longer any animation to his features.

James felt as though he was wading through a sea of red haze with weights attached to his feet. He knew where to go to get out, but he couldn't seem to get there. He wanted to talk to Paige. Tell her everything. He was so consumed by the *Red* that it was in full control of him. Slowly, he began to free himself. The *Red Times* were happening more often now.

"Hey," he said softly and slowly.

"Hey, James. How are you feeling? You were far away for a while."

"I'm okay."

She tried to speak again, but her voice was trapped. When she was finally able to release it, it was shaky and very soft but audible. "James. They're saying that you did some pretty terrible things. That it was you who killed Bryce and Karol."

He met her eye to eye. She mustered up all the

strength and resolve she had to stay put. She knew that a guiltless person would be protesting, screaming from the rooftops of their innocence. He just sat there, his glare boring into her and paralyzing her with fear.

Very softly, he asked her a question, but Paige could not hear him. "I didn't hear that, James." He said it again, but it was no louder than the first time. She shook her head to indicate that she still didn't hear him.

He stood up and towered over her sitting in that small chair. He bent over and put his hands on either side of her and rested them on the desk behind her; locking her in place. He took a deep breath and boomed, "Why – can't – you – LOVE – ME? Why – can't – you – LOVE – ME?"

Paige tried to get up from the chair, but she couldn't. She struggled to budge but could not even move. Finally, she heard Carl and Arabella coming up the stairs.

Carl grabbed James by the shoulder, pulled him away from her, and yelled, "James, stop. What's happening to you?"

James was breathing rapidly, his cheeks puffing out with every exhale. He was losing control.

Arabella went behind him and cuffed him.

Paige was a crying mess; even Carl could not hide his tears.

"I took them so you'd love me." He shouted at Paige. "Now, I have everything you love. Love ME!"

The pieces were falling into place and sadly

beginning to make sense. None of them could have prepared themselves for the grotesque picture emerging. They filed into the SUV for a long ride back to Rhode Island.

++++++++++++

Paige was taken home and Carl, Arabella, and James went to the CPD. Paige couldn't get warm. Her body was hyperalert from the sheer dread she felt deep within her bones. She wanted to be able to turn back time. Fix this. It felt as if she was watching a movie of her life, but one she could not edit for the outcome she wanted.

James was placed in the conference room at the station. No one knew how to react or what to say to Carl. When Anika saw that he had arrived, she came out of her office and called him over.

"Carl, I know that this is your case, but you need to step away where James is involved. I'm not removing you from everything, just this."

He nodded in agreement. He couldn't think straight, let alone pursue this avenue of the investigation.

Captain White walked by and stopped to offer Carl his sympathies. He told Carl that he would be the one to conduct the interview with James.

Carl was thinking like a father and not a cop. "That's great. I appreciate it. Listen, I know it looks bad, but there are many things that just don't add up, like . . ."

Samuel stopped him saying, "We'll get to the bottom of it, don't you worry."

The desk officer interrupted them by giving Carl several phone messages from Lydia. "She's been calling for hours. Tried to get me to tell her what was happening. Told her it wasn't my place." He patted Carl on the shoulder and went back to the front desk.

Carl knew what his next move had to be and could not have dreaded it more.

He drove into Lilly Pad Estates, arrived at the house, and knocked on Lydia's door. The air around his old house felt different somehow, almost unwelcoming. He immediately heard a canine stampede approach the door. When he entered the house, he was greeted with wet noses, kisses, and wagging tails hitting his legs. A feeling of nostalgia washed over him. She had painted the walls different colors, but overall, not much had changed. Lydia sat on the couch in the living room and waited for Carl to fill her in on what had happened. He couldn't find the words to say what he needed to say. Every time he began, he had to stop. He noticed that she tried to hide the fact that she had been crying. Her tense ashen skin was full of worry. He decided that the best thing would be to look down at his hands. He sat in the seat across from her and tried his best to summarize the entire devastating tale.

"Lyd, you know that because this investigation is continuing, I can't really give you too much detail . . ."

"Detail? How about any information at all?

You've kept me in the dark and I knew it had something to do with our son. Detail?"

"I know. Look, it all happened so quickly. I just brought him to the station and came right here. All we know for sure is that it looks pretty bad. It seems like James might be one of the killers we were after."

"No. What are you talking about? They caught the two killers. I saw your boss on the news. Both killers died."

"It was all pretty clear cut at first. All the pieces seemed to fit. Arabella . . . well, she was working a different angle. When Fiona Hansen was found dead, everything changed. She was killed after the Hoover's were already found dead." He finally looked up to see if he should go on. She seemed like she was following along. "Then, Paige came to the station and saw something that looked familiar and the next thing I knew I was chasing my son up to the cabin."

"Carl. There has to be another explanation. He could never harm anyone, let alone kill someone. You can't believe this. I don't believe this."

"There is proof. Lots of it. I can't say what. I would never put us through this if I wasn't sure. There are a few things that need to be figured out, but I'm almost positive it's him."

"Where is he? I need to see him. I need to talk to him and have him tell me if he did this. I need to hear it from him."

"He's at the station right now being questioned. Lyd, there's something else you should know. When

I found him at the cabin, he was . . . in a trance. Like when he was little, after we split. It was so bad. Paige was able to snap him out of it. He went after her. He pinned her and screamed at her. We had to pull him away. He hasn't said another word since."

"Oh, my God. James. It's all my fault. I've been working so much. I wasn't there for him. He tried to take care of me. I should have been there to take care of him!"

Carl moved over to the couch and put his arms around Lydia. They cried and comforted each other. He told her that as soon as it was possible for her to see James, he'd let her know. He headed back to the station.

FORTY-FOUR

Paige

Sloane heard the car stop to let Paige out. She met her at the door. Paige came in, flew to Sloane, and melted in her arms. Heavy, violent sobs wracked her body. Sloane felt so helpless. There wasn't much she could do. She just held her and let her take her time to recover.

"Mom. It's all my fault. James killed Bryce, Karol, and Mrs. Hansen. All because of me." She sounded so spent. It seemed as though every last fiber of energy in her was being used to string together these words. Sloane ushered her into the living room and they sat down on the couch.

"He read through my journal and it made him snap."

"Journal? What journal, honey?"

"The one I kept at the hideout. We found an underground storage bunker years ago and would go there to hang out. It's in the woods behind our house near the reservoir. We cleaned it up and brought things there to keep us occupied. I had taken some of my journals to doodle in or whatever. One of them was filled with the people I loved. I would write about why I loved them. I had photos and sketches and listed different likable things about them. The thing is, I didn't put everyone in it. You, dad, and Timmy aren't in it. It was just people outside the family who I didn't automatically love. I always felt that James was a part of the family. He wasn't in it. When he saw that I didn't include him, something inside of him shattered."

"Paige, listen. You can't take responsibility for someone else's actions. The fact that he did what he did does not fall on your shoulders. Do you think that Bryce would have reacted the same way if he had read it and James was in there and not him? Listen. Love can quickly turn into something dark and unnatural with someone unstable. The fault does not lie with the object of that dark desire."

Sloane could see that Paige was mulling this over. She had to find a way to get through to her daughter so that she could see it wasn't something a normal person would do. Most importantly, she needed her to realize that it was not her fault. She knew that there was only so much a teen could handle before permanent damage was done to their psyche. Seeing some of the worry and self-loathing vanish from her face, she thought that logic was winning over her tragically believing she'd somehow played a part in this chilling horror story. Looking at her face, Sloane realized how mature her daughter had become. Gone was any trace of innocent naiveté. She was looking into the eyes of someone who understands the cruelties of this world. Her youthful cheeks were strewn with red blotches and streaked with salted droplets.

"Paige, how did they all of a sudden come to think it was James? I thought they had found the killers?" Paige informed her mother about how the last pieces of the mystery were put together. She then decided she needed to take a long, hot shower and go to bed. She hoped that she would sleep for days.

FORTY-FIVE
Carl

Back at the station, Captain White was trying his best to get James to talk to him, but it wasn't working. "James, you need to answer for what you've done. If you don't, it will only make it harder for you."

There was still no reaction from James. He sat before him with lifeless eyes and spittle running down his chin. There was no reaction at all to any of the questions asked of him.

Carl had called his cousin, Colin Holt, who was a lawyer, to represent James. He now sat next to James and tried to cajole a response. He also had no luck. The door to the interrogation room opened and the chief ushered the captain into the hall.

"Why don't you let me give it a try? It might help to have a maternal figure coax him out of his trance."

"Sure. I was just about to call it quits anyway."

Anika walked into the room and took a seat across from James and his attorney. "Hi James, it's Chief Haverhill. I have some questions to ask you. "James, I know there must be a lot you want to get off your chest. Don't you always feel better when you tell your mom things that upset you? I promise, once you start opening up, you'll feel a lot better." There was no response so she decided to try a different approach. "Can I get you a soda or something to eat?" Still no reaction from James.

She opened the folder she brought in and placed photographs of a dismembered Bryce on the table in front of him, along with Paige's "LOVE" journal. "James, we've confiscated the journal you took from Paige. If you see here in this photo, the body parts removed match perfectly with the things written in the journal. We also have your fingerprints in the journal where you smeared Bryce's blood over here and here." As she pointed out what she was talking about, she looked for signs that James was listening and understanding what she was saying. There were none.

The three of them were seated in the conference room. With respect to Carl, they didn't want to bring James to an interrogation room. Everyone on the force felt that James was a family member. This was not an easy situation. Carl was a terrific sergeant, but there was no coming back from something like this.

When Anika looked up from her notes, she saw that James's lawyer was visibly uncomfortable and was picking at the lifting Formica that was coming undone at the edge of the large conference table. He met her eyes and she motioned to the attorney to follow her and left the meeting room. They looked for Carl.

Anika found him and said, "Carl, we need to get him some medical help. He is completely beyond reach. I'm afraid if we keep him here much longer, it could do permanent damage. I'd like to bring in a specialist. It's getting late, I don't know what we can do before tomorrow. I'd hate for him to be like this in a cell."

Carl looked as if he'd aged 20 years in the last 24 hours. There were big, dark bags under his eyes, his hair was disheveled, his clothing was wrinkled and untucked, and he needed a shave. "If you think that's best, that's what we should do."

Anika looked sorrowfully at her colleague.

Colin said that he knew of someone he thought would be good to take a look at James. "She works over at the Briarcliff Hospital for the Criminally Insane. Let me make a few calls and I'll get back to you both." He stepped out to make the call.

Arabella came over to the group and read some notes from her pad. "I spoke to Dr. Gildan at the hospital. The only loose end to try to tie off was how James could have killed Bryce if he was at the same hospital and drugged with the rest of them. He said that James was the last to wake up. It took him significantly more time to come to. He thought at first it was because he ingested more of the alcohol-laced with the drugs, but that wasn't the case. He double-checked the records and he had the least amount of drugs in his system. It could mean that while the others were unconscious, he took Bryce, killed him, left him at the Vales' home, and then went back before they were found. It's a jump but the only thing that I can come up with."

Carl said, "Okay, that might fit. The question that remains is how he could carry that off. His truck wasn't there. He was picked up that night."

"Right. I thought of that too. I went back over my notes from when we interviewed the partygoers." Arabella flipped some pages until she found what she was looking for. "Ah, here. Sade made a comment that didn't quite ring alarm bells but could explain that piece. When I went back and interviewed them at the school, she said that when she was taken to the Angeli residence to retrieve her car, she had to adjust the seat and rearview mirror before she could drive it."

They all exchanged looks and let it sink in.

"Arabella, you truly have an exceptional gift for seeing the big picture. You will be going places."

Anika looked at Carl realizing he might have taken what she just said the wrong way and added, "She has learned from the best, that's for sure."

That was only partly true. What Arabella had was a God-given gift. She graduated top of her class, she was the one to always think outside the box and find the most obscure clue to solve a case. She was exceptional.

Colin came back in and told them that he had arranged transportation, this evening, for James to be taken to Briarcliff Hospital. "Dr. Eva Wright will be waiting to do an assessment right away. She's the best, Carl. I told her about what James has been accused of and the state he's in. She will help him to be able to interact with the world again. He'll get a chance to tell his story."

+++++++++++++

Carl needed caffeine in the worst way. By his calculations, he had gotten about three hours sleep over the last three days. He knew that Lydia was most likely in the same boat this morning. He stopped at her favorite coffee place. It was a little hidden gem where most of the locals would go. He ordered a large steaming regular for himself and a medium iced French-vanilla decaf with extra cream and one sugar for her. It did not matter that the air was changing its ways and traveling from the north to chill this quaint New England town, it could be ten degrees out and she always liked her coffee iced.

When Lydia saw Carl pull up, she quickly ushered the dogs inside and locked up the house. They drove together in silence. They were both very apprehensive and exhausted. There was heavy traffic in all the usual spots on the busy highway. It seemed as though because they wanted to get there as quickly as possible, it was taking twice as long. After exiting the highway and making a few turns, the building finally came into view.

Carl and Lydia entered the hospital for the criminally insane. They found the directory plaque hanging on the wall and made their way to Dr. Wright's office. Lydia announced their arrival with the receptionist and they took a seat in the waiting room.

They were called into an office that mirrored the architecture of the building. It was full of deep nautical colors; golds, greens, and blues. Dr. Wright sat behind an oversized mahogany desk while Lydia and Carl sat in teal upholstered seats with scalloped backs. The wall behind the doctor's chair was laden with shelves filled with books.

"Hello, Carl and Lydia. I'm Dr. Eva Wright."

She looked at each of them. She was an attractive woman in her late 30s to early 40s. She had long dark brown wavy hair that framed her oval face. She wore a cream-colored silk button-down blouse that contrasted her mocha skin beautifully. When she spoke, it was evident that she embodied the perfect blend of intelligence, compassion, and forcefulness needed to be good at what she does.

"I've met with James a few times and ran some tests. There is no brain trauma or infection; all his scans so far are normal—I'm still waiting for a few more. He is exhibiting what we call a psychogenic coma—specifically, a reactive psychosis that we hope will be temporary. This can happen shortly after a trauma or a major stress event. The presentation mimics a coma but without an organic cause. It is more of a psychiatric illness. Patients who suffer these will be in a state of unresponsiveness and may experience hallucinations, confused thought processes, strange speech patterns, disorientation or confusion, and memory trouble, among other things. Did you notice any of these before he became unresponsive?"

Carl interrupted her, "Wait a minute. Do you think James is nuts? He was perfectly normal a few days ago. Did he just snap? Is that what you're saying?"

Lydia reached over to him and rested her hand on his arm. "Carl, let her finish. You aren't with him every day. Some things have been out of the ordinary. What about all those 'episodes' he used to have?"

Dr. Wright picked up where she left off. "Yes, I was about to address that. I see from his medical records that there was a span of almost four years where you both had sought out neurological help for James. He would black out and lose periods of time."

Lydia answered that she was correct. "It started when Carl and I split. It was very traumatic for James."

"Yes, you could say that was the first major stressor he experienced. The brain can perform extreme protective mechanisms to shield us and safeguard our psyche. I'm sure you've heard of dissociative identity disorder?"

"Wait a minute. You think he has split personalities?" Carl was acting out of character. He was usually quiet and introspective. He would always wait to hear what someone had to say, process the information, and then respond. Although this was atypical of his behavior, it was most likely due to the lack of sleep and the pressure that he had been under as of late.

"No. Not at all. I was just trying to point out that

DID is one way the brain copes with trauma. Psychogenic coma is another."

Carl and Lydia looked at each other. This was worse than they thought. They were hoping for a diagnosis with an easy, quick remedy. They did not think they could withstand a long stretch of James being unresponsive. They both felt that the sooner James could explain what had happened, the sooner they would know the trajectory of their lives—for the best or the worst.

Lydia asked, "What's the next step?"

"I will administer a high dose of antipsychotic medications to see if we can arouse his consciousness. It is my fervent hope that this will work. Some studies have had good results and I am hoping for the best with James. I do have to warn you, it doesn't always work the first time. He may need several doses before he is cognizant of his surroundings. I don't want to get your hopes up. While it is rare, some never come out of psychogenic comas. If the trauma that caused it is too much to bear, the brain will never allow full consciousness."

Carl asked, "When can we see him?"

"I will arrange for you to both be present when I administer the medications. Colin and a member of the police force will also be there. If he is able, he will need to be questioned about the murders." She stood, indicating that the visit had ended, and walked them to the elevator. "I know this is very hard for you. Stay strong. He will need both of you to get him through this."

FORTY-SIX
Paige

Paige awoke and went downstairs. She sat in front of the television staring at a black screen. Sloane asked, "Want to watch a movie?"

She replied in a monotone voice, "No, thanks."

Sloane was worried. She knew this would eat away at her daughter. She decided that a distraction would be good.

"I have an errand to run. I'll be back soon, okay?"

Paige nodded and continued to stare at the TV.

Once Sloane was in her car, she sent a text to Amber and asked her to round up the group and head over. She laid out her plans and Amber told her that she thought it would be great for Paige.

Sloane then headed to the local apple orchard and picked out eight different-sized pumpkins. They also sold acrylic paints so she bought several colors as well. When she arrived home, the girls were just pulling up to the house. They helped her carry everything inside the house.

When Paige saw everyone, a look of confusion washed over her.

Sloane said, "I had them come by to help us paint some pumpkins."

A knowing look quickly replaced the confusion. She knew what her mother was doing and was very grateful for it.

Sloane cut some trash bags and taped them to the dining room table to spare it from being ruined. She then set it up with the paints she purchased, brushes, and craft supplies from her stockpile, and brought in the pumpkins. She told everyone to head in and get started. She set up her Bluetooth speaker and played her Halloween playlist, brought in snacks and drinks, and left them to it.

"I need to pick up Tim from Cookie's in a bit. He's been there getting over his ear infection. Let me know if you need anything else. You know he'll want to join you so be prepared."

"Okay, but I think we're good, Mom."

They were busy creating stencils and selecting what they would need to work on each pumpkin.

Sade was the first to ask what they were all wondering, "Paige, how are you doing? I mean, really doing?"

The girls stopped what they were doing and looked at Paige with wonder in their eyes.

"I'm good. Really. I'm fine."

She couldn't look at them directly. She knew that they would see right through her, but there wasn't anything else she could say because there wasn't anything else they could do.

Brooke cleared her throat and said, "Ms. Zenun has been so helpful. Um, she asked me to give this to you." She handed Paige the flyer.

Counseling available at Cumberland High School

The Cumberland School District will have counseling sessions available for students at Cumberland High School this Thursday following the recent loss of two students.

Counseling will begin during first lunch and will also be held after school. Call 401-555-5239 for an individual appointment.

Lyght Zenun,
Counselor, MA, LMHC

Paige read the flyer and said, "You can tell her that my mom has been sending me to someone since, ah, since Bryce. Timmy goes too. He's really nice and very easy to talk to. When I'm ready to go back to school, I'll talk to her too."

Jenna told Paige that she knew Ms. Zenun would be very happy to hear that, and then said, "Paige, is it true that you drew out the sketches he used to kill everyone?"

"Jenna!" Everyone shouted.

Paige told them it was all right. "What happened was that I had a journal where I wrote down the things that I loved about certain people. He used that against me. In a horrible way. In the worst way possible." Paige's voice began to quiver.

Amber asked, "Why? Why did he do it?"

Jenna said, "Why? Cuz he's nuts! Why else?"

Paige shook her head. "No. I caused this. It's my

fault. I didn't include him in my journal. It sent him over the edge."

"Paige, do you hear yourself? You can't think you're responsible for the actions of that psycho. What you did was an innocent thing that many kids do. Hell, I did something similar when I was younger. It was harmless and he turned it into something evil." As Sade said this, a tear rolled down the side of her dark brown nose.

"You know what I mean. If I hadn't made that dumb journal, or if I had just included him in it, none of this would have happened. I know that on some level it's irrational to think that way, but it's how I feel."

Everyone grew quiet and was unsure where to look or what to do. Unpleasantries out of the way, they all got back to their projects.

FORTY-SEVEN
James

Carl and Lydia entered the Briarcliff Hospital together again that afternoon. When they arrived on the second floor as instructed, they were hit by an intense odor of industrial-grade disinfectant that did a poor job of covering the stench of despair. They wanted to leave immediately; to run and never return. The thought of their son in this place made them ache. They knew that they had to be strong and push through for his sake.

They waited for Dr. Wright and Colin in the designated waiting room. As they looked out the window, the sky mimicked their mood; it had turned dark with banners of moisture-laden clouds gathering across the morning sky, waiting to burst at any minute. Eva arrived and briefed them on everything that would be happening. Colin came in shortly after. Someone in scrubs and a white lab coat came to the door and said that they were ready to begin. They all got up and went into room 222. James was propped up in the center of the hospital bed. Both hands were restrained to the side railings. He had a thin tube in his nostril. There were two bags on a tall metal pole at the side of his bed. One was half full of a clear liquid leading into his arm, and the other was smaller and empty but for some light brown residue that was attached to the tube that entered his nose. There was also a Foley catheter exiting his body and finding purchase in a bag attached to the bottom of the railings at the side of his bed.

Dr. Wright saw Lydia looking at the IV bags with a frightened gaze. "Because he is unable to eat or drink, we are giving him electrolytes to keep him hydrated and there is also a feeding tube entering his stomach through his nose. The food just finished so we are ready to administer the medications."

Captain White and Chief Haverhill entered the room. After some introductions and pleasantries, Eva announced that it was time to begin. The person who ushered them to the room went to the IV bag and injected the tube adding some yellow-tinted medication from a syringe.

Dr. Wright said, "He is getting a high dose of antipsychotics and epinephrine. If this works, he may be able to interact with us."

They watched the injection work its way through the tubing and into his arm. They waited in silence; an ear-piercing silence. Carl took Lydia's hand. If this worked, they'd have their boy back. If not . . . he didn't want to think about that.

The administrator of the drugs took James's wrist and held it feeling for his heart rate. She looked to Dr. Wright and nodded.

Eva walked over to the bed and called his name.

"James. James, do you know where you are?"

He blinked and took in a very deep breath, still staring straight ahead.

"James, your parents are here."

She looked at them and signaled for them to go to him.

They were together on one side of the bed. Lydia put her hand on his forehead and kissed him. Carl followed suit.

"Hey, son. It's dad."

James turned to look at them. He tried to take the tube out of his nose but realized that he was restrained.

"Hold on, James." Dr. Wright said as she stopped him.

The other woman stepped up and told him to take a deep breath and to exhale out his nose. While he did, she removed the tube. He gasped and coughed.

"Why did you do that?" His voice was raspy. He cleared his throat. "Mom. Dad. What's going on? Where am I? Where's Paige? She was just here." He tried to free his hands but couldn't.

Carl answered, "James, you are in a hospital. Do you remember me getting you from the cabin?"

"The cabin? No. We were there?"

"Yes. You drove there. That's where you saw Paige, not here. We followed you there. You ran away because you . . ."

Anika cleared her throat, "Carl, why don't you let us take it from here?"

He looked at her with confusion and pleading in

his eyes. Lydia took him by the arm and walked him into the hall with Dr. Wright.

Colin stepped up to the bed and said, "I need a minute with my client first."

Everyone stepped out into the hall.

"James, my name is Colin Holt. I'm a distant cousin of your father. Your parents have hired me as your attorney. I highly suggest that you don't say anything yet to the police; especially in the state you're in."

James looked at him. "I'm remembering what happened now. I have to tell. I know what I did. I need to get this off my chest. I don't want to wait anymore. I know it's your job to tell me not to, but I'm going to." He hoped that if he relieved himself of this burden, it would keep the *Red* away.

"If that's your wish, I can't tell you not to, but be advised, it is not in your best interest. What will happen next is that they will come back in and officially arrest you. Then, they will ask you a series of questions. You do not have to answer any question you don't want to."

"I understand. You can call them back in."

Colin brought the officials in while Carl and Lydia were ushered to a waiting room. James looked at the two representatives from the police department and recognized them as being people his father worked with. They were his bosses. The *Red* was trying to take over once again. It brought Paige with it. He stared at her so strongly that when he closed his eyes, she was still with him beneath his very lids. He had to fight to remain in the present. He knew why they were there and he didn't want to face what he'd done, but it was over now. They knew.

"James, I'm not sure if you remember me, I am Captain White and I work with your dad."

James nodded that he remembered.

"We will be recording this session for credibility."

He nodded his approval again.

"Please state that you agree for the record."

In a raspy voice, James said, "I agree."

Captain White spoke for the recording, "The interview with James Lowden is beginning at 2:16 pm. Present in the room with James Lowden is me, Captain Samuel White, Chief Anika Haverhill, and James's lawyer, Colin Holt."

"I need to read you your rights."

James nodded his understanding.

"You are being arrested for three murders. The murders of Bryce Walker, Karol Romano, and Fiona Hansen. You have the right to remain silent. Anything you say can and will be used against you in a court of law. You have the right to an attorney. If you cannot afford an attorney, one will be provided for you. Do you understand what was just said to you?"

James said that he understood.

Captain White placed the recording device on the bedside table near James and took notes while the chief spoke to James directly.

"James, I'm going to ask you some questions. It is very important that you answer them honestly. We can't help you unless we know exactly what happened. Can you do that for me?" she asked.

James nodded in compliance.

"Please state that you understand for the recorder."

"I understand."

"James, do you know what happened to Bryce Walker? Can you tell us how he died?"

It took some time, but James found his voice and was able to tell his grisly story. "I killed him," he confessed in a monotone statement. It felt freeing to say those three little words. More freeing than anything he had ever uttered before.

"Okay. Start at the beginning and tell us everything that happened that night. The night of the party after the homecoming game."

"I took some Acepromazine, Gabapentin, and Ketamine from the veterinary clinic where I work. Paige's friend, Sade picked me up. I had it on me then. We went down to the basement where Jenna lives. Some of them were making a punch. I went to help. I added the crushed pills. When everyone drank it, it knocked them out."

"There were traces of the drugs in your system as well. Did you drink the punch?"

"Not then. I did later to make it look good."

Samuel and Anika shared a look that said a riddle had just been solved.

"When everyone was out, I took the keys from Sade's pocketbook, unlocked the doors to her car, carried Bryce up, and put him in the back seat."

"Did you do anything when you first got into the car?"

"Um, well, I couldn't fit behind the wheel, so I had to move the seat and fix the rearview mirror. That's all. I knew I only had a little time to do what I needed. I drove to Paige's neighborhood and stopped at the beginning of the cul-de-sac. I took out some insulated gloves, heavy-duty bolt cutters, and climbed up a telephone pole. I cut one of the power lines. Once I did, the power was off for the neighborhood. I didn't want to be seen on anyone's security camera."

He looked tired and sighed heavily.

"I went to the Vales' house and took the scarecrow. Bryce slept peacefully in the backseat. His rhythmic breathing was soothing and it calmed me a bit. I knew if I got too anxious, mistakes would be made. I needed to stick to my plan."

James looked out the window of his hospital room and could see over the tops of some trees with pointed wine-colored leaves. He could hear rain tapping rhythmically against the dirty windowpane. Something was perplexing to him and he couldn't quite pinpoint what. As he continued to look, he realized that he was looking through bars on the windows. He thought that was odd since he was told that he was in a hospital. He was trying to work out the puzzle when . . .

Anika said, "Go ahead and continue, James."

He stopped trying to work out what he was seeing. "I took him to a hideout near the reservoir. I can take you there if you want."

"We have been there, James."

He attempted to figure out what it meant for his treasures. "Oh, okay."

It struck Anika as if a ton of bricks had fallen on her. How can this boy she knew for so long be telling this story as if he were discussing a hobby of his; she remembered him telling a story of a fishing trip with more emotion.

"Once I was there, I went down to my laboratory."

Again, looks passed between the two officers.

"I had been bringing all the tools and supplies I would need down there for days before the party. Once everything was there, I swear the equipment called to me." He trailed off for a bit. "Anyway, I used rope and duct tape and strapped Bryce to the table to keep him in place. Then I covered up in the trash bags that were down there so my clothes wouldn't get bloody."

James continued, "When I brought him down there, that's when I killed him. It took several slices to his chest to wake him up, but when he did wake up, he was fully awake. Bryce screamed and tried to get free. He tried to get a glimpse of his chest to see where the pain was coming from."

James thought back to that night. As Bryce was taking stock of the situation, James retrieved a metal contraption that resembled a table vise and put it into his chest—it was technically called a chest spreader—the name coming to him all of a sudden. It

298

looked like Bryce was experiencing fear, as he had never known before.

"His ribs bulged and snapped. I used a chest spreader to open his chest and I ripped his heart out. Then he closed his eyes and he would never open them again." James looked as if he were struggling for the right words to say. "Then, I took them too. The tricky part was trying not to squeeze too hard so they wouldn't be damaged. Once they were out, I cut off his hands with an ax. When all the necessary body parts were removed, I put them into mason jars and buckets with some formaldehyde."

James tried to reach for the glass of water next to his bed but then he remembered his hands were bound.

Anika realized what was happening and put the glass up to his mouth.

He drank from the straw and then continued. "I removed the clothes from the scarecrow and then put them on Bryce. I put him back in the car on the tarp I had laid out on the seat and drove back to the Vales' house. On my way there, I tossed the original scarecrow stuffing, blood-splattered garbage bags, and Bryce's bloodied clothing in a dumpster, the one at Habibi's gas station. You know that one?"

Anika nodded that she did, and stared at Samuel to make sure that he jotted that down. He did.

"Once I was on the porch, I placed Bryce's body in the spot where the scarecrow was, made sure it looked correct, put the tarp in a neighbor's trash can, and returned to the car. That's when the transformation was complete. Then, I drank some of the punch when I was almost at Jenna's so it would hit me when I got back inside the house. I went back down to the basement and laid on the floor, with the cup in my hand, where I had been standing, earlier, and went to sleep. When I woke up, I was at the hospital."

Anika was terrified of James's absolute emotionless tone as he chronicled the very dark acts he committed. Every word he spoke deepened the fractures in her heart. She needed to get out of this room.

"Okay, let's take a break. I'll send your parents back in. We'll be back in a bit."

"Can you not let my parents in yet? I don't want to see them until I finish telling you everything. I'm afraid if I see them, I won't be able to continue."

"Okay, sure. We won't be long."

Samuel, Anika, and the attorney left briefly.

"Samuel, I want you to call the station and get someone to look into the trash collection for the dumpster at Habibi's gas station, and the Vale's neighborhood. See if they can track down the discarded items James listed. And, have Arabella talk to the young lady about the car seat again just to verify. We need to have everything laid out perfectly for the timeline."

Anika went to the nearest ladies' room and splashed some water on her face. She got a bottle of water and then the three opened the door to go back into the hospital room. They were perplexed and disturbed to see James talking to himself in a strange way. They went in quietly and observed.

"You can't have me. No. I won't let you. Paige, I can't find you. Where did you go?" He was violently turning his head left and right and making a strange noise. "I'm stronger than—I am. No more. Red. Red."

Colin cleared his throat and James looked at them. "Shall I call in the doctor?"

James stopped what he was doing, sat up straight, and shook his head no.

"Okay, James. Let's continue." Samuel turned the recorder back on and spoke into it, "Interview reconvening at 4:39 pm."

Anika asked, "What happened to Karol Romano?"

"Well, I knew that she was going to the vigil for Bryce so I followed her home from school that day. I was about to knock on her door when her mother came home with groceries in her car. Karol came out to help bring them into the house. One of the times she came out, I called to her. I told her I needed help with something in my truck. She came over to me and I used chloroform to knock her out."

Samuel interjected, "Hold up. How were you able to get chloroform? I worked in a veterinary clinic for a time and I don't remember them using that on the animals." He looked quizzingly at James awaiting a reply.

"Dr. Hogan is a large animal specialist. He had to work on a sick horse right around that time. He uses it on horses."

Captain White jotted that down as another thing

to look into, then nodded for James to continue.

"Once I got her into my truck, I injected her with Acepromazine, Gabapentin, and Ketamine and then I brought her back to the hideout," he looked down in apparent shame. "You know what happened next."

"Let me ask you something, James. Did you honk your horn as you drove away?"

"What? Oh, yeah, when I was inserting the needle into her neck, I bumped it by accident."

"Okay. Please, continue."

James closed his eyes and remained silent.

"James, we need you to continue, for the recording."

He struggled to speak though his lips moved. He was having a conversation with himself that was inaudible. Then it looked as though he might be sick, and then his face changed and he was normal again. It was all very odd.

"I strapped her to the table in the hideout the same way I did with Bryce." He looked like he was thinking. He shook his head a few times. He stopped for a bit and said, "No. No, Paige, please!" He closed his eyes for a beat and then opened them. He looked up at the other people in the room. He continued as if nothing just happened.

"I prepared everything like before. Once I was ready, I took her eyes out first. I already did that so I knew what to do. After that, I got a hammer and banged out some of her teeth and then I sliced her lips off. She wasn't fully unconscious and she wouldn't stop moving and screaming, so I picked up the ax and swung it into her neck. Then she was quiet. I wrapped her in a tarp and brought her up to the truck and I drove to the high school. I helped set everything up. Once the vigil started, I went back to my truck and got her out. I carried her to the D.A.R.E. car, squished her in behind the steering wheel, then went back to my truck and stuffed the tarp in the back. Then I joined Paige and the others."

It was clear that James was struggling more frequently to stay focused and present. He stopped often in his reminiscing of Karol's story and would call out to Paige. It seemed as though he thought that she was in the room. They needed him to continue or risk losing his confession if he retreated within himself again; he could stay there indefinitely.

"Thank you, James, you're doing great. Now, tell us about Fiona Hansen. What happened to her?"

Colin spoke up. "I think the boy needs a break. He doesn't seem well."

Anika objected. "I'm afraid we need to keep going."

She went to James and gave him another drink.

After he took another sip of water, he began, "I knew she was in that old folk's home near the veterinary clinic, um, Healing Angels, I think. It's near the reservoir and pretty close to the hideout." He stopped for an exaggerated pause. He didn't blink; it looked as if he wasn't even breathing. Anika cleared her throat and he began again. "I would go there with Paige and her family to visit an aunt. One day we were there and we noticed Mrs. Hansen was there too. She was in a wheelchair sitting outside near her aunt. We went over to say hi and she recognized us. The person with her said she was having a good day. He said that it comes and goes. He said it was a shame that she was struggling with dementia at such a young age." James shook his head in a sorrowful way. "When I thought about my plans to get Paige to love me that made me think she'd be easy to take. I wanted to go through the whole book. To get everything she loved. If I had everything, there would be no way she wouldn't love me, right?"

James looked at the three with desperation in his eyes. They just looked at him and didn't give him an answer.

James stopped and stared off again. There was a loud noise coming from the hallway that snapped him out of his trance. "I had a lab coat from the clinic. A car hit a dog and I carried him in and got my clothes dirty, so Doc Hogan gave me one. I kept it in my truck. I knew they'd be outside at a certain time, so I went there with the lab coat on. It was easy. I walked up to her and said, 'Hi.' She smiled, and I wheeled her over to my truck and put her inside. I put her wheelchair in the back of the truck. Once we stopped, I used some chloroform on her and took her out in the wheelbarrow I brought. I put her in it and brought her to the hideout."

A nurse coming in to check James's vitals interrupted them. Anika asked her to come back in thirty minutes. She was not too happy about that and left in a huff.

"I didn't want to hurt her too much. I gave her a drink with the same drugs I used in the punch. She drank it all. When she was out, I sliced her throat at the main artery first. Then I took the ax and chopped off her arms. I put them in the containers. I brought her back up and I took her to the Monastery and covered her with leaves and twigs. I dumped her wheelchair in the back of the Monastery where the dumpster is near that Cumberland Highway building. That's pretty much it."

"Thank you for your honesty, James. I have some questions before we wrap up. First, why did you remove those specific body parts from each person?"

"I don't want to talk about that. I did it. That's all."

"Can you state for the recording that it has something to do with the journal we found in your truck?"

Colin stepped in and said, "My client does not wish to answer that at this time. Move on."

"Okay, James, that's fine. One more question. Why those locations? Why was each body left at those specific locations?"

Colin began to intervene once again, but James indicated that he would answer that question.

"For Bryce, it was so Paige would need me. I wanted her to be scared. The family made a big deal of scarecrows every fall and I wanted it to make her unhappy. For Karol, I knew I wanted it to be where people who were at the vigil would see her. I saw the crashed car and thought that would be a good place. With Mrs. Hansen, I didn't know what to do with her. I thought about a time when she took my class on a field trip there. It was a nature walk or something." James began to mumble incoherently once again. His eyes were moving left and right in very jagged motions. It was an extremely unsettling scene.

Samuel ran out to the hall and called for help. The nurse from earlier ran in and pushed a button on the inside of his bed. Soon after, several medical professionals ran into the room to attend to James. He was mumbling about something red but wasn't making much sense. They ushered Anika, Samuel, and Colin out of the room and continued to work on him.

Colin, Anika, and Samuel were brought to Lydia and Carl in the patient lounge.

Anika said to Carl, "We're sorry Carl, the guilty knowledge information has been confirmed and he's admitted to everything."

Lydia asked what that was.

Carl said, "Lyd, it means that he has information that has not been disclosed to anyone but those involved in the case. Information that only the actual killer would have."

They hugged each other and sobbed once again.

Samuel tapped Carl on the shoulder. Carl looked up at him.

"The doctors are working on James right now. He started zoning out, talking to Paige as if she were there, shaking, and mumbling things . . ."

Before he could finish, Lydia broke away from Carl.

"What? Why didn't anyone get us?" As she uttered the last word, she dashed toward room 222.

Once inside the hospital room, Lydia attempted to run to James. The nurses deflected her attempt. Carl ushered her to the far end of the room where they would be out of the way of the staff working on their son.

After a brief time, Dr. Wright came over, "I'm sorry. James has slipped back into a psychogenic state. We were hopeful that his respite would last, but we are in unchartered territory with this syndrome. We just don't deal with it enough."

Carl felt his whole world implode. On one hand, he was devastated to think that James could be perpetually locked inside himself. On the other hand, he was almost relieved because that meant he would be remanded to this medical facility instead of a prison.

She walked Lydia and Carl to James's bedside while the others cleaned up and left. With silent tears falling from his eyes, Carl bent over and whispered to James that he loved him. Lydia stood in silence with a vacant look in her light blue eyes. The first thing that came to him was that she was broken. He thought he had broken her all those years ago, but he was wrong. This did the job.

He took her by the hand and led her out to the car. After several minutes of driving in silence, she droned, "I should stay with him. He doesn't look right. Did you see him? The light in his eyes disappeared like a candle that was snuffed out."

"Lyd, I'm so sorry. This has been quite a shock. You need to go home and rest. You can go back later. Um, you should check to see if there are certain times when we can visit. It's not like a regular hospital."

Lydia began to take large, heavy breaths. She grabbed the dashboard and turned to face him. Through clenched teeth, she said, "I know very well that he's not in a regular hospital. I know he's reverted back into his shell where he can't be hurt anymore. Where YOU forced him into all those years ago! This. Is. All. Your. Fault!"

"Lyd."

"Don't you call me that. You lost that privilege years ago!"

"You're right. It's all my fault."

Carl took the onramp and was driving home while thoughts raced through his head. He knew she was right. This all started when he left them. Could that really make a kind, loving child grow up to be a murderer? There were lots of children of broken homes who grow up to be fine, normal, productive members of society. He wondered if he'd ever learn the answer.

While he was deep in thought, a call came through. He answered. It was Paige. This was a call he was certainly dreading.

Paige's voice was heard in the car. "Hi, Mr. Lowden. How did everything go?"

"Hey, Paige. You know there's not much I can

say, but all our suspicions were correct, unfortunately."

It took a while for her to respond. With a shaky voice, she quietly replied, "So, it's all my fault. I knew deep down it was. Okay, I have to go." With that, the call ended.

Carl didn't have a chance to tell the poor kid it wasn't her fault but his. He went back and forth about calling her back but thought he'd give her some time. He'd call Mitch or Sloane later to check on her.

Lydia broke the silence and said that she would call Sloane later to make sure that Paige was okay. She didn't say anything else until she was at her house. "I might have overreacted. I need some time to cool off." She didn't give Carl time to respond. She closed the car door and went inside.

FORTY-EIGHT

Paige

The afternoon sun was finally absorbing the previous day's precipitation. Paige ended her call with Carl and was dispirited. She wanted to talk with her mom, so she went to find her. As she was following the sounds of her mother rustling about in the kitchen, her phone rang. It was Sade.

"Paige. I'm glad you answered. Have you heard the news?"

"I did. But, how did you hear it so soon? I just hung up with Mr. Lowden."

"Did he tell you James used my car?"

"What? No. That's not what I'm talking about. Can you come over? I need to talk."

"Okay, let me hit up the girls and we'll come by."

"Okay, thanks."

Paige sat at the kitchen island and announced that the girls were on their way over. "Mom, I spoke with Mr. Lowden. He said James did those things because he was angry that I didn't put him in my "*LOVE*" journal."

"Paige. I know you are upset right now, and rightfully so. But I also know that you are a bright young woman. When you think long and hard about this, you will realize that no rational person would be so upset over not being mentioned in a journal, that they would embark on a killing spree as a result."

Paige looked as though she was searching for a rebuttal but just exhaled and went back to sulking. Sloane massaged her neck and shoulders to try to release some of the tension. A text alerted her that the girls were there.

She let them in and the group went upstairs to her bedroom. She always felt at home and the safest in her purple and gray haven. It was such an expression of her. As she sat on her bed, she grabbed two of the throw pillows. She longed for the feeling of safety within her home but mostly within her sanctuary. She hadn't been able to get that back since the night they found Bryce on her porch. Paige saw Sade watching her closely. Even though she was new to the *mean girls*, she seemed to have a deep understanding of each of them. Sade moved to Cumberland when she was 15, so she didn't have the history the others did, but her personality meshed with theirs instantly. Paige asked her to share her news with everyone.

She began by saying, "This is so weird meeting together without Karol. The rest of us have brushed up against someone dangerous and came away unbroken. She wasn't that lucky. It doesn't feel right."

They all nodded in agreement that they felt her conspicuous absence.

Amber spoke up after a time and said, "You know my mom works for Dr. Sheftel. She said that Karol's mom calls there every day worried about her husband. She thinks he is having a breakdown. It's just awful." She paused, looked around, and said, "Okay, Sade, I can tell you really want to tell us your story. Hopefully, it will get our minds off of her."

Sade looked as if she would burst if she didn't speak right then. "So, Officer Luthor called me. I thought we were finished with questions, but, nope. She wanted me to think back to the night of the party—so, I did. She asked me if anyone other than me drove my car. I told her no. Then she asked me to think about when we left the hospital." She looked up and saw the girls enticing her to speed things along with harsh looks and hand gesturing.

Trying to speak faster, she blurted out, "She wanted me to tell her, step-by-step, what I did when I picked up my car from Jenna's. I did, and then she asked me if I had to adjust mirrors or anything. When I thought back, I remembered that I had to adjust my seat—which is wicked weird, right? I brushed it off and never thought about it again. Weird though, right?"

"Is this leading somewhere?" asked Jenna.

"Uh, yeah. It. Is! It's the reason why I had to readjust my seat. She said that James used MY CAR to take Bryce to his messed-up murder hideout! MY CAR!" That revelation seemed to change the demeanor of the group. They sat there with their eyes fixed on her and their mouths hung slack.

"Then, he took him here to pose him on the porch."

After Sade finished bubbling over like an opened bottle of champagne, Amber was the first to break from her shock. "How could that be? He was brought to the hospital with us."

"I have no idea. I'm sure we'll find out all the details soon enough."

Paige tried to keep her composure, "This is all my fault. I'm so, so, sorry. If I hadn't brought him to that party, none of this would have happened. If I hadn't forced him on you all, Bryce and Karol might still be alive!"

She moved off the bed and ran into the bathroom, visibly upset.

"Paige, come out. No one blames you. His own parents didn't even know what was going on with him. This isn't on you." Sade looked to the group for additional words of encouragement.

Sloane knocked on the door and opened it to see everyone huddled around the bathroom door. She saw that Paige was missing and could infer what was going on.

"Girls, why don't you go down and meet us in the music room."

The girls took the cue and left Sloane to speak to Paige.

"Paige, let me in."

Paige opened the door and hugged her mother. "Mom, Sade just found out that James used her car to . . . do what he did to Bryce. I brought him into this group."

Sloane stroked her head. Her heart was breaking for her daughter. "Listen. Would you have done so if you knew what was going to happen?"

"No, of course not!"

"Well, then if you're so certain that you wouldn't have, you need to be just as certain that you had no way of knowing this would be the outcome and that it wasn't in any way your fault. Can't have it both ways."

She stepped back and wiped the tears from her daughter's ivory cheeks.

"Paige, people ebb and flow like the tides. And, just like the tides, you can't control them. Now, let's go downstairs."

Sloane and Paige went into the music room. Tim was showing off on his guitar. Sloane's phone began to ping excessively.

Tim looked at his mom with an annoyed expression, "Hey, you're messing me up with those beeps."

"Sorry. I added some more cameras outside and they need to be adjusted. They're picking up cars that drive by the house and I keep getting notified."

He looked at his sister and they both rolled their eyes, silently agreeing that their mom was going overboard as usual.

+++++++++++++

The next afternoon the group met back at Paige's.

She told her friends she wanted to go for a ride and told her mother that she'd be back soon. They all piled into Jenna's car.

Jenna asked, "Where do you want to go?"

Paige answered, "I want to see him. Take me to that hospital."

They drove in silence for what seemed like a very long time. Amber was the first to speak. "Paige, I don't think this is a good idea. You shouldn't go anywhere near him. This is crazy."

Jenna pulled the car over and put it in park. "Paige, first of all, you can't just walk into a place like that. There are criminals in there. I'm sure it's locked up tight."

Paige thought about this for a minute and asked her if she still had the materials from the vigil in her trunk.

Jenna said that she did.

"Well, that solves it then. I'll go in with the clipboard we were using. If you are holding a clipboard, everyone thinks you're in charge."

Paige took out her phone and after a bit, made a call. "Yes, hello," she said in her most adult voice. This is Lydia Lowden. I'm checking to see if my son, James, has been moved into a different room. When I was there, I told the staff that the one he was in was unacceptable. I'll be heading there soon and I want to make sure I have the right room." She paused. "Huh, okay. Well, I'll have to straighten this out when I get there—to room 222." She smiled satisfactorily.

FORTY-NINE
James

The Head Nurse called for transport to take James to the basement for an MRI of his brain. He felt terrible for his patient in 222. He knew that all the patients at this facility were there because they had broken the law and were deemed psychologically unfit to be brought to prison. Seeing the young man propped up in bed, drool running down the side of his mouth, with a vacant look in his eyes, he wondered what would ever become of him. He felt called to try his best to help every patient, no matter what brought them here. He believed that many of these patients never experienced an ounce of kindness or compassion, so he made it his mission to give all he could.

He decided to tell James what was to happen, knowing that there was a chance he could still understand what was going on within his surroundings.

"James, you are going to be taken for a scan of your brain. It will be an MRI, which is very noisy. They will give you earplugs, but you will still be able to hear loud, banging noises and feel the vibrations of every sound. They will be injecting a dye in your

IV that is used to show any possible abnormalities within your brain. I'm going to disconnect you from the IV pole and the catheter here and when you get back, we'll hook you right back up."

As he was finishing up, two orderlies came in for the transport.

"James, your ride is here. You'll be in good hands. I'll be here when you get back."

He patted James on his shoulder and unfastened the wrist restraints so that the orderlies could move him onto their gurney. He watched as they wheeled James into the elevator.

The bell sounded alerting them that they were on the ground floor. The orderlies exited the elevator and wheeled James to the MRI department. Several stretchers were waiting in the queue. Their orders were to stay with him and then immediately return him to his room.

One of the orderlies looked at the long line of patients waiting to be scanned, and said, "I need a smoke. You?"

The second orderly looked very pensive.

"Come on," the first nudged him with his elbow. "He's a droolin vegetable; nothin's gonna happen if we step out for two minutes." He snapped his fingers loudly and vulgarly in front of James's face, very close to his open eyes.

James remained there and did not flinch, staring off into nothingness.

"Okay, let's go, but we need to be quick."

They checked up and down the hallway, saw no

one was watching, and left.

++++++++++++

James tried to shove his way through the red mist that was as thick and as dense as a wall. It had been bad at times, but this was the worst by far. He was trying to regain control of himself when he realized that he was moving. He was lying down—he was on a moving bed.

It came back to him. He was in a hospital—then he remembered why. He wished that the *Red* had still consumed his consciousness. It was a respite not to be himself for a while. He liked it better there with Paige. He couldn't work out how, but she was there with him. While he was struggling to break free from the fog the *Red* left him in, he overheard people talking—it sounded as if he were underwater and they were above. They were in an elevator. The doors opened and they wheeled him up against a wall. He overheard one of them say he was a drooling vegetable, and then snapped his fingers in front of his face. He remained still to see where this was going. The anger he felt at this moment helped him to cut through the fog for which the *Red* had imprisoned him. The men left through a small room to take a cigarette break.

James was pushing himself through the red veil enclosing him. All at once, he realized that this was his chance. He took inventory of his surroundings and realized that he was no longer restrained to the bed. He sat up, swung his legs over the side, and stood up. He looked to see if there was anyone around and searched for a way out. There was nothing but rooms. He knew it would be risky but decided to take the path the two orderlies used to head outside. He knew it would eventually lead him to freedom.

The room was a small, dark custodial utility room. There was a sink with mildew-smelling mops spewing out of it along with rusty buckets, dirty rags, and empty cans strewn everywhere. There was a set of tall metal staff lockers at the east corner of the room. He went over and opened one. He saw a dark blue custodial jumpsuit with a name patch that read *Glenn*. He was about to put it on when he heard the men coming back in from their smoke break. He hid behind the open door of the locker. They walked right through never looking anywhere else in the room.

He rushed to put the jumpsuit on—he ripped the IV needle out of his arm and replaced it with a piece of masking tape he found. He looked around quickly for shoes of some sort but could not find any. He was wearing the token hospital socks with the non-skid treads on the bottom—that would have to suffice.

He went out the same door the two men entered. It emptied into an alley adjacent to a loading dock. It was very narrow; the walls lining the way were made of old, degrading concrete blocks. The three large, wide steps he went down fed into the loading dock area. He was hoping for a vehicle he could commandeer or hide in; he was fresh out of luck. He knew it was only a matter of time before they came looking for him. He made his way to the main road and began walking north; taking a circuitous route that would keep him concealed.

FIFTY
Paige

Paige entered the main lobby of the hospital, clipboard in the crook of her elbow, and pushed the up button for the elevator. She felt pretty self-assured until she heard a deep voice say, "Excuse me, Miss?"

She tried to play it cool and pretend that she didn't know he was talking to her. She stared straight ahead. His deep voice was now at her side in the form of a seven-foot-tall security guard. He had a clipboard of his own and asked her to sign in. She did so with a shaky hand. He was about to say something more when there was a ding and the elevator door opened. Paige smiled, shrugged her shoulders, and entered.

She pushed two and tried to come up with a script for what she would say in case she was questioned before she reached her destination. The doors opened quickly and she got out. She decided that no matter what, she would turn right and make it look intentional—no matter where his room was. While walking, she kept looking at her clipboard with purpose. She came to room 222 and entered.

While standing inside the room looking at an empty bed, a female voice asked from the doorway,

"Are you here from transport? Have you found the patient?"

Paige turned around in shock.

"Oh, who are you? You shouldn't be here. You don't have a visitor's badge. You need to go back to the main entrance to get one."

"Sorry. I will. Um, what did you mean when you asked if I found the patient? Do you mean James?"

"I'm sure it's nothing but a miscommunication. Don't worry." The nurse's words did not match the panicked look on her face as she quickly rushed to the station area and spoke with other panicked-looking staff.

Paige did not expect this and was torn as to what she should do next. She decided to go back to the car. On her way to the elevator, there was an announcement over the loudspeaker that gave a code that put everyone in a flustered mode. All patients were brought to their rooms and the doors were shut, and most likely locked. People were running up and down the halls. She knew she had to leave soon or she might be locked in herself. She made her way out and got to the car without incident.

Paige got back into the car. "Drive. NOW! He's gone. He escaped!"

No one said a word as Jenna drove. Paige knew that everyone was most likely thinking the same thing she was; about their families and what could happen now that James was on the loose. She wanted nothing more than to burst through her front door, hug her mother, father, brother, and then run far away to somewhere he would never find them. Then reality set in. She knew that she needed to contact Carl immediately.

FIFTY-ONE
Carl

The daytime was being swallowed up into evening faster with every passing fall day. It was barely after four o'clock and the sun was already on the lower part of the seesaw in the sky's vast playground.

Carl didn't much like the hot weather, but he missed the longer days. His phone rang. "Hi, Paige."

Paige's voice boomed through the speaker, frantically shouting, "He's gone! He escaped!"

"Slow down, slow down. What? Are you sure?"

"I was just at the hospital. I snuck into his room. They're going crazy looking for him."

"Oh, my God. Okay. Thanks. Go right home. Tell your parents to get you all somewhere safe until further notice." He ended the call.

"Carl, what the hell? What should we do?" Arabella looked as confused as he felt.

"We have to go to Briarcliff and get some answers."

She asked, "Missing? What does that mean? Like misplaced or taken or what? Someone in a coma can't just get up and leave, right?"

"I have no idea. With everything he's done, I wouldn't put it past someone to want revenge. I'm just really surprised. I thought that facility was safe. I want answers."

Carl pulled over and turned the car around to head to the hospital.

"Carl, Lydia needs to be told."

"Shit. You're right."

"I can call her if you want."

"Yeah, that would be best. We didn't end on great terms the last time we spoke."

Arabella placed the call. She moved the phone away from her chin and told Carl, "Got her voicemail." She quickly moved it back and said, "Hi Lydia, it's Arabella. I need to tell you some troubling news. Carl just got a call from Paige who tried to sneak in and visit James. She said that he is missing. The hospital cannot locate him. We are on our way there right now. I'll call you back as soon as we know more."

She was lost in her thoughts, questioning all possibilities. Until they knew exactly what happened, there could not be any definitive answers. If he was taken, that had its own set of troubling ramifications. If he escaped, which was more unlikely, all bets were off.

"Carl, we need to call this in."

"I think we should wait until we get there. We don't know what's happening. She could have misheard what she thought she did. If he is really missing, I can't believe they wouldn't have phoned me or Lydia by now."

When they got to the hospital, there was

electricity in the air that wasn't there the last time he walked the halls. Everyone was doing a good job at keeping their terror at bay, but he knew how to read people. What they were witnessing was the epitome of controlled chaos. They were told to wait in one of the waiting rooms and they did. A few minutes later, Dr. Wright came in and looked distressed. She sat down next to him—Carl knew that this tactic was meant to make the other person feel like they were on the same level. Police officers often used this approach.

"Carl. I'm so sorry. I still don't know how this could have happened. I was just on the phone with the security department. They are reviewing CCTV footage right now and will be contacting me soon."

"Why didn't you notify me or Lydia right away? Or the police for that matter?"

"I needed to have the facts before I did that. I should know everything very soon."

"Do you at least know the basics? Was he alone? Did he wake up and leave, or did someone else remove him? Could someone have him right now?"

"All I was able to learn was that he was brought down for an MRI and he was left in the hall by the orderlies. When it was his turn, he was nowhere to be found. I'm sure the security footage will help resolve the issue."

Arabella snorted, "Issue? Really? I'd say that the footage will reveal the major screw-up perpetrated by this very hospital." This was the time when Carl would usually step in and try to deflect her overly direct commentary, but he was grateful to have her on his side. When she did not get the signal to stop, she continued, "You trusted a dangerous criminal to a couple of orderlies? Is that how this hospital operates?" Once the words escaped her mouth, she wished she could stuff them right back in. Sometimes her anger got the best of her and she hurt other people. Carl didn't need to hear the obvious. She was relieved to see the grateful look sent her way.

Eva looked terrible. She had deep, red veins running through her bloodshot eyes, and the frown lines around her mouth and on her light coffee-tinted forehead were much more pronounced than the last time he saw her. He swore that even her long, dark brown hair had lost its shine. Her phone pinged, and interrupted his thoughts. She looked at it.

"They have the video ready. Why don't you both come with me?"

They walked in silence to the security department. The guard directed them to a monitor and readied the feed. James could be seen on the stretcher coming out of the elevator and then he was next seen in the hall of the scanning unit. The orderlies appeared to be having a conversation when one of them snapped his fingers right in front of James's lifeless face. Dr. Wright winced when she saw hospital employees behaving like that. A few seconds later, they were seen leaving James alone and exiting into a custodial utility room.

"Incompetent . . ." Arabella stopped herself this

time. She was thinking of a more tactful line of conversation when they saw James turn his head on the video. He was lucid and looking up and down the hallway. He sat up, got off the stretcher, and went through the same door the orderlies did moments ago.

"Son of a bitch. If I didn't see this with my own eyes . . ." Carl looked at Eva. "Was he bluffing this whole time?"

"No. He wasn't bluffing." Dr. Wright looked as if she were trying to choose the right words to say next. "You said that when he was young, he would have these episodes, correct?"

Carl nodded in agreement.

"And he would always snap out of them eventually?"

Carl nodded again.

"I believe that James fights his way to come out of the state he works himself into. It's a form of reactive psychosis. As I said before, I think that it started as a coping mechanism for him to retreat from stressful situations. Now, I think that he is having a hard time reconciling his actions and it is more stressful for him. He is having trouble distinguishing what is real. It seems likely that the delusions and hallucinations are worsening. I also think that it is getting harder and harder for him to control this dissociative fugue when it takes over."

The security guard cleared his throat. "There's more if you want me to proceed."

The group refocused its energy on the original

goal. The camera view changed and they were looking at an outdoor loading dock. The area was empty and then a door opened. James walked through it wearing a set of dark blue coveralls. He looked around and walked out of frame.

"That's it. There's no more."

"My son could be anywhere by now."

"Carl, he couldn't have gotten too far unless he was picked up."

"Why do you say that?"

Arabella asked the guard to back up the footage and stop it when she asked him to.

She answered, "Look, he's only wearing socks on his feet. He would most likely stay on the main roads and not risk walking on a dirt road laden with rocks and other sharp objects. The grassy areas will also still be wet with the rain we had."

Carl was continuously amazed by her ability to analyze any situation. She truly was the best cop he ever met.

"Let's go find my son."

FIFTY-TWO
Paige

"What do we do now, Paige?"

"Let me think. Oh, my gosh. I don't believe this is happening. How is this happening?"

Paige couldn't stop shaking. Every fiber of her being was rocked with waves of sheer and utter terror. Whom would he come for next?

"Take me home. I need to go home."

Jenna didn't think it was a good idea.

Amber spoke her mind, "I don't think it's safe there, Paige. It's getting dark. What if he's coming for you?"

Sade shot Amber a look in the rearview mirror that made her stop talking.

"Home it is—you should probably call and give your parents a heads-up before we get there."

Paige agreed with Jenna and called. She spoke to her dad. Her mother was at Tim's karate lesson. He told her to come home and that they'd figure out a plan.

The closer they got to her house the more anxious Paige became. The familiarity of the winding roads could not steady her nerves. She had read great poems that spoke of the soothing feeling of going home. She thought back and realized that it was usually true and not just something people wrote, who lived far away. She wished she could have that feeling back now.

Paige made sure that everyone was going directly to their respective houses and would tell their families everything that had occurred and would head somewhere safe. They all promised they would. When she left them, she prayed that it wouldn't be the last time they would see each other.

Her father met her at the door. She ran up the porch steps and into his arms.

"We need to move away, Dad. We can't stay here."

He wrapped his arm around her and brought her into the house.

"Don't worry about that now. I'm sure they'll find him soon."

"You don't know him like I do, Dad. He won't stop. He's so angry with me and he's taking it out on everyone I love. No one is safe!"

"Let's wait until your mom and Tim get back and we will discuss what to do. I've already called Cookie. We can stay with her again."

"No! Dad, you're not listening. He knows where she lives. She has to leave too. WE ARE NOT SAFE! We have to go somewhere that he won't ever think to look for us. And Cookie has to come!" She sat there feeling dejected. She looked at her father. "Dad, you didn't see the pictures of what he did to them. They were my friends. He used my words against me for pure evil."

"Okay, listen. Why don't you go upstairs and pack some things? As soon as they get back, we'll head out and stay in Newport for a few days. It's off-season so I'm sure we won't have a hard time finding somewhere to stay."

Paige hugged him and ran up to her room. She checked her phone to see if there had been any news updates about James escaping. There were none. She wondered what was taking them so long. The public needed to know.

As she was packing, yet again, she noticed that the motion detector spotlight was set alight in the backyard. She began to shake. She was sure it was him. She couldn't move. She tried to cry out but to no avail. She made her way to the window. She plastered herself against the wall to one side and carefully looked out in-between the slats of the blinds. She scanned the yard. All looked still. Then, she heard a crash near the trashcans and saw the culprits. Two raccoons were looking for a free meal.

She felt her pulse slow down. She turned the wand and shut the blinds tight. She repeated this for the other three windows in her room. She finished gathering her things to vacate the house once more.

Paige knew that her mom and Tim were back by the telltale sound of Jasper's welcome home barks. She bounded down the stairs and flew to her mother, hugging her fiercely.

"Paige, what's the matter?"

She was sobbing so much that she couldn't get a

word out.

Mitch came into the kitchen and told Paige to get Tim upstairs and help him pack.

Tim and Sloane said, "Pack?" in unison.

Mitch said, "Go on you two, I need to talk to your mom."

Paige took Tim upstairs and Mitch filled Sloane in on the new developments.

"I started packing, but you know how terrible I am at that. I'm going to make sure everything's sealed up tight and ready to be empty for a few days. Why don't you go up and finish?"

"Okay. I'll finish up there, then I want to check the cameras. I moved most of them so that if he ever came by again, he wouldn't know where to look."

"Don't even tell me you had a premonition about him escaping," Mitch teased.

When all was packed up, they dropped Jasper off at their neighbor's and they were ready to leave. Sloane called Cookie to say they were on their way for her.

The family arrived at Cookie's. Cookie came out wheeling two carry-on cases and two overnight bags. Once loaded into the SUV, there was barely room for her.

At the hotel, the family vowed to treat themselves to luxury and relaxation. Mitch could see the worry fading away from them all—all but Paige. He knew it would take more time with her, but that was to be expected.

FIFTY-THREE
Carl

Carl and Arabella were driving up and down the highway in hopes of spotting James in his blue jumpsuit. This was the fourth time—Arabella knew this was the fourth time because it was four times now that she saw the giant witch's hat on Nibbles Woodaway, the massive termite mascot for a local extermination company. The Big Blue Bug was always dressed in holiday themes.

"Carl, we should head back to Cumberland. He must have hitched a ride from someone. Otherwise, we would have run into him by now."

"I'm going to take some side streets and head that way."

He took the next exit and made his way north by way of main roads and side streets he thought James might have taken. He thought about how scared James must be. He knew that there was something fundamentally wrong with him but also knew that somewhere deep down, his son was still there. He knew that James wouldn't want to be all alone like this.

He remembered a time when James was having a birthday party at an arcade and got lost for a few minutes. He and his friends had just driven race-car-themed bumper cars. They all exited and made their way to the table for cake and gifts. He was following his friend who wore a red shirt and had curly dirty-blonde hair. When the boy sat at a different table, he realized it wasn't his friend at all and that he didn't know where his table was. In a matter of minutes, Carl was calling for him while Lydia was searching frantically. Afraid that he would get into trouble, he hid between the end of the snack bar counter and a popcorn machine. His aunt spotted him. He had nightmares about getting lost for weeks and would bring it up all the time.

Carl's phone rang. It was Lydia. She asked him if he had an update. When he told her that there was no news, she asked him if he thought she should leave work and go home. He told her to stay put, that he'd go by and check the house.

Arabella said, "You know, I was thinking that we might want to check the kid's hideout. He might have gone back there."

"I thought that too. We can go there after I check out the house. First, we need to contact the captain."

Arabella called Captain White and filled him in on what was happening. He said that he would send out an APB for all units to be on the lookout for James. She gave him a description of what the jumpsuit looked like and said that he was on foot as best they could tell.

"Ask him to get officers stationed at the places he's likely to turn up."

"Did you copy that, Cap?"

"Loud and clear. We'll get a detail to his residence, the Vale home, and for each of the teens who were at the party."

Arabella suggested that they also put a crew at Cookie's and the hideout in the woods. "If I can get some extra manpower, I will. I'll do my best."

"Roger that."

FIFTY-FOUR

James

James was thinking and constantly moving the hair from his eyes as he walked. He hated the fact that there was another person out there killing at the same time he was. He wanted what he was doing to be special. He wanted Paige and everyone to see the lengths he would go to just to be hers.

After walking for almost an hour, James came to a gas station. It was dark and he didn't want to be on the road with the temperature dropping. He saw a woman filling up at a gas pump. She was driving a Mac truck. She whistled while she completed her task. James walked up to her slowly so that he could think about what he would say.

"Um, excuse me, ma'am, could I borrow your cellphone to make a call? You see, I was at the convenience store down the road buying some lottery tickets, and I was robbed. They took my car, wallet, my cellphone, the lottery tickets, even my shoes."

"Oh, no. You poor thing. Guess it wasn't your lucky day." She chuckled but noticed that the pun escaped the young man standing before her. "Let me call the police for you."

"You know what, that won't be necessary. They called them at the store. The police came and took my statement and left because there was some emergency. I never had a chance to ask to use their phone."

"Oh, sure. Here you go." She gave him her cellphone.

James dialed his cellphone number knowing full well that it wouldn't be answered.

"Oh, no. She must be at work already." James tried to make himself look as pained as possible. It seemed to be working. He handed back the phone and hoped she would offer him a ride.

"Thanks. I'll just walk. Nice meeting you."

He began to walk away from the woman.

"Hold up. Isn't there someone else you can call?"

James turned around, still sporting his crestfallen look, "No. It's just me and my mom. I'll be fine. Thanks again." He started to walk away a second time.

"Look. I can get you a cab. You shouldn't have to walk home after what just happened to you."

James looked at her with utter relief. "That would be great. If you give me your address, I'll pay you back, honest."

"No need. I think the universe owes you a kindness right about now, Glenn." The woman asked for his address and called the taxi company. She asked him if he wanted her to wait with him and he declined the offer. She finished gassing up the truck and drove off.

Shortly after, the car arrived. He was blinded by the bright headlights that surrounded the license plate E D B T Z. James climbed into the back seat. He looked through the dirty, scuffed plexiglass shield at the driver who had a kind face. It matched the face on the ID card dangling from the rearview mirror announcing that his name was George.

James felt a mix of emotions. He wondered if anyone was looking for him. He wondered if Paige knew he was free. Free to go back to the way things were. Sure, he would need to prove his love so that she would finally understand and put him on the top of her list. He was sure that she would create a new journal—maybe they could even make one together. It would be filled with things they each loved about one another.

The address he gave was a block away from his house. He was sure there would be patrols casing the place by now. He came into his yard from the back, crossing through the yard that bordered his. He was relieved to be home and ashamed and afraid to be there as well. He walked to where his bedroom was at the rear of the house and opened the window. He always left it open because he often forgot or lost his keys. He also liked to sleep with the window opened a crack all year long. It made him feel free because he could breathe fresh air.

Once in the house, the dogs began to bark and welcome him home. He didn't want anyone to be alerted so he gave the command for them to sit and be silent. That was followed by treats to keep them quiet. He checked the front window and saw a strange car parked across the street. He was happy that he made the decision to come in through the back.

He didn't put any lights on when he got in. He took a shower, put on some clean clothes, and work boots. He made himself some food then fed the dogs. He knew that today was his mother's scheduled double shift at the casino. She worked one every week, and she would not be home until later tomorrow. He couldn't risk her coming home early when she heard he left the hospital. He didn't want to see her yet.

He grabbed a key from the ceramic bowl on his bureau and headed out to the camper that Dr. Hogan kept at Dr. Doolittle's. The doctor often slept there if there was a touch-and-go situation with an animal and he didn't want to be too far away. James had used it twice before while he was planning and carrying out his scheme. He just hoped that there was no emergency going on at the moment.

James was careful to take back roads and keep out of sight. He arrived at the pet clinic without incident. He let himself in, set the alarm clock on the shelf beside the slim foldout bed, and trailed off to sleep. When he awoke, he was groggy and didn't know exactly where he was. He knew there was somewhere he needed to be. There was so much swirling around in his head that he had to focus on what to pull to the forefront. Paige. Of course. He needed to go to her to talk about things . He just knew she'd understand. He would make her understand. While the other thoughts were struggling to take center stage, he had to focus. These thoughts were wrestling with each other; he could feel the red mist trying to envelop him. He knew he didn't have much time before he was trapped within himself again.

James knew if he were going to accomplish his task, he would need to head out right away. He knew that the Vale family would be eating breakfast right about now. He opened the door and noticed a damp crispness to the air—the kind that settled deep into the bones. He went back and grabbed a thermal sweatshirt that Cookie had given him as a gift. This made him wonder if they would be at home or at Cookie's again since he was sure they heard the news of his escape. Hmmm, where to go first . . .

He decided to start at the Vales' house and take it from there. James opted to use the route that would place him in the woods to the back of their property. He would have a clear view of the kitchen at the back of the house. If they were there, he'd know.

He made it there in good time. He had to be careful because he knew that his father and the rest of the police force would be anticipating his every move. He did not walk on the cleared, direct path but veered off in different directions that were not frequently traversed.

When he arrived, he could tell at once that the house was empty. He stood there at the edge of the property glaring at the back of the majestic home that he so loved. He wanted so much to be a permanent part of it and the family that dwelled within. James wanted to be certain that they were not there. He hunched down and stealthily made his way to the swing set where so long ago his love for Paige had grown. From there, he brazenly made his way to the side of the house. He could see most of the front and saw what most certainly was an unmarked police car. He would expect no less.

James went back around to the yard and made his way to the door that led to the garage. He knew that the code to enter was Cookie's birthday. He wondered if they had the presence of mind to change it. He entered 03-22-39 and it worked! He opened the door and noticed that two of the cars were gone. He knew where the cameras were so he made sure to stay out of the frame for each of them. He decided to see if Paige or the family left any clues as to where they might be. He strategically made his way into the main house avoiding the places where he knew Sloane had cameras set up.

Once in Paige's room, her familiar scent immediately filled his lungs. She always wore Dolce & Gabbana Light Blue. Her room smelled of that and fresh linen. He walked around looking at the things she left behind. He looked for her laptop and as he expected, she had taken it with her. He opened drawers and checked everywhere in her desk. He couldn't find anything that would help to find her. Anger and rage were coming to a boil within him. This was making it even harder to keep the *Red* at bay. He quickly went to the study to search there but again, no luck. He didn't want to spend too much time there in case someone came back.

James decided that he wouldn't find what he was looking for. He thought about going to Cookie's house, but he figured that if they were keeping the Vales' somewhere, Cookie was most likely with them. He knew that there was only one place where he would feel balanced and where he could collect his thoughts. He headed for the hideout. He hoped that wasn't being surveilled.

FIFTY-FIVE
Lydia

Lydia did come home early. She couldn't concentrate at work knowing that James was out there somewhere. As worried about him as she was, she was also worried about what he might do next. She knew that he wasn't in a good frame of mind. It was still so difficult for her to acknowledge the fact that her son was so damaged. She knew that she should have pushed harder for someone to help him when he was young and experiencing those episodes and blackouts. It seemed that everywhere she turned she hit a brick wall.

After she pulled into the driveway, she saw a familiar face in an unmarked car across the street. She waved to the plain-clothed officer and he waved back.

She went into James's room and looked around. She saw the jumpsuit Carl had described in a heap on the floor. She looked around to see if anything else was disturbed but didn't think so.

She went into the bathroom next. The shower area was wet, as well as the floor mat. The scoop used to feed the dogs was on the counter and she did not leave it there. It was evident that he had been home.

She looked around in the other rooms but he was not there.

Lydia called Carl. "I left work early and came home. He's been here. The jumpsuit is on the floor in his room and he took a shower. I checked; he's gone."

"Was there an officer at the house?"

"Yes. He was in the front. James must have come in through the back."

FIFTY-SIX
Paige

Paige awoke to shafts of sunlight coming in through a gap in the blinds of the hotel room window. The rays were like golden daggers piercing her heart at the thought of what had recently happened to her world. She wanted to stay in bed all day but knew that her parents and her grandmother would be overly worried about her if she did. She had to put on a happy face and go with the script for the hardest acting role she would ever have to play.

A restless and hungry Timmy, who was doing his best to rouse his parents from their slumber, awakened Sloane. She looked at her phone and saw that it wasn't even seven o'clock.

"Timmy, really? You couldn't let us sleep in?"

"I'm hungry. And I want to go to the pool!"

"It's awfully funny how it takes me forever to get you up for school, but now that you can sleep, you're up at the crack of dawn. Just give me a few more minutes."

"Cookie is up. I texted her on your phone. She's gonna take me to the pool. She said I can even eat my breakfast there!"

"Okay. Have your sister bring you. We'll meet

you there in a bit." Sloane put her head back on her pillow and then felt Mitch get out of bed.

Paige saw what was happening and ran into the bathroom ahead of her father.

"Hey, that's where I was headed," Mitch said.

"I know," Paige yelled through the door. "You're too slow, old man."

Mitch went into his bag and grabbed the things he would need when he could get in and get ready.

Sloane groaned, "Okay, okay, I'm up. Why should I be able to sleep in this beautiful hotel?"

Paige came out of the bathroom with her long hair pulled back into a ponytail, wearing a bathing suit and flip-flops. She went into her bag and pulled out an oversized sweatshirt to use as a cover-up. She rummaged for the Stieg Larsson book that she was reading and put it in her tote. "We're heading to the pool. Come on, squirt." She scooped Timmy toward the door. "We'll see you there." She left and headed to the pool with Tim. She walked him there, left him with their grandmother, and then headed to the gift shop to see if she could find a newspaper with any additional information she couldn't find online. There was no story anywhere.

When she arrived back at the pool, she found her grandmother and brother.

"Hey, Paige! Guess what? They're bringing me pancakes. Cookie said I could eat them while I'm in the pool! Isn't that wicked awesome?"

"Sure. But, if you think I'm swimming in maple syrup, you're mistaken. You'd better be careful!" She smiled and went to sit on a lounge chair near Cookie.

"Hi, sweetie. I ordered pancakes for everyone. Don't tell your brother, but they are Lemon Blueberry Ricotta Pancakes. If he heard that, he probably wouldn't eat them. I ordered them to be brought out in batches because I didn't know when everyone would get here. I texted your mom to let her know."

Paige thought that was a brilliant idea and hoped that she would have that much wisdom when she was that old.

She made herself comfortable and took out her book. She read a few pages when the first batch of pancakes arrived. She heard Tim's excitement when he came up for air and saw the waitstaff wheeling the food cart over to them in the humid, chlorine-smelling pool area.

Just as they were setting up the three orders of pancakes, bacon, and hash browns, Sloane and Mitch arrived. Cookie looked at Sloane and said, "You look tired. Rough night?"

"Yes. Pretty rough. Then someone couldn't contain himself over the thought of eating pancakes in the pool—thanks for that by the way. I read the texts."

Cookie laughed. "Well, it's not every day I get to stay in a fancy hotel with my family."

"Mom, can you bring my breakfast to me?" Tim went under again and came up. He let the water out from under his goggles and smiled a goofy, proud smile.

Sloane thought that she couldn't remember the last time everyone was this relaxed and happy. She was relieved that they could feel free here.

"Sorry little man, but this plate has my name on it." She began to eat one of the three meals. She made a big show of how delicious and satisfying it was.

"No fair!" Tim looked on in disbelief.

"Hey, you woke me up, now you pay the price."

Paige and Cookie were also eating their meals in between laughing at what was playing out in front of them.

Mitch sat next to Sloane and said under his breath, "You're really going to eat the kid's breakfast?"

"That I am, my love." She took a large bite out of the bacon. "I have to leave soon, so I'm eating now. You all can stay, so you can wait for the second round."

They all yelled, "Leave?"

"Yes, leave. I have an optometrist appointment. I will go there and come right back here." When she saw the frightened looks on their faces, she added, "Scout's honor!"

Mitch spoke up, "I'll go with you."

"No. That's crazy. When was the last time you were able to just sit back and relax? You stay here. I'll only be gone for a bit. It's not like he knows my schedule. I'll be fine."

FIFTY-SEVEN
Sloane

Sloan arrived for her appointment at Vision Care of Cumberland and was seated in the comfortable, welcoming anteroom while she filled out her patient information form. Her name was called and she was taken into a small room and had her pre-test screening. Once that was completed, she was told to go back into the waiting area and that Dr. Cliff Howard would be ready for her soon.

She was looking at the selection of frames and trying to decide which pair to get next when her phone vibrated. She was sure that it was a text from the kids—probably a picture with everyone in the pool having fun without her. She grabbed her phone and unlocked it. It wasn't a text at all. It was an alert from her home security system. There was a breach in the woods behind the house. She froze, paralyzed with fear. She checked the video feed and saw him. It was James. He was now entering her yard and stopped at the swing set. There was a cry forming at the back of her throat that she could not let erupt to the surface.

She had to work to get her limbs moving. She ran over to the reception desk and told the staff that she had to leave because of an emergency and to tell Dr. Howard that she would reschedule. Then Sloan ran out the door and into her car. She checked the recording and there he was. He was entering the house. She started the car and headed home.

+++++++++++++

Driving home, Sloane tried to tell herself that she was doing the right thing but knew that no one would see it that way. As soon as she crested the slight hill leading to the cul-de-sac, she knew that she had to talk to him. She'd known James for so long that she felt as though she could reach him and have him turn himself in to the police.

If not, she knew where the pistol was kept. She would use it if she had to. Her phone was pinging like crazy with security alerts. She knew that meant he was moving throughout the house. Why was he there? Did he really think we would be waiting like sitting ducks? It dawned on her that she didn't think to change the alarm passcodes to enter the house. She remembered that he knew them. What he didn't know was that she had increased the cameras—there were at least two in each room, capturing windows and doors.

Once on her street, she parked a few houses away from hers and checked the footage—he was downstairs now. She was playing out how she would get into the house without the officer spotting her. Just as she was about to get out of the car, she saw a figure in her yard. It was James. He had left her house. With no time to think, she exited the vehicle and bolted through her neighbor's yard and into the woods after him. She had several cameras set up in the woods. When she came to the end of her property, she engaged the live feed from them on her phone. That way she could follow from a distance without him knowing. Hopefully, a plan would come to fruition as she closed in on him because right now, she had no idea what she was going to do. The trees seemed to whisper to Sloane urging her to turn back and abandon this crazy pursuit, but she pressed on.

From the bits and pieces of what she had heard about the murders, she believed that he was going to the hideout where he carried out the gruesome acts on those poor unsuspecting people. She had never been there so she couldn't say for sure, but it made sense. James slowed down and then stopped. He started to speak, but she couldn't make out what he was saying. When she stopped, her feet sunk into the earth. It had rained a lot a few days prior and the earth was still soddened with excess moisture that the plant roots below the soil had not yet absorbed. Sloane inhaled and stepped behind a tree. She could feel the rough tree bark and a falling leaf kissed her cheek. She continued to watch the woeful scene in front of her.

James began to punch at the air and hold his head. It was the saddest thing she ever witnessed. She wanted to go to him and hug him. She was close enough now to make out the word red. She didn't know what it meant but thought it might be important when she had to confess that she did this reckless, dangerous thing.

He began to walk again but was continuously blurting out incoherent fragments of sounds and words. He stopped when he came to an area with yellow police caution tape around the perimeter of what looked like an old abandoned fire pit. She thought that if the tape wasn't there, she would have never noticed the mossy, charred wood among the leaves and tree debris of the forest floor.

She watched as he crouched down, hoisted it up, and pushed it to the side. Once moved, it uncovered a large opening. James descended into his home away from home that he shared with Paige for many years. She felt a mixture of sadness and anger at the thought of him desecrating this place with his perverse murders. She knew children needed a space to call their own. She was just very surprised to learn that Paige came here all those years and she had no clue.

Sloane tried to think of what her next move should be. She knew that she should call the police. She didn't want James to escape once again. She could feel her heart racing. She knew that she had to calm down and get control of herself. The scent of the damp earth was beginning to soothe her. She did a few deep-breathing exercises and began to regroup. She walked over to the underground fort's cover and placed it over the opening as quietly as she could.

Once it was in place, she gathered up the largest boulders and rocks that she could move and placed them on top of the cover. She heard a crash from below. At least now, there was no way for him to escape. She called Carl.

FIFTY-EIGHT

James

When James looked up past the tops of the trees, losing the battle to remain clothed in their fine leaves, he saw the sky was a brilliant deep blue—the kind of blue that only came with a New England sky in the fall.

Once he arrived at his destination, he removed the lid. The distinct scents of nature's normal decomposition changed to a methanal, metallic, and iron stench of a completely new decomposition that assaulted all his senses. It wafted up the aged steps. He knew this was the aftermath of his handiwork. He went down the steps noticing that they were beginning to crumble. He thought it must have been due to all the traffic going in and out once the police discovered that this was the place where Bryce, Karol, and Mrs. Hansen died. He found his way to a lantern. He turned it on. He turned the others on as well. James inspected the place with a feeling of foreboding. He wasn't sure if it was nostalgia or the fact that his prized possessions were taken away as evidence.

Those parts were special. They were the things that Paige loved. He needed them to transfer her love to him. As he became angrier, he felt the familiar throbbing taking hold of him. His vision was blurring with each beat of his heart and was followed by a ringing in his ears. He knew he would lose the battle this time. When the *Red* was this strong, there was no use in fighting it. He wanted nothing more than to let go so that it would encompass him completely.

As he was focusing on his thoughts, he noticed that the entrance light from above was put out all at once. Then he heard what sounded like someone putting something on top of the lid over the opening to his sanctuary. He thought that he should be concerned about it, but the feeling of letting go was too overwhelming, and the thought quickly abated.

The *Red* was becoming more resilient. It was almost as bad as it had been at the hospital. He heard it calling out to him. It was telling him to come willingly, coaxing him to acquiesce. The *Red* was showing him beautiful things. He wanted to see more and he was trying everything in his power to stay James for a while longer. He picked up one of the crates and smashed it against the table. He looked around for other things to destroy hoping it would hold him in the present. He needed to quell the pain. Then he saw Paige's shelf. He tried to swim his way through the red mist to revel in her possessions and keep his conscious mind at the surface of the *Red*.

Her things. They were a part of her. He got up and focused hard as he sorted through electronic toys, and mixed colored pencils—and there it was. The book. Romeo and Juliet. She loved the story— said there was nothing more romantic than star-crossed lovers.

"Yes, James. That's right. I always said that. You know, I think that *we* could be star-crossed lovers too."

Paige! It was Paige! She looked so beautiful. She shimmered in the glistening red mist that surrounded her like a full-body halo. Even her skin sparkled. He could feel her presence in every cell of his body. She began caressing his face, neck, and shoulders. Her hands glided down to his and found their resting place.

"Do you really think so, Paige?"

"I do. I really do, James."

She reached out and began to trace the features of his face with her fingertips, beginning with his eyes, moving down to his nose, then his mouth. It felt cool and soothing. Time seemed to stand still; thick and all encompassing. It filled every nook and crevice of the subterranean room like an expanding red foam. James could never remember feeling this happy and free.

"Listen, James. We should make a pact like Romeo and Juliet so we can also be together forever."

Even though Paige had never before expressed these feelings to him, James always knew her true heart. He knew she would come around especially once she learned about what he had done to win her love. He knew that all his pain and suffering would eventually culminate in a blissful reward. The misery had to be endured in order for him to end up at this moment.

"Yes. I'll make it happen, Paige. I'll find a way." James stood and looked through the boxes and shelves for something that would speak to him. He needed some way to tie their lives together, always. He came upon some rope and laughed thinking that it was a little too literal. He continued searching. He thought that the police must have confiscated all of the items that would be useful to him in this instant.

Paige called to him, "James."

When he turned to look, she was hanging from one of the hooks used to cure meat long ago.

"That's it!"

He went back to procure the rope and made his way over to one of the menacing-looking meat hooks beside her. He fashioned a noose with the rope, brought one of the crates over, and stepped on it to affix it to the hook. He looked over at Paige for her approval. She sparkled and glowed with the biggest and brightest smile, signaling her encouragement.

James put the loop around his neck, tightened it, and kicked the crate into the table, shattering it. Paige was now floating before him showing him the way. She became one with the *Red*, which was incredibly strong now. It was thicker and more enticing than ever. He let it envelop him and knew that it would be for the last time. He would be with Paige forever. There she was, waiting for him with open arms. He felt at peace.

FIFTY-NINE

Carl

Carl got the call from Sloane about what had occurred and he told her to go back to her house. He and Arabella notified the captain and they headed over to the woods. They followed the markers that were previously set up. When they neared the site, they could spot a figure standing idle near the caution tape.

Arabella looked and said, "She didn't go home."

Carl said, "No, she did not."

They walked the remaining way and drew their weapons, signaled for Sloane to move away, and took stock of the situation.

Sloane was shaking. She said, "There was a crash."

"What?" Carl asked.

"A crash. I put those boulders and rocks on top of the entrance cover so he couldn't escape until you arrived. He was talking and laughing for a bit. There was the first crash, but afterward, I could hear him talking more. It was hard to tell what he was saying. He was even doing that while he was walking through the woods. After the last crash, I didn't hear him at all. I've called down to him, but he hasn't answered."

Carl looked panic-stricken. He ran to the cover and threw the boulders and rocks off the lid. He slid the cover to the side and was about to enter. Arabella grabbed him and told him to stop.

"That's my son down there." He ran a hand through his hair and made a move to descend so Arabella stepped in the way once again.

"All the more reason not to do this. You need to wait for backup, Carl."

He turned away from the hatch and went over to Sloane.

"How did you end up here anyway?"

Sloane looked down at the ground searching for the right words. Either way, she knew that she'd be chastised for her actions. "I have security cameras all over my property and even some in the woods. I received a notification that someone was there and it was James. I went home to see if I could talk him into turning himself in. He was in my house! In Paige's room!" She met his eyes and at that moment, they were just two worried parents. "By the time I got out of my car, he was walking into the woods, so I followed him. I know it wasn't smart."

"Not smart? That was reckless, Sloane. You could have been hurt. You know what he's capable of." As Carl was admonishing her, they heard footsteps trampling over crunching twigs and branches.

It was Samuel and a crew of five others. Arabella went up to the captain and filled him in on what Sloane had told them.

The captain went over to Carl.

Before he could speak, Carl told him, "Cap, there was no patrol here when James and Sloan arrived."

"Lincoln was arranging to send us someone. They are scheduled to be here in an hour or so. I'm sorry it wasn't sooner." He looked so sad. "You can't be here, Carl."

"I'm staying, Cap."

Samuel knew it was a losing battle but said, "Listen, no matter what we find down there, it's not going to be good. Just go be with Lydia and we'll catch you up as soon as we know what we're dealing with."

Almost on cue, Lydia came running through the woods to them. She saw the puzzled look on Samuel's face. "I still have a police scanner at the house. I followed the markings. Once a cop's wife, always a cop's wife."

"That settles it." Carl walked over to Lydia and put an arm around her. "We're not going anywhere."

Sloane walked over to both of them and ushered them to stand aside with her. She filled Lydia in on what had occurred and waited with them. The outward display of muddy-colored tears streaking down her cheeks explained the internal collapse of Lydia's world.

The captain and the officers went down the steps. There was no air entering Carl's lungs as he waited for the news. He was hoping that the news would allow him to breathe normally again.

When Samuel came up Carl could read him

immediately. A shudder wracked his body and he couldn't keep his composure. Lydia saw this happening and knew exactly what it meant. She turned to face him and they cried with one another for a while.

Sloane moved closer to them and tried to console them. Carl moved away and left the two women.

He went over to Samuel. "Tell me."

"He hanged himself. I'm sorry, Carl."

Carl went back to console Lydia.

Sloane suggested that they come back to her house to rest. They agreed. They were too shaken and didn't want to see James brought up in that state.

SIXTY
Sloane

"**I**'m putting a little something extra in this to take the edge off." Sloane delivered drinks to Lydia and Carl as they sat in stunned silence in her living room. She had ushered them to the soft cream-colored leather loveseat.

Carl moved a pillow and Lydia took it to hold to her chest. It was as if she couldn't breathe without it. He was so wound up that Sloane could see the muscles of his jaw pulsating because they were so clenched.

Sloane didn't know what to do. She didn't want to sit and invade their privacy, but she also didn't want to leave them alone at a time like this. She decided to sit across from them in the very chair James sat in countless times in the past. "Is there anyone you want me to call for you or anything I can do?"

Lydia made eye contact, but it looked as if she didn't understand the question. Her pretty blue eyes were full of pain.

Sloane felt the full weight of them. "Why don't you just rest for now?"

Again, neither one said anything in response to her statement.

Sloane excused herself and called Mitch. "Mitch. It's over. You can all come home soon."

She braced herself for a peppering of questions and sure enough, he fired away one after the other. "What? What do you mean? I thought you were at the eye doctor!"

Sloane chose her words carefully. "I was. I'll explain everything when you get home. Mitch, James is dead. Carl and Lydia are here. I think they're in shock."

There was a long silence on the line. "You have a lot to explain, but I'll leave it until we get back. It's going to be hard to tear Tim away from this place. Everyone's treating the kids like royalty."

Sloane knew that she would be cast as the villain in this vignette, but she wanted nothing more than to have the whole family back where they belonged. "Okay, well, I'll text you when they've gone. Have them pack up now."

"All right. Love ya. I'll wait for the text."

There was a heavy feeling of trepidation within the house; it was as heavy as death itself. She went back in to check on them. She refilled their drinks and placed them down on the Carrara marble coffee table. Carl nodded his appreciation. He seemed to be regaining a little of his composure, but it was taking longer for Lydia. She was wearing a sweatshirt when she met up with all of them, but when Sloane came into the room, she had Carl's jacket on as well. Even so, she was shaking and her lips had a bluish tinge to them.

"Lydia, why don't you come upstairs where you can rest in the guest bedroom?"

The vacant look continued to fill her eyes, but she stood up acknowledging what was being asked of her. Carl began to rise to help Lydia.

Sloane touched his shoulder and he sat back down. She helped Lydia up the stairs and into the room.

"Is this where James stayed when he was here?"

Sloane wanted to kick herself for not thinking about that. "Yes. This is where he slept when he was with us. I'm sorry, Lydia. Why don't you come to my room? You would probably be more comfortable there anyway."

Lydia went over to the bed and slipped the baby blue comforter down exposing the pillow. She reached for it and brought it up to her face, inhaling it.

"I can smell him. No. I'd like to stay here if that's okay."

"Of course. Stay as long as you like."

"Sloane, I need to thank you for all the times you looked after him when we couldn't. Not just lately. You were an important figure in his life. He always spoke fondly of this family. I want you to know it meant a lot."

Sloane thought that at this moment, Lydia looked so raw and vulnerable it hurt. She couldn't imagine losing a child, no matter what they had done. She knew that Lydia didn't think very highly of her and it made her second-guess every instinct to try and comfort her. She wouldn't wish this pain and devastation on anyone.

"Lydia, we loved James like one of our own. He was a very special young man. That's how we will always remember him."

As Sloane turned to exit the room, Lydia added, "I also need to apologize to you. At times, I questioned your motives and felt jealous of your relationship with James. I know it was petty and I want to get it out there."

"You don't need to apologize for anything, Lydia. Every mother feels that when there is another maternal figure in her child's life. It is perfectly normal."

Sloane went back down to find Carl outside on his phone. She decided to busy herself with anything she could think of. She thought of Paige. She knew that Mitch would not tell her there. This would be one of the most difficult conversations she would ever have.

Carl came inside and asked Sloane if she thought he should go check on Lydia. "I don't know what I'm supposed to do."

"You sit. I'll go up and check."

As soon as she finished speaking, Lydia came down. She had a little more color in her cheeks. Sloane thought that was a good sign. She wished that she could remember everything else you were supposed to do when someone was in shock. Carl went to Lydia and embraced her.

To see two adults before her who were so shattered and dejected try to make sense of the things that have unfolded, was unbearable. What was even worse was that she knew how they should be. They were both energetic, jovial people. She wondered if they would ever regain an ounce of that normalcy again.

Lydia stated that she was ready to leave. Carl called Arabella and told her that he was leaving with Lydia and that she should keep him apprised of all new developments. They thanked Sloane and left in Lydia's car.

SIXTY-ONE

Arabella

To say that confusion and disbelief filled the small Cumberland police station would be an understatement. Officers and detectives alike were walking around in a daze. The events of the past weeks were hard to understand. They all tried to reconcile what had occurred. It seemed as if they were living within a bad movie. The actual events that shook the town they lived in—the town they loved were far worse than any movie.

It was time for the video conference call between the FBI and the other joint task force members. Everyone filed into the conference room for the final update. As one of the young officers was working her magic to connect the calls, Anika, Samuel, and Arabella walked in. You could hear a pin drop. They took their seats as photos of the many other law enforcement leaders were projected on the large screen that was pulled down on the wall.

ASAC's face appeared front and center. He cleared his throat and asked what had happened.

Anika moved so that she was directly in line with the computer camera. "I think the best way to say it is that we had it wrong." She looked at Arabella and corrected herself, "Well, *most* of us had it wrong. There were two killers, but not the husband-and-wife team as we first thought. The fact that a third player working alone and killing while the couple was also killing was the piece most of us missed. The problem, as you know, was that their killing styles were very similar, leading us to believe that it was one person who sometimes varied from their routine."

ASAC shook his head. "I must say, this is one for the books. I've checked around and this is a first for sure. It doesn't fit the copycat serial. It's in a whole new category. You were just the unlucky district to have a pair of twisted people living among you. He shook his head in disbelief. "When you said that most of you had it wrong what did you mean?"

"One of our detectives, Arabella Luthor, was working on a different angle from the rest of us. She believed there were two separate killers. She came to me with the information right before we knew the boy was involved. She has proven herself as a valuable member of our team since her arrival."

ASAC boomed, "Luthor, front and center."

Arabella walked over to Anika and looked into the camera.

"I'd like to see your case file on this once everything is wrapped up. There is always room here, at the bureau, for someone with sharp, divergent thinking."

She replied, "Yes, sir."

"Okay, wrap it up with a bow. What has happened since the task force dismantled?"

Arabella went back to her seat and Samuel moved into camera range.

"Hello, sir. Soon after you left, we discovered another dismembered body on the grounds of an old local Monastery that now serves as the town's library. Her throat was sliced at the carotid artery and both arms were removed. This happened after the Hoovers were deceased, leading us to believe that there was another killer out there—copycat or no."

The Chief of the Lincoln police department moved to the front of the screen when he added, "We sent some officers to that crime scene because Cumberland was still running short. We have almost completed the reports and will send them out ASAP."

"Thank you. White, how was the boy identified as a player?"

"As you know, he is the son of Sergeant Lowden and a friend of one of the girls at the party where the teens were drugged. The girl, Paige Vale, came into the station to deliver some pastry to everyone during the wrap-up. Until that point, she had only heard that all of the victims had body parts removed but nothing more. As we've just discussed, Luthor was working her own hunch and trying to piece it together on her case boards. Paige saw it and something clicked in respect to the exact body parts that were removed."

"Well, if she could ascertain all that from someone's case board, we should recruit her as well!"

Samuel flagged Arabella to the front once more and told her to continue filling in the blanks.

"When Paige was younger, she had a journal where she wrote about the people she loved and why she loved them. She and James had been good friends since they were very young. His feelings for her went a lot deeper than friendship but were not reciprocated. Paige and the third victim, Bryce Walker, were an item. James was not happy about that. He found said journal and realized that he was not in it. Somehow, he snapped. He decided to systematically take all of the things that she loved about everyone listed, thinking that eventually, it would make her love him."

"That seems a little extreme to say the least."

"From what we can tell, James had some neurological problems when he was a young boy and he was never properly diagnosed."

"Well, I still have a lot of unanswered questions about this one, but I'm sure everything will become clear to me when the reports are completed. At least we know it's finally over. Good work, everyone. If things hadn't played out the way they did, I shudder to think how many more bodies there could have been." He ended his connection leaving the remaining members there.

Anika asked if anyone had anything else to add. When no one did, she ended the call.

"All right. Arabella, have you spoken to Carl?"

"I went by his place before I came here and spoke

with Tara. She said that she gave him something to help him sleep. He is sleeping right now. She'll take good care of him. I also stopped by Lydia's. The officers were just arriving to go through the house. I talked her into boarding the dogs and going to a hotel. She'll stay there until she's ready to go home. I don't know how anyone comes back from this. Especially a cop's family."

SIXTY-TWO

Paige

Mitch arrived with the kids after taking Cookie home.

When they came in, as expected, Tim's first words were, "Can't we go back, Mom? It's not fair! We were having a blast in the game room."

"We'll go back. Just not right now. The next time dad has some time off, Newport, here we come!" That seemed to appease him for the time being.

Paige came in with her bag, placed it down, and went up to her mother. She threw her arms around her. Mitch saw what was happening and took Tim upstairs so they would have some privacy.

"What happened? Did they find him?"

"They did, Paige. Let's sit down." They went into the living room and took the spots that hours prior held the forms of James's parents. "When I was at my appointment with Dr. Cliff, events transpired that led me to come here. I came home to find that James was here. I followed him into the woods. He went to your hideout. I . . . I blocked him inside once he went down. Then I called his dad."

As she recalled the incidents, a lone tear streamed down Paige's cheek. Sloane was expecting waterworks and braced herself for it, but somehow this was worse. It was like all her sadness and pain were coming out in slow motion. It twisted Sloane's heart and left her with a pain she never knew before and hoped she would never know again.

"How did he die?"

"That's not important right now."

"Mom, after everything, you know I don't need to be babied."

"He hanged himself, Paige." She held her daughter until the shock of the situation subsided and then said, "I feel so awful. I wish I knew how deeply disturbed he really was. Maybe I could have gotten him some help."

Paige let loose and began to shudder and sob some more. Her mother embraced her until she was over the worst of it. "Mom, do Carl and Lydia know?"

"Yes. They were there when the officers went down and found him. They came here for a bit while they composed themselves. It will take some time, but I'm sure they'll be all right."

"I need some air."

Paige got up and went through the kitchen, out onto the deck, and down into the back yard, taking in the brilliant blue cloud-strewn sky. She took in the fresh air that was now maintaining an icy nip to it. The Indian summer was no more.

This yard held so many memories of James. They would hang out here together when they were younger, playing for hours on the swing set. James was always included at family gatherings and holiday barbecues. Everything would feel so wrong without him. Her new reality felt more like a dream that she wished she could awaken from and have things back to normal.

Paige noticed the swings swaying in the breeze, again like an evil pendulum. She remembered that fateful day long ago when he chased her into the house because she had a wounded knee and scraped elbows. Her life would never be the same; it was forever changed. Where she once saw the beauty and possibilities in life, she now only saw shadows and death. She went over to the swings and sat on one. The urge to pump so hard that she'd make it over the bar was even stronger right now. But who would be there to catch her if she fell? Her eyes burned, brimming with the threat of more tears. When the swing went back, she noticed something. She and James had carved their names into the metal poles of the swing set ages ago. The letters had rusted and faded. Now, there was a fresh cut. She got off the swing to get a closer look. Above his name was the word Red.

------FREE BONUS!------

If you would like Paige's story to continue, email me at **sharynhaddadvicenteauthor@gmail.com** and type **Novelette** in the subject line. I will send you a novelette about how Paige's trauma left her in a very dark place and how she rose up from it, fought her demons, and won.

Acknowledgments

First and foremost, I'd like to thank my husband, Joe Vicente, for his meticulous proof-reading time and time again. I would tell you to do this professionally, but I don't want to lose your expertise for my own selfish needs. Thank you for trusting my voice, knowing what I'm trying to say, and helping me get there when I couldn't always see the light.

I owe sincere thanks to my daughter and son. Kaitlyn Vicente, without your feedback, this book would not hold the story I wanted to tell. As always, you helped me find my way. Thank you for also lending me your talent for the perfect design for the cover of this book. Your creativity knows no bounds. I am forever indebted to you. Nickolas Vicente, in your typical honest, loving way, you helped me to see a way to make my story better.

I am very fortunate to have some wonderful family and friends who also supported me along every step of the process. My mom, Patricia Haddad, and good friend, Gail Kelley, read early revisions and were my biggest cheerleaders! I cherished your feedback.

This wouldn't be the book it is without the sage advice of my fellow partners in the macabre—Caren Koropey, who gave me some great guidance—thank you so much! I owe a heartfelt thanks to Anna and Loui Fernandes, Ben Miller, and Lauren Nagel, who read an early draft and gave crucial feedback.

My friends and family mean the world to me. Thank you for you love and encouragement. New England holds a very special place in my heart and I am so very lucky to share the same bit of sky with each and every one of you.

And to my readers: I wholeheartedly appreciate you taking the time to read my story. I hope you fell in love with the characters and their story as I did.

About the Author

Sharyn Haddad Vicente grew up in New England. She was raised by her parents in the smallest state in the country, Rhode Island, with her sister, and brother. She still resides in New England today with her husband of 35 years, and her adult daughter and son.

She attended Rhode Island College where she received a degree in psychology. She then went on to the University of Rhode Island to earn a degree in adult education. She works at the Community College of Rhode Island where she is employed in both the psychology and English departments.

Sharyn's love of storytelling goes back to when she was a young girl. She has always had a penchant for psychological thrillers. She loves how the power of a good thrill can encourage the mind.

If you enjoyed this book, Sharyn would be eternally grateful if you took the time to leave a review at Amazon. No spoilers, please.

Visit: sharynhaddadvicente.com

Made in the USA
Middletown, DE
20 August 2023

36984439R00219